WRENCHING FATE

BRIDES OF PROPHECY
Book 1

By Brooklyn Ann

Dedicated to Karen Ann
6~11~62 – 2~14 ~09
You were the best mom that I could ever wish for.
I'll never stop missing you.
Thanks for believing in me.

Acknowledgements

Special thanks to Rachel Faircloth, my best, best, best friend, for always being there!

Thanks to Christa Scovel for reading my first handwritten pages and asking what happened next.

Thanks to all the people who read some or all of the work. Dean Chamberlain, Wayne Bird, Margaret Bail, Erica Chapman, Jamie DeBree, Rissa Watkins, Sterling Smith, Gabriel Rees, Michel King, Shelley Martin, Bonnie Paulson, Asa Maria Bradley, Millie McClaine, Layna Pimental, and Ashlyn Chase.

Thanks to Danae Ayusso for help and advice with the cover.

Thanks to Kent Butler for all your help with the process of bringing this story into the world. You just can't stay out of my acknowledgements, can you?

Thanks to my friends at Gus's Cigar Pub for your friendship and enthusiastic encouragement.

And thanks to my friends and family for their never ending support!

Chapter One
Coeur d'Alene, Idaho

Akasha Hope had one foot out the window and on the roof when there was a knock at her bedroom door.

"Damn it," she muttered and hid her smokes before admitting the group home director.

Mrs. Kenzie smiled tightly. "You've been assigned a legal guardian," her keeper announced calmly as if relating the menu for tonight's dinner rather than ripping the rug from under Akasha's feet.

"What?" She couldn't have been more surprised if the woman had stripped and danced naked around the room.

Though most residents of *Bright Future* were sent to foster care within months, Akasha had been a permanent resident since the cops found her wandering on the shoulder of Highway 95 three years ago. Besides the deterrent of her questionable age and foul mouth, she'd acquired a juvenile record of smoking, drinking and breaking curfew. Akasha encouraged her portrayal as "unfit for adoption." Though her state assigned identification declared that she was seventeen, Akasha was really almost twenty and soon on her way to abandoning this pseudo childhood.

At least she'd managed to get into what Idaho residents called the "dual enrollment" program, simultaneously earning college and high school credits at the North Idaho College campus. Not only did that get her out of the demeaning, oppressive environment at the high school, it was also her first step towards getting a business degree and opening up her own automotive repair business. Now Mrs. Kenzie was telling her that some asshole was going to ruin her plans.

"Why the fuck did they assign me a guardian?" She practically growled.

Mrs. Kenzie rolled her eyes. "Your caseworker didn't say. And it's too late to argue. Your guardian's on his way to pick you up so you better pack now."

"Hold on." Akasha stopped the woman. "Which of the 'shoppers' was it?" A few men stared at her when they visited over the years. Their gazes were far from parental.

"None. The man declined to come at visiting hours." The group home director snorted. "If he had, I think he would've thought better of his choice when hearing your smart mouth. Still, one would assume your file would be enough to deter any prospects." Mrs. Kenzie gave her one last derisive look before striding out of the room, nose so high in the air it was a wonder she could see where she was going.

Akasha sank on the bed, her mind reeling from shock and her body quivering with fury. *How dare this son of a bitch fuck things up for me!* The nicotine craving became too much. She scrambled out the attic window and onto the roof. Taking out her pack of Camels, she lit up with a growl.

A bright orange harvest moon rose in the cloudy sky, glimmering molten gold on the orange leaves of maple trees lining the street. Her mind raced as she smoked. *Why the hell would someone waste time and money on paperwork to be my legal guardian for less than a year?*

There were only three possible options.

One: a charity case. It'd hurt her pride, but she could deal.

Two: slave labor. She worked her ass off in the group home anyway.

Three: her so-called guardian wanted a sex toy. She rotated her ankle, smiling as she felt the reassuring weight of the knife in her boot. The bastard would be in for a surprise if he thought it'd be easy.

Akasha crushed out the cigarette and slipped the butt under a loose shingle before climbing back to the window. The wood frame cracked under her grip.

"Fuck." She hadn't lost control of her unusual strength in a while. Akasha grinned bitterly. *This asshole has no idea what he's getting into.*

After maneuvering the damaged window closed, it took all of two minutes to pack. She only had four changes of clothes, her school stuff, and seven books. One backpack, one duffel bag. That was it. That was her life.

Mrs. Kenzie opened the door and sniffed the air. "You were smoking again."

Akasha gave her best poker face and threw on her leather biker jacket.

"Oh well, it's not my problem anymore." Mrs. Kenzie grabbed the duffel bag off the bed. "He's here, so let's get going."

Akasha swept a last glance across her small attic room. Would she miss it here? It was frigid in the winter, sweltering in the summer, and as stifling as a cage. However, the room had been her home for almost three years and it was better than most places she'd slept in. What lay ahead was unknown. *Who the hell is this guy?*

He had to have some clout to gain guardianship over her, which implied no one would help her if he turned out to be a sicko. If things went bad, she'd be back on the streets with no hopes of a high school diploma or getting into college.

As she followed Mrs. Kenzie down the stairs and to her future, Akasha wondered how much negotiating had gone on and how much money had changed hands behind her back.

The man waiting for her in the parlor wasn't what she expected. For one thing, he looked younger than the other prospective foster parents. For another, he was *gorgeous*. His long straight hair, blacker than hers, framed a perfectly chiseled face. And his green eyes... *holy crap*. Like twin arc welders, they bored a hole through her.

With heated cheeks, Akasha dropped her gaze to his tailored black clothes, then looked down at her ripped jeans and faded shirt, resisting the urge to pat down curls more messed up than the wiring harness of a Jerry-rigged Pontiac. She drew herself up to her full height of five-three to meet his eyes once more.

He extended his hand. "It is a pleasure to meet you, Akasha." His deep, slightly accented voice gave her a strange shiver. "I am Silas McNaught."

Power radiated from every inch of him. When Akasha was on the streets, she'd seen drug dealers and pimps who seemed to exude supremacy, but none had come close to the absolute authority which this man wore like a mantle. *Was it just his obvious wealth, or was it more?*

Taking pains not to squeeze too hard, she shook his hand. She was so torn between rage and confusion that she didn't know whether to punch him in the throat or demand an explanation for his intrusion into her life.

McNaught's eyes widened. "You have a very firm handshake."

If only you knew I could crush your hand with the slightest effort. Akasha suppressed a glare. If she did, she'd be thrown in jail, or worse. A memory of armed, uniformed men chasing her superimposed itself over her vision. She shook it off with a shudder.

The man seemed to sense her frustration. "I'll take your bags if you are ready."

Her hostility depleted slightly by his politeness. Akasha followed her new guardian out into the night, wondering why he chose to pick her up this late in the evening.

All thoughts ceased when she saw his car.

"Holy *shit!*" She gasped. "Is that a '68 Barracuda?"

McNaught nodded. On light feet, she ran to the car, forgetting that her backpack was supposed to be heavy. The gleaming black convertible was one of the most magnificent things she'd ever seen.

"It's beautiful," she breathed reverently. "What's it got under the hood? Is it a 318, 440, slant 6?"

"I don't know."

She gaped at him. *How the hell could he not know which engine this beauty had?* Why did he buy it without knowing? He had the decency to look ashamed as he unlocked the trunk and put her bags in.

Her eyes closed, lips parted in pleasure as she heard the engine start and he pulled out of the parking lot, heading north on Government Way. As Akasha silently struggled to absorb the shock of her new situation, the only sounds were the purr of the 'Cuda—it sounded like a 440… maybe even a 383— and the crunch of dead leaves under the tires. She opened her mouth to ask him why he had taken her, and flinched when her stomach growled.

"You didn't have dinner," he accused.

Damn, it starts already. "Nope."

He whipped the car left, oblivious to the honking horns. "We will have to get you something." He turned on Appleway, A.K.A., 'fast-food alley.' "What would you like?"

"Um… McDonald's is cool." She tried not to sound too excited at the prospect. It would be humiliating if he knew she hadn't been to a McDonald's in over three years.

Her belly rumbled again when she smelled the deep-fried goodness in the drive-thru. She ordered two Big Macs, large fries and a root beer. He ordered nothing.

"Don't like fast food?" she asked. *He probably thought his rich ass was too good for it.*

"I dined earlier." McNaught's tone was unreadable.

He paid and handed her the steaming bag. She salivated and hoped for a short drive.

"Go ahead," he said as he pulled back on the street.

Akasha's gaze whipped over to him in shock. "Are you kidding? You don't eat in a car like this! Do *you?*"

He chuckled. "No, but as you are my charge, I think I will put your needs above those of my automobile."

Not knowing what to say to that, she shrugged. "Well... maybe I'll just eat my fries."

They tasted better than she remembered and were gone by the time he turned onto Cherry Hill Road. McNaught had to downshift to second gear to continue up the steep incline. As the road curved, Akasha saw many huge houses. *Crazy rich people. This road's gotta be deadly when it's icy.*

When they reached the top, Mr. McNaught took out a remote, opening wrought iron gates surrounding... a castle. It was a no-shit, honest-to-God castle, made of stone and complete with turrets.

"Here we are," her guardian said with a wry smile as she gaped.

They parked in the biggest garage she'd ever seen. It could fit four cars with room to spare for toolboxes and engine stands. When she got out she noticed how freakishly clean and unused it was. It smelled like fresh paint, not *garage.*

He unloaded her bags and led her inside.

Her new home was modern on the inside and screamed luxury with its hardwood flooring and plush carpets reeking of austere newness. Despite the gleaming mahogany furnishings topped with objêts d'art and expensive paintings on the walls, it seemed like no one lived here.

He led Akasha into a dining room with a table that could seat twenty, complete with a humongous chandelier glittering overhead. Her sack of Big Macs was out of place on it. Hell, *she* was out of place here.

"What do you think so far?" Mr. McNaught asked. His voice had a slight lilt, almost musical. Where was he from?

"Um… it's very… fancy," she said.

He gave her a look as if he knew that wasn't really a compliment. "You may eat while I get your things. Then we shall talk and I'll tell you what to expect."

She nodded and unwrapped a burger. When she took a bite a sudden memory assailed her with an intensity that almost choked her.

Max burst into the shop with a grin on his grizzled face. He held a McDonald's bag in one hand and a case of Coors in the other.

"Big Macs n' Beer!" he announced. "C'mon, spark plug, you've tinkered with that damn car long enough. Time ta eat up so we can beat the boys at poker tonight!"

Dammit, she missed that old man. He was the closest thing to a father she'd had since her own was murdered. Her eyes and throat burned with unshed tears. Akasha took another bite of the burger, resolving not to be too depressed to savor the food. She soon devoured both Big Macs with the ferocity of one who'd gone hungry too many times to count. Still, it wasn't the same without cold beer to wash it down.

McNaught returned as she was wiping the last of the ketchup from her lips. This polished gentleman was the polar opposite of the coarse biker-turned-mechanic who'd "raised" her briefly. How the hell was she going to get along with this guy?

"Will you join me in the living room?"

She looked at the garbage left from her meal on the table. *So out of place.*

He seemed to read her mind. "Leave it for now."

The living room looked like it belonged on the cover of a home magazine. She sank into an overstuffed pine green couch. McNaught turned on the gas fireplace and sat in a burgundy chair on her right.

He grabbed an ashtray from the end table and set it on the granite coffee table. "You may smoke if you like."

Akasha's gaze darted to his, surprise and suspicion roiling in her gut. "How did you know I smoked?"

"I read your file. Though I disapprove of the habit, I shouldn't like to fight you about it. You're intelligent enough to quit eventually. Would you like a glass of wine as well?"

He was letting her smoke *and* drink? *Maybe this won't be so bad after all.* She nodded and dug in her jacket for her smokes. One of the end tables concealed a mini fridge from which he removed a bottle of Chardonnay and a glass. It was one of the coolest things she'd ever seen.

He filled the glasses and began. "First, you must know that I'm away all day. The kitchen is already stocked, but feel free to make a list of anything else you'd like."

O...kay? He went through all the trouble and paperwork to get her and he wasn't even going to be around most of the time?

McNaught continued in the same business-like tone. "You will be given an allowance of one hundred dollars a week. If that's not enough, please inform me. Also, I'll be taking you to buy clothing and other necessities tomorrow evening."

"Wait," Akasha interrupted. If she didn't get this straight now, things were only going to get more awkward. "You didn't take me to be some kind of sex toy, did you? 'Cuz if you did, we're going to have problems no matter what you buy me." She reached for the knife in her boot, watching him carefully.

McNaught's lips curved in a smile so wide that dimples formed in his cheeks, eyes shining with admiration and respect. His laughter tickled the air.

"Somehow I find it hard to imagine you being a 'toy' to any man. You can keep your weapon sheathed, Akasha." His eyes locked on hers and his expression turned solemn. "I swear, on my honor, that I will never take you unless you ask me to."

The sound of her name on his lips made her shiver even as his promise sent waves of heat cascading over her body. The confusing reaction brought her anger back to the surface. *Wait, did he mean he would if he had the chance?* She searched his expression for any sign of a perverted leer at the thought of "taking" her. There were none.

"Why did you take guardianship over me?" she asked, quivering with frustration. "What the fuck do you want with me?"

He frowned at her language. "I merely wanted a companion who could tolerate my odd hours and in return I hoped to help someone in need."

She didn't buy that. Though for some reason she believed he didn't want her to be his 'barely legal' playmate. She sipped the wine slowly this time. It tasted like brake cleaner.

"Why me, though? I'll be free in less than a year. It seems pointless."

"Your record intrigued me. You're incredibly intelligent, though somewhat of a troublemaker. Other than that, you're a mystery. You told the authorities you're a runaway from California, but nobody ever claimed you." His eyes narrowed. "In fact, the state declared you to be two years younger than you really are."

A tremor rushed through her at his scrutinizing gaze. "How did you know about that?"

The corner of his mouth rose with a smile. "Would you believe me if I said I was psychic?" At her frown, he sobered. "It was in your file. I don't see a reason for you to have lied to the authorities. However, I also don't see why they bothered with taxpayer money to, in effect, trap you like they did. It must be some secret you are hiding." He leaned forward, green eyes seeming to glow as they tried to capture her gaze.

"I won't talk about it." She finished the wine, pursing her lips.

"You don't care for the wine?" he asked.

She was so grateful for the change in subject that she blurted, "Actually, I prefer beer."

McNaught lifted a brow. "Really? What brand?"

"Coors."

He threw back his head and laughed, covering his mouth. "The 'Silver Bullet!' I should have guessed."

What the hell is so funny about that? Akasha shook her head. This guy was being way too generous. Max wasn't half as kind when he took her in. Of course, his gruff demeanor turned out to be a front. Was Mr. McNaught's kindness a front? Her head ached. "Where's my room?"

He blinked at her sharp tone. "So you will stay then?"

Akasha sighed and nodded. *What choice do I have?* Fixing him with a stern stare, she warned, "But if you pull any shit, I'm out of here."

He led her up a grand curving staircase right out of "Gone with the Wind," then down a long hallway and into a room meant for a princess.

"What do you do, Mr. McNaught?" she asked.

"I ah…" He gave a strange half-smile. "I'm in finance. Very boring, I'm afraid."

Akasha struggled to keep her eyes in her head at the mind-blowing luxury surrounding her. "Obviously lucrative."

He blinked in surprise at her reply, obviously not expecting her to be literate. "I hope you'll be pleased with the room."

The room was huge. Her feet sank into the royal blue carpet. A queen sized four-poster bed dominated the area. On the other side of the room was a vanity of deep dark wood and a matching dresser. A sliding glass door opened to a balcony.

"I left the walls bare so you can decorate. There's a robe and slippers in the closet." He pointed to one of the three doors. "The bathroom is there."

Akasha's mind swam. Her own closet? Her own bathroom? *A pair of slippers?*

McNaught inclined his head respectfully. "I'll leave you alone now. Goodnight, Akasha."

"Good night Mr. McNaught," she replied, unnerved by his formality.

"Please, call me Silas." Warmth tinged his voice before he closed the door behind him.

The moment he left, Akasha fled to the bathroom and locked the door as she changed into an oversized t-shirt. But once she was snuggled under the covers of the heavenly soft bed, sleep was impossible.

This guy is way too nice. Silas McNaught was so polite it made her teeth hurt. Yet he was the first person to believe that she was nineteen. Should she have lied? Now he knew she was legal.

She watched the sliver of light under the door and clutched her knife, waiting for him to come into "her" room and do something terrible, something to disprove his kindness. She waited and waited until her eyelids drooped and she succumbed to the bed's luxurious comfort.

Chapter Two

Her boots were tiny. The Lord Vampire of Coeur d'Alene stared at the worn things, marveling at how light they felt in his hand. He set them down and lifted her leather jacket from the floor, inhaling the myriad scents of it. Leather, motor oil, tobacco... and woman. He hung the garment up— careful not to rattle the many zippers— and approached the bed.

Silas stood over Akasha, fists clenched at his sides, resisting the urge to touch her. Had he made a mistake in bringing her here? Instead of embracing him with teary gratitude, she radiated fury at his rescue. *Had my visions been wrong?*

In his mortal days people had called Silas McNaught "the mad laird" because he sometimes fell into trances and awoke being able to foretell the future. After five centuries, McNaught paid little heed to his prophetic visions, except for one in which he held a beautiful lass with amethyst eyes and raven curls as she cried. Silas believed this woman was to be his bride. He finally found her last month. To his surprise, she'd been under his nose for three years.

Yet one look into those cold purple eyes and he was almost certain no tears had ever been shed from them.

Still, he hadn't realized how irresistible she was. Akasha looked innocent and vulnerable as an angel as she curled up in a ball, one fist resting against a round cheek. Her other hand clutched the knife she'd threatened to stab him with. An admiring smile tugged at his lips. *An avenging angel, perhaps.* Dusky curls reflected the moonlight and her bowed lips pouted. He leaned down to kiss them... then stopped. That would be wrong. He would have her willingly, or not at all. Instead, he began the next step of securing her.

Silas locked in Akasha's mind, willing her to stay asleep. Pain burst in his skull as her mind fought him. Doubling his effort he increased his psychic grip. If he didn't move fast, he would lose her.

Quickly, he bit down on his finger, drawing blood.

With his other hand, he coaxed her lips open to let the blood drip in her mouth and whispered, "I, Silas McNaught, Lord of Coeur d'Alene, Mark this mortal, Akasha Hope, as mine and mine alone. With this Mark I give Akasha my undying protection. Let all others, immortal and mortal alike, who cross her path sense my Mark and know that to act against her is to act against myself and thus set forth my wrath as I will avenge what is mine."

He repeated the ancient oath in his Gaelic tongue and reached out with his senses. The Mark flared between them, warmth rushing up his body. At last, she was his. Satisfied with the night's work, he placed a kiss on her forehead and slipped out of the room.

Suddenly, thunder sounded, powerful and ominous enough to make his bones ache. His skin electrified with tension,

Silas strode down the stairs to glance out the window at the calm sky and the October harvest moon.

As he dreaded, the thunder came from within. He massaged his temples to ease the violent reverberations in his skull. Something was coming... something ancient and bloated with enough power to shake the earth.

He took his sword down from the wall as the front door opened of its own volition and a tall cloaked figure strolled in. The very air shivered from its presence.

"You will not need that." A low voice came from the black velvet folds of the cloak.

Silas fell to his knees, eyes wide with recognition, though his grip remained firm upon the steel hilt of his weapon. "Greetings, my Lord Delgarias. You honor me with your presence."

The Thirteenth Elder, rumored to be the oldest of their kind, nodded and bade Silas to rise. "I have come to discuss this mortal you Marked."

Silas blinked. A Lord Vampire didn't need permission to Mark a mortal, he only needed the Elders' approval if he intended to Change him or her. Delgarias's visit couldn't bode well. If he intended to harm Akasha— He bit back a growl at the thought.

Quelling his trepidation, Silas returned his sword to its honored place above the marble hearth. "Very well, please have a seat." He stepped aside to allow Delgarias to take his favorite burgundy recliner— and to further block the way to the stairs. "Would you care for some wine, or perhaps a shot of *Glenlivet*?"

The Elder moved the latest issue of *The Wall Street Journal* to the coffee table and nodded. "You always have the best scotch. But first, tell me, McNaught," his voice low and silken as he leaned forward, blue eyes glowing like lightning. "If I had attacked, would you have fought me?"

"Yes." Silas's reply was instant. Perhaps he should have kept his weapon.

"You would have died."

Silas nodded, wondering where this was going. "I must defend my lands and people, even if I die doing so. That is my first obligation as a Lord." His eyes narrowed. "Or have you forgotten that in your frequent periods of absence?"

Degrees chuckled, but there was an edge of steel beneath. "Careful, McNaught, not to try my temper. *I* have not forgotten, but I believe others of your rank have. It is good you remember. Good that I was not a fool to have chosen you—" He shook his head as if to clear it. "About that drink?"

Silas headed to the bar as the other vampire's power prickled his skin. He regarded Delgarias as he poured the drinks. He'd only been in the Elder's presence once, back in 1926 when he became the Lord of Coeur d'Alene, at the Elder's enigmatic suggestion...or command. No one knew how old Delgarias was, or where he came from. The vampire was like a phantom, appearing out of nowhere to settle a dispute or issue the occasional command.

Delgarias pulled back the hood of his cloak and Silas, as usual, tensed at the vampire's odd appearance. His skin seemed poreless in its luminosity. The Elder's long hair was made of translucent strands with black cores, like shafts of feathers. The waist-length mass hid his pointed ears tonight, but Silas had seen them before. And his fingers were an inch longer than normal. Sometimes he suspected Delgarias had never been human.

He handed the Elder his drink, watching those long fingers curl around the glass with morbid fascination. Silas took a sip of scotch, rolling the fiery liquid across his tongue before allowing it to trace a hot path down his throat.

Delgarias didn't bother with such care. He quaffed half his drink in one swallow as if he were a mortal man. Unlike other vampires, food and drink didn't seem to affect his digestion. He set down the empty glass and rested his hands in a steeple beneath his chin.

"The circumstances with this mortal are quite unique," Delgarias interrupted Silas's thoughts. "She was in the state's custody."

"But she's not a minor. The state merely thinks she is," McNaught replied, fixing him with a rigid stare. "I know our rules and I handled the mortal laws through the proper channels."

Delgarias leaned back in his chair and regarded Silas intently. "Did you ever stop to wonder what put this woman in such a strange situation? Why would the authorities make her younger than she truly is? It seems a waste of time and money to me."

McNaught sighed in disinterest. "Perhaps she will tell me."

The Elder's lips twitched. "And perhaps she will not."

Silas shrugged. He didn't care too much about the woman's mysterious background or lack of it. What mattered was that his centuries of searching for her had at last come to an end. "Why are you concerned with the matter?" He prodded.

"As I said before, the circumstances are unique." Something in his tone implied that he wasn't talking about Akasha's being a former ward of the state. "If you want to keep this woman, you must obey two commands. First, you must not Change this woman until *I*, and no one else, give you permission."

Silas nodded. "I can live with that... As long as you don't make me wait for too many years." It was strange that

Delgarias was taking such a personal interest in such an insignificant affair. "What else?"

"I want you to guard her friends," Delgarias said. "But under no circumstances are they to learn what you are."

"Her friends?" Silas frowned, recalling the nights he watched Akasha sneak out the window of the group home to join a car full of black garbed teenagers. He was alternately amused and annoyed with the so-called "Goth" trend. It didn't occur to him that he would have such persons under his roof.

"What am I to be guarding them from?"

Delgarias leaned forward. "There are those of our kind who will find them to be quite... interesting; one young lady in particular." He fell silent for a moment, his expression unreadable. "Her mother recently passed away, so she may need extra supervision and, at the least, a little more patience." There was something off in his tone.

"What of her?"

"She is the daughter of Mephistopheles," The Thirteenth elder said calmly.

Silas winced as the glass shattered in his grip. Oblivious to the blood and liquor dripping on the plush carpet, his voice dropped to a whisper. "The old legends are true, then?"

It was long whispered that vampires had been created by a dark god of another world and then banished to the earth realm for displeasing him. Could such a phenomenon be real?

Pain contorted Delgarias's smooth features before they settled back into complacent lines and he nodded. "Mephistopheles himself made me what I am."

"What is he? When were you... created?" Silas whispered, reeling in shock. "And what has this to do with the woman I Marked?" He knew it was unwise to question the Thirteenth Elder, but his mind spun with the news.

"I do not feel the time is right to address your first questions. As for the last, your pet mortal might have very little to do with Mephistopheles," the vampire said noncommittally. "Or perhaps much. I only ask that you guard her and the others and keep them out of trouble."

"So I am to be a nursemaid, then?" Silas asked, his Scottish brogue creeping into his voice in irritation, as he plucked shards of broken glass from his hand.

To his vexation, the other vampire laughed. "You may call it what you wish, just see that you do it." His voice took on a steely edge. "Unless you wish to relinquish Akasha to me? After all, I can find some other vampire up to the tasks I require."

"No!" Silas flashed across the room and seized his sword, every cell of his being roaring to protect Akasha.

Delgarias raised a brow at his impetuous move. "I should chastise you for that. But now all I ask is that you do as I asked."

"I will, I swear it on my honor." He lowered the blade.

The Elder bit his finger and placed the bleeding tip to Silas's wounds, healing them instantly. "I must be going now. Thank you very much for the drink. I wish you luck with your mortal woman."

"Wait!" Silas said. "How did the daughter of Mephistopheles get here? And what does it mean for our kind?" He stopped, eyes widening as he faced the Delgarias, realization sparking his senses. "You *knew* Mephistopheles's child would be here. That's why you encouraged me to take this city."

The Elder had a way of knowing what was to come with frightening accuracy.

Delgarias's face was impassive. "There will be time enough to discuss that later. Just watch over Akasha and her friends and keep out of trouble. That is my command."

With those parting words, he vanished from the spot.

Silas sighed. *Why did the Elders have to be so infuriatingly vague?* He bent down and began to clean up the broken glass.

At least Akasha was safe. And how hard could supervising a few teenagers be? He frowned and put the shards in an ashtray. One of them was the daughter of the creator of vampires and the circumstances of her presence were baffling enough to give him a headache. But he supposed he would have to deal with it. God willing, his experience as Laird of his clan and later as the Lord Vampire of a city made him up to the task.

Chapter Three
Phoenix, Arizona

Major Frances Milbury of the Covert Operations Assassinations Team— COAT for short— clenched the arms of his chair so tightly that the stumps of the severed fingers on his left hand were as white as the intact knuckles on his right.

He spoke slowly to keep from screaming at his former university rival. "You mean to tell me you've been sitting on this for *three years* and it didn't occur to you to notify me?"

FBI Agent Joe Holmes, head of the Abnormal Investigation Unit (AIU), reclined behind his desk, blue eyes twinkling at the man's ire. "I didn't have to. The body and evidence we found is so far outside COAT jurisdiction it's laughable."

Milbury sneered. "You don't have the 'jurisdiction,' nor the security clearance to decide what is and isn't a concern to our department."

Holmes grinned with his usual obnoxious cheer. "Come now, I'm doing you a favor in revealing our findings. A little gratitude should be forthcoming."

"The lateness of this 'favor' could have compromised my investigation!" Milbury slammed his good fist on the desk. "Who knows what crucial evidence was lost?"

Holmes sighed and ran a hand through his unruly white hair. "I say again, the victim was a civilian. He was, in fact, a serial killer the FBI had been trying to catch for years. More than that, he was beaten to death by a creature with supernatural strength, which is why my department was called rather than yours. What connection to the military could be seen in this?"

Milbury rolled his eyes. "So you thought one of your 'monsters' killed him."

The AIU investigated crimes committed by what they believed to be supernatural beings such as witches, vampires, and God knew what else. Milbury saw it as a waste of taxpayer dollars.

Holmes gave him another superior smile. "Yes, we did. But the DNA didn't match a vampire's. Too many red cells and too... *engineered*, for lack of a better word. Which brings me to a question: What has your department been cooking up that has you looking for a nineteen year old female with no military association? And why are you so interested in the remains we've stored?"

Milbury's temper receded as triumph and anticipation seeped in. "Was the DNA found on the victim female?"

"It was," the scientist admitted in a cautious tone.

Francis smiled tightly. "I could tell you the information's classified, but I'll humor you and ask, why did you call to inform me of this victim when I sent out memos describing the girl? The remains are of an older male, correct?"

Holmes chuckled and adjusted his horn-rimmed glasses. "You're lucky I even read your note. Runaways aren't our specialty. However, the COAT letterhead piqued my curiosity. All that aside, let's say I found a possible connection."

"I want everything you have released to me immediately," Milbury demanded.

Holmes shook his head. "Not so fast. It's still my property. I can, however, give you full access to my lab and all files and evidence pertaining to this case... *if* I feel like it."

Milbury wanted to knock him in the teeth. "What do you want, Joe?"

"I want in on this." All of Holmes's usual cheer was abandoned, giving way to implacable determination.

"You want in *how*?" Francis knew, but had to ask. He couldn't afford misunderstandings.

"I want to perform the research and testing on this woman. I want to know how this mutation works." Holmes's gaze filled with scientific zeal.

Milbury's eyes narrowed. "What makes you think I'd be authorized to let the Feds in on this?"

Joe smirked. "Because *you* came. Not a scientist or even a doctor. I'm willing to bet you don't have either on your staff. In fact, I'm not so certain your superiors even know we're having this conversation."

Francis sighed in an effort to hide his prickle of unease. Damn the rat bastard, he was right. Milbury's department was a cleanup crew for "loose ends." All Francis had were paper pushers and assassins— and since the budget cuts, very few of those.

Holmes had him by the balls and he knew it. Somehow, the slimy Fed had done his homework and knew how low the COAT had sunk in this last decade. Still, Holmes didn't know everything.

Like what happened to the scientists who'd engineered the serum with which the girl's father had been injected.

"The technology in my lab is superior to all others," Holmes insisted. "And as for finding the girl, I have connections you don't. *Civilian* connections."

Milbury pretended to agonize before snarling, "All right! But we must involve as few people as possible. Now show me what you've got."

Holmes donned his lab coat, resembling a mad scientist with his bug-eyed glasses and unruly white hair. "You sound like a drill sergeant when you're pissed, you know that? Now, if you'll follow me, I'll show you all, explain it to you in laymen's terms, and even tell you what we should do next." His shit-eating grin grated on Francis's nerves.

They headed down a long corridor, jostling other employees who rushed by, tapping clipboards against their hips as ID badges bounced on front pockets.

When they reached a door adorned with warnings and authorized personnel signs, Holmes pushed a few buttons by the handle. A laser scanned his retinas before the door opened with an unassuming click.

The lab was pristine with its gleaming stainless steel tables and gurneys. Several computers lined one wall, white cupboards and file cabinets stood against another. The far end contained drawers right out of a morgue. Holmes pulled a file and went to a computer, fingers flying across the keys, looking far too cheerful in such sterile surroundings.

"Where was the body found?" Milbury asked when the scientist began whistling.

Holmes didn't look up from the screen. "In a ditch, off a road near I-90, just outside of Bozeman."

"She was last seen in Colorado, almost twelve years ago." Milbury said, shaking his head in wonder. "I thought she'd have gone further by now."

Agent Holmes eyed him intently, waiting for him to continue. When Francis didn't speak, he shrugged and got back to business. "I think I'll show you the crime scene photos and files first, before we move on to the bone and tissue samples."

Holmes laid glossy photographs on the desk. The body was depicted at every possible angle, with a close up on each part of its anatomy. The colors were bright against the lab's white and silver background.

At first it was difficult for Francis to make sense of the images. It was as if his brain wouldn't accept what his eyes were seeing.

Eventually the colors and shapes came together. In place of the victim's head was a shapeless blob of bone shards, brains, blood and skin. It looked like his grandmother's goulash. He made out what might have been a nose. Bile rose up in his throat. He forced his gaze down to closeups of other parts. The torso and upper arms looked strange, like deflated balloons. The corpse's pants were down, revealing a flaccid penis coated with dried blood.

Francis gagged and wiped his brow, turning away from the grotesque photographs. The room seemed hot despite the low hum of the air conditioner.

"Fascinating, isn't it?" Holmes seemed to enjoy his discomfort. "This girl must have had immense strength to cause such damage to a man that size."

Milbury quivered in outrage. "Haven't you any respect? This was a human being!"

The AIU agent shook his head, expression sobering. "Not this one. Despite his species being *homo sapiens*, this man was a monster. His DNA was linked to twenty-seven murders. His victims were brutally raped; some were children. And with all the hymeneal blood and tissue we dug out of his pubic hair, I'd say the bastard got what he deserved."

"God, that's disgusting!" Milbury could feel his face turning green.

"That's forensics, and it's how we catch bad guys." Holmes retorted.

Hymeneal blood.... Francis tensed. "Wait. You mean he raped the girl? She would have been about sixteen."

Some of the pity Milbury felt for the man drained away. He had a niece that age. Still, he wondered if anyone deserved to die like that. And the evidence in front of him proved how dangerous this girl could be when provoked.

With a traumatic thing like rape happening to her, who knew how unstable her state of mind could be?

"How did he overpower her immense strength?" The thought leapt into his head.

"We found a gun nearby with the victim's prints on it. He must have threatened her with it. She likely disarmed him while he was pulling up his pants."

Milbury's mind raced as he made plans on how to subdue the girl once he found her. "Tell me more."

Chapter Four

BANG-BANG-BANG! The deafening noise made Akasha jump out of her chair, knocking the plate of remaining birthday cake to the floor.

Her eyes snapped to the window.

A shower of bullets assaulted her parents. Blood- bright red and angry, spewed everywhere, splattering the trailer and staining the snowy ground. A bullet struck her father's shoulder and he screamed. Another went through his stomach, making him fall to his knees. There was another bang. The side of his head exploded and he collapsed.

"Akasha run!" A bullet pierced her mother's throat and with a feeble gurgle, she fell.

Ping-Ping-Ping! Bullets assailed the trailer. Akasha saw a group of men in black uniforms wielding guns. They came closer. While they examined the bodies, she ran. One of the men shouted. Footsteps pounded behind her. Her spine tensed and burned as her stomach roiled with terror, but still she ran.

***

Akasha awoke upon a tear-soaked pillow, aching from the memory. Panicked, her eyes darted across the room. *Where the hell am I?* The lavish furnishings were so alien, she might as well have been in a spaceship. Chest tight, she struggled to remember. As the last vestige of the dream bled away, she remembered Mr. McNaught with his suspicious kindness— and unnerving good looks.

It seemed she'd survived the night in his dubious care... and most of the day as well from what the bedside clock read. It was a little after noon.   Torn between gratitude and confusion that her new guardian didn't wake her, she climbed out of the massive bed. Grabbing her backpack, she headed to the bathroom, double checking the lock on the door.

Once dressed, she cautiously opened her bedroom door and headed downstairs, eyes darting in all directions. McNaught was nowhere around. He'd said he was away all day, but it was strange that it applied to weekends as well.

Akasha shrugged. *The less I have to deal with him, the better.* As she grabbed a banana from the fruit bowl in the massive marble-adorned kitchen, a thought gave her pause.

I better search this place. See if he has any dead bodies in the basement, or torture porn under his bed. Her stomach roiled, whether from guilt or fear at the thought, she couldn't tell. The rising tremor of curiosity about the handsome prince of this fairytale castle was harder to ignore. Finishing the banana, she headed back upstairs, deciding to work her way down.

As she walked down endless corridors, it occurred to her that there was something she had to do tomorrow, but with her world being turned upside-down last night, she couldn't remember what it was. The nagging feeling continued as she opened door after door to empty rooms. A surge of fury roared through her at the blank white walls and uncarpeted floors. *How the fuck am I supposed to learn anything from this?* The vacant spaces seemed to mock the blank in her memory.

Whatever it was she had to do, it was important.

Grinding her teeth in irritation, Akasha had to concentrate to avoid crushing the next doorknob.

"Finally a room with something in it." As soon as the words left her lips, Akasha's eyes widened.

From the mega king-size bed, masculine furnishings, and swords on the walls, this had to be Silas McNaught's bedroom. Heat filled her face as she stepped further. She'd never been in a man's bedroom before. Well, except for Max, but he didn't count.

The bed was as pristine and militantly tucked as one in a luxury furniture store. One could almost think he didn't sleep in it. Still, Akasha ducked to peek underneath and swept her hands under the mattress. No dirty magazines there, not even a freaking dust bunny.

She checked the end table drawer and found nothing but paperback novels, issues of *The Wall Street Journal* and various business magazines. No *Hot Rod* or *Motor Trend* for him. But at least he was a Stephen King fan. That was one of her favorite authors.

Further exploration only turned up a closet full of designer clothes likely worth more than her life and a luxurious bathroom with a Jacuzzi tub she could almost swim in. The only sense of a personality in this decadent suite was the books and the swords.

Elaborate decorative and obviously medieval antiques, the blades simultaneously complemented the décor but gave a warning. Lines from a Rolling Stones song played in her mind.

Please allow me to introduce myself. I'm a man of wealth and taste.

"But don't fuck with me," she added on her way out of the room.

The main floor was at least fully furnished, and with a little more personality. The entertainment center held a collection of war movies and historical documentaries as well as an impressive collection of eighties music. Akasha shook her head. She would've never taken McNaught as an *Oingo Boingo* fan.

The exploration nearly cut short when she encountered the library. Floor to ceiling books filled the room and a pair of overstuffed recliners surrounding a cheery fireplace beckoned her to curl up and escape from her confusing situation.

"No." Akasha straightened her spine, resolving to keep looking. "I don't trust him."

She hit the jackpot when she found the office... or rather she would if she understood anything she saw. The calendar on the wall listed only initials and times. McNaught's file cabinet was impressive with all the stocks and bonds it held, but she already knew he was rich... okay, she didn't know he was astronomically rich, but that didn't explain his motives.

Her file was incredibly out of place amongst the account statements and certificates of accruing wealth. Akasha flipped through the pages. A lot of meaningless "ward of the state" documents, her mug shot, criminal record, health records— and her psych evaluation.

"Anxiety, chronic insomnia, night terrors, possible mood disorder..." she muttered, fighting off a pang of humiliation. "Yeah, I sound like a real angel."

The file barely scratched the surface of her dirty secrets, yet it painted her character well enough. Akasha thrust it back in the cabinet with a shiver of self-disgust. *How could McNaught want me under his roof after reading that?*

She froze, terror uncurling in her belly. *Could he have something to do with the cocksuckers who killed my parents?* Forcing back a drowning tide of panic, she willed herself to remain practical.

If there was anything to be learned, doubtless it would be on the computer. Akasha glared at the cold gleaming monitor. Computer class was the only damn subject she struggled with in school.

Akasha's breath came out in an irritated sigh. "Where's a fucking computer whiz when I need one?" If only her best friend Xochitl was here to at least show her how to log onto the damn thing.

Eyes widening, she whispered, "*Xochitl*," drawing out the syllables of her friend's name slowly: "*So-she.*"

How you get that out of such a fucked up combination of letters, I'll never know. Closing her eyes, she remembered the night she'd made her first friend in the group home.

Akasha had just snuck back into her attic bedroom to find a small form huddled on the usually vacant bed next to hers. It had been none other than Xochitl Leonine, aspiring rock star and one of the few other students in the dual enrollment program.

"My mother died tonight," Xochitl had explained numbly before sobbing in Akasha's arms. A strange sense of rightness had marked the moment, and never left. Bound by mutual pain, the two had been inseparable since then.

Now, Akasha dug her wallet out of her pocket and found the crumpled scrap of paper with Xochitl's new number. Xoch' wasn't a techno-geek by any means, but surely she'd do better with McNaught's computers than Akasha could.

Taking the cordless phone from the mahogany desk, she dialed her friend's number.

"Hello?" A gruff voice answered. Bill, Xoch's new foster father. He'd had "asshole" written all over his face the first and only time Akasha saw him.

She struggled to keep her voice polite. "Is Xochitl there?"

"Who's this?" he demanded. A football game cranked to full volume in the background made it hard to hear.

"Akasha," she bit back a curse, wishing she'd lied. "I just need some help with my homework."

Silence stretched over the line, punctuated by some loud sports announcer. "You're not the one at the group home, are you?"

His tone implied he'd hang up if that was the case. At least she was able to answer honestly. She wasn't there any more. "Nope."

She could feel Bill's hostility as he bellowed, "Xochitl! Some gal named Akasha wants to talk to you."

At last, Xochitl's voice came on the line. "What's up?"

In case someone else was listening over the line, Akasha measured her words carefully. "I need help with the computer, can you come over?"

There was no computer for the inmates of the group home. Sure enough, Xochitl picked up on that. "Um, sure. Where are you?"

"You know that big hill off of 15th street by the freeway? I'm at the castle on top."

Xochitl sucked in a breath. "Oh my God—"

Bill's voice cut her off with another bellow. "Don't say the Lord's name in vain!"

Tremors overtook Akasha as a memory roared through her.

"You will learn the Word of God if I have to beat it into you, demon spawn!" Over and over, the heavy bible rained blows upon her head and back until she lost consciousness.

"'Kash?" Xochitl's voice was tinny through the phone's earpiece. "You still there?"

She swallowed back a load of bile. "Yeah, so you'll come?"

"Yeah, I'll be there in a few."

After flicking random buttons on the electronic panel in the mudroom until the front gate opened, Akasha smoked and paced outside.

Ten minutes later, a light blue Datsun puttered up the hill, blaring hard core thrash metal. Xochitl's grin was a balm on Akasha's nerves. Tentatively, she smiled back, watching her friend maneuver the gearshift and steering wheel while holding a can of Red Bull in one hand and a cigarette in the other.

Xochitl pulled up in front of the garage and leapt out of her car in a flurry of black and purple hair. She waved off a cloud of blue exhaust smoke with a grimace. "Damn, Little Beast does not like hills."

"The piston rings are probably shot." Akasha eyed the car. "Probably your valve stem seals too."

"Enough about the car unless you can fix her," Xochitl wagged a scolding finger, displaying purple nails adorned with little black bats. "What the hell are you doing here?"

Akasha bit her lip, remembering her situation. "Apparently, I live here now. I was assigned a legal guardian."

"No fucking *way!*" Her friend gaped. "Is your guardian here? What's she like? Besides having killer taste in real estate?"

"So far I have no idea what *he's* like. I only met him last night and he's away at work all day." Akasha lit another cigarette and explained the situation.

Xochitl's eyes widened with dawning understanding. "So you want to search for dead bodies and kiddie porn and stuff?"

Akasha nodded, relieved that she wasn't being paranoid. "I don't trust him. He acts way too nice."

"Well, I say we check out the basement first." Xochitl scampered back to her car and popped the hatchback.

Before Akasha could ask what she was doing, Xochitl emerged with a deadly looking rifle, complete with bayonet. Black and white spots obscured her vision as ice filled her lungs. Her friend's black trench coat was superimposed with the black uniform of her parents' killers.

"Xochitl, what the fuck? Why do you have a gun?" She sputtered, cringing against her will. "Put that thing away!"

"Dude, it's deer season." Ignoring her plea, Xochitl loaded the rifle with long, lethal bullets and slid on the shoulder strap, adjusting the gun on her back. "What's wrong, 'Kash? You look like I busted out an A-bomb. Chill. I passed hunter's safety four years ago, and if there's anything dangerous here, we're gonna need it."

Swallowing a lump in her throat, Akasha nodded. "Okay, but as soon as we're done with the basement, you gotta put it back."

"All right. But damn, I never would have thought you'd be so freaked out. We're in Idaho, for fuck's sake, and you're acting like some kind of—" Xochitl's rant ceased as they entered the house. "Holy wealth, Batman!"

Akasha chuckled at her friend's reaction, trying to ignore the rifle. "Okay, let's check out the basement first, then I can give you the full tour."

As they slowly made their way down the stairs, her body broke out in shivers at the way Xochitl pointed the gun forward like a trained sniper.

If she actually fires the thing, I swear I'll lose my shit.

Thankfully, the basement was fairly empty. Besides a bathroom and a few storage closets, it was mostly cavernous space with a lonely pool table in the corner.

"Sweet!" Xochitl pointed the rifle at the floor and unloaded it with an expert hand before returning it to her back. "You totally gotta get a dart board down here."

Akasha's nerves remained tense until the gun was back in the car. For the next half hour she showed Xochitl the rest of the house, smiling as her friend exclaimed over everything.

When they reached the office, Xochitl fired up the computer.

After at least ten minutes of clicking the mouse, she leaned back in the cushy office chair and swiveled around. "No porn, no freaky things in the search history, not even any funny YouTube videos. Just boring stock market stuff." Xochitl picked up a business card from the silver tray on the desk.

"McNaught Finances, LLC... yup, he sounds boring as hell, despite having a bitchin' sword collection. No offense, but I bet he became your guardian just to land a tax break or something. That's what my foster parents did."

"Hmm," Akasha murmured. Should she be disappointed or relieved?

Xochitl cocked her head to the side, looking like a curious cat. "Still don't trust him?"

She shrugged. "Nope." *A tax break? Yeah, right.*

"Why not?"

Akasha lit a cigarette, avoiding her gaze.

Xochitl lifted a brow, her silver piercing gleaming in the lamplight. "Is he hot?"

Heat rose up through her body, setting her cheeks on fire as the words he'd said danced through her mind. *I won't take you unless you ask me to.*

Xochitl's honey brown eyes widened. "Oh my God, he *is!*"

Akasha looked away and changed the subject. "How are you getting on with your foster parents... and everything else?"

Her friend immediately slumped like a kicked puppy. "They're horrible, 'Kash. All 'your soul better belong to Jesus, 'cause your ass belongs to me' kinda thing."

Guilt suffused Akasha down to the marrow of her bones. Guilt, and a fierce protective worry for her friend. "You be careful, Xoch'. Zealots can be dangerous. If they hurt you, I won't be averse to running away with you."

"I can't leave the band. Besides, I have less than a year before I'm eighteen." Xochitl shook her head. "So how do you know about zealots?"

Akasha sucked in a breath. It had been years since she'd told anyone about the horrific Mrs. Steele. "I lived under the dubious care of one once. She used to beat me and the others and half-starved us in the name of 'fasting.' The others were like dead-eyed drones. I took off before that could happen to me."

Xochitl gasped and placed a warm hand on hers. "Where'd you live after that?"

"A lot of places. Most not so great." Waving off her friend's curious look, she glanced at the clock. "Anyway, you better go before he gets back."

"Okay." As they plodded back downstairs, every vestige of Xochitl's hunched form screamed reluctance to return to her foster home. "You coming to the funeral tomorrow?"

"Fuck! I completely forgot." Another wave of wretched remorse choked her. "I'm sorry, Xoch' but yeah, I'll be there, I promise."

"It's okay. In the face of all this," she swept a gesture at the opulence around them, "one could forget anything."

Akasha stiffened as Xochitl hugged her goodbye, still unused to affection. As the sound of the Datsun's worn out engine and the stereo's wailing guitars faded, she made her way to the liquor cabinet.

"No beer," she grumbled, eyeing the bottles of expensive wine and scotch. "I so don't belong here."

Another twinge of guilt niggled in her heart. So far it seemed Xochitl had far more cause to complain. Her friend didn't belong with a pair of bible-thumping assholes either.

Chapter Five

Silas breathed a sigh of relief as he detected Akasha's Mark still in the house. Despite her hostility and suspicion, she'd remained under his roof. Every cell of his being longed to see her at once, but the blood thirst reigned supreme. He left his secret lair under the basement to hunt. A lad vandalizing the freeway overpass made a speedy meal.

As he walked up his driveway, an acrid smell broke through the perfume of autumn leaves. A small puddle of motor oil stained the concrete in front of the garage. Someone had been here. A low growl rumbled in his throat at the thought of an interloper.

His predatory instincts rose when he entered the house and detected a strange, alien scent. Whatever had been here had not been human. It reeked with power. The odor of gun oil further added to his worry.

Again, Silas reached out for Akasha's Mark. She was in the library, displaying no sign of distress. Fangs bared, he left her there to search the house for more signs of the intruder. The scent of it permeated every room, but it lay thickest in his office. The creature had spent some time on his computer. Though nothing was there of concern, he resented the invasion. What had it been looking for?

More interesting was Akasha's heavy scent all over his file cabinet. Silas's lips curved in a wry smile. Her mistrust had driven her to snoop, and the mysterious visitor appeared to have aided Akasha in the endeavor. Thankfully, one sense of the Mark upon Akasha implied that they failed to find his lair. Calmness radiated from her presence.

On his way downstairs, Silas pondered the evidence the visitor had left behind. Oil stains from an old car, fingerprints on his keyboard, and— he picked up a cigarette butt and a Red Bull can off the coffee table.

If not for the scent of inhuman power, he'd assume it had been one of her friends. Silas stopped in his tracks, remembering Delgarias's words. It *was* one of her friends.

"The daughter of Mephistopheles," he whispered in awe, quickening his pace to the library.

Akasha looked so content and cozy curled up by the fireplace that at first he was loath to disturb her. A light, whimsical smile played across her lips as she turned the pages of her book.

"Good evening," he said gently.

Still, she flinched. Her delicate features molded back to the usual cautious mask. Silas suppressed a sigh. She was like a feral cat. It would take endless patience and care to tame her.

Slowly, she closed her book and met his gaze. "Um, hi."

"You had a visitor today," he said carefully.

Those amethyst eyes narrowed. "How do you know?"

He held up the cigarette butt. "You don't smoke this brand. Also, my car doesn't leak oil, the last time I checked."

"Yeah, I had a friend over. Even poor little orphans like me have social lives. You got a problem with that?" Despite her attempt to sound glib, he could see her hands trembling.

"Not in the slightest, I assure you." Silas assured her. "I would not want you to be lonely when I am away."

Akasha eyed him quizzically, as if such consideration was alien to her. At first she seemed at a loss for words, then her lips curved in a sardonic smile. "We were checking to see if you were hiding dead bodies in the basement."

Ah, so that explains the smell of the gun. Silas couldn't help but grin. It seemed she was a practical lass. Raising his hand to cover his fangs, he laughed in delight that she at least had a sense of humor as well as the courage to tease him. "I certainly hope you didn't find any. My cleaning service would be quite upset."

For the longest time she gaped at him. Obviously she'd expected him to be vexed at her remark.

He laughed again. "Well, now that you know I'm not a serial killer, shall we go shopping?"

As she followed him into the garage, he once more observed the blatant admiration in her eyes as she looked at his car. *Would that she'd look at me like that.* A self deprecating smile curved his lips. *Jealous of a car? Perhaps I am mad after all.*

Akasha remained silent the entire drive despite his attempts to lure her into conversation. At the mall, he could see Akasha's skin prickling from the stares she received. Silas could well imagine what people were thinking as they ogled the bedraggled girl with the well-dressed man. Yes, a new wardrobe would be just the thing.

She picked out a few pairs of jeans, and with crimson cheeks, bras and underwear. Nothing pretty and feminine seemed to appeal to her. T-shirts depicting classic rock bands seemed to please her mightily, however, so Silas also bought her a music player and a gift card to load it up.

When he purchased a phone and handed it to her, she stared at it as if it was an artifact from another world. A pang of sympathy struck him. Most people her age were tethered to those things like a lifeline. She appeared to never have touched one.

Sparing her from admitting her ignorance, he asked if she were ready to depart.

Her voice shook as she looked up at him. "I need to get something formal. I'm supposed to   go to a funeral tomorrow."

Silas raised a brow. *What was this?* "Who died?"

"My friend's mom." Akasha held her breath, as if awaiting his protest.

The daughter of Mephistopheles, it has to be. Delgarias said her mother died recently. "Your friend... was this the one who visited?"

Akasha nodded solemnly. "Her name's Xochitl. We're both in the dual enrollment program at the college."

"Xochitl," Silas repeated. "A strange name... She had no other family? Poor girl." He was surprised to feel genuine pity for the creature. "Well, I daresay she'll need a lot of comfort. Will your other friends be there?" *The ones I am commanded to guard?*

Her eyes narrowed once more. "Yeah."

Silas opened his mouth, but shut it before his questions made her suspicious. "Very well then. You better wear your new coat tomorrow to the funeral. It's going to rain. Now, shall we go to dinner?"

Akasha let out an audible sigh of relief.

At dinner, she devoured her meal with unladylike haste. Rather than disgust, Silas once more felt sympathy. She had known starvation. He longed to offer her his plate as well. After all, he couldn't eat much of it, but he sensed the offer would offend her.

On the way home, he bought her a six pack of beer, joy infusing him at her pleasure with the offering. Once settled in the living room, Akasha almost warmed up to him as she opened her fourth can. Alas, he ruined it.

"Where did you live before the group home, Akasha?" *And who hurt you so badly?* He added silently.

"I told you, I don't want to talk about it," she snapped, rising to her feet. "If you ask me again, I swear I'll leave."

He blinked slowly and frowned. This threat would not do. "And go where? You're considered a minor under the state for the next four months. And I would have to report you missing or risk people thinking I did something nefarious." Fighting back dread at the prospect of losing her, he continued with bland logic. "Even if I did let you leave, wouldn't you end up in the same situation you were in when I found you? Or perhaps worse?"

Her eyes sparked in unmistakable fury. "So I'm fucking trapped, then." Her fists clenched, doubtless with the urge to punch him.

Silas nodded and remained firm. "I'm afraid you are, for now. But surely you can consider me the lesser of evils?"

She crushed her beer can with the flat of her hand. "That doesn't mean you have the right to interrogate me."

Before he could respond, Akasha fled to her room, tripping on the stairs. Silas sighed at the hostile retreat. She was nothing like he'd imagined her to be. It was bad enough that she seemed to loathe him, no matter how he tried to be kind to her, but the mystery surrounding her drove him mad.

Her file implied she held some tragic secrets, and Silas had been prepared to coax them from her, but in the face of such unnatural hostility, he suspected Akasha's story went much deeper than his worst imaginings.

***

Pisa, Italy

Selena, Lord Vampire of Pisa, lifted languid eyelids and rolled her head on her shoulders in a display of prophetic zeal. Her worshipers sighed in rapt devotion. She leaped to her feet, arms outspread, to address her audience.

"I have had a vision!" she shrieked, red tresses billowing. "The King has died in the world with twin moons as foretold. Rejoice! For soon the sun shall vanish and our promised land will be made ready for us!"

With deafening cheers, her subordinate vampires crowded forward, kneeling to kiss her feet. Selena basked in the adulation like a reptile upon a sunny rock.

She motioned for silence with a languid sweep of her hand. "Now let us pray." Raising her arms to the vaulted stone ceiling of her lair, she continued. "Oh, Mephistopheles, revered creator of us all, please feel our devotion and forgive us for the transgressions of our ancestors so we may be welcomed back into your almighty presence."

The Order of Eternal Night repeated the words solemnly, bowing their heads. Selena let them remain on their knees a while longer before bidding them to rise.

"Bring in the sacrificial vessels. We will now feast." Her command rang throughout the chamber.

The doors opened and ten terrified humans were led into the chamber. Selena licked her lips, reveling in the taste of their fear. She strutted around them with the discerning eye of a connoisseur. Her gaze fixed on a sultry Italian girl, jealousy burned through her skull at the human's youthful beauty. It would be a pleasure to destroy that one.

Selena took the quivering adolescent in her arms and gestured for her followers to commence feeding before sinking her fangs in the girl's throat. She swallowed the blood in greedy gulps, visualizing the youth and beauty of her victim rushing into her. When the blood ceased to flow, she thrust her hand into the body's rib cage and tore out its glistening heart. As she sucked the organ dry she recalled the vampire who had taught her the trick.

Oh, my beautiful Silas, she thought with a pang. *Why did you leave me?*

Selena had encountered the handsome Scot back in 1520. Her spies informed her that the vampire, Razvan Nicolae, had Changed another psychic in an attempt to find his brother. Selena made a habit of examining these fledglings when Razvan was finished with them in hopes of finding a link to an ancient text she'd acquired. It depicted a prophecy of another world.

Silas's powers had proved to be even more formidable than she'd anticipated. She'd wasted no time in seducing him and convincing him to join her in Italy. Unfortunately, the honeymoon ended shortly.

Selena's followers mocked the Scot's thick accent and she could tell Silas disapproved of them. He was disgusted with her human sacrifices as well. She couldn't comprehend why. Didn't he see that this was their divine right? She read to him the scrolls she'd stolen from the oldest vampire in the land.

They spoke of a world with two moons in which the sun would die. This would be a world in which vampires would thrive! Silas didn't see it that way.

"Selena," he'd said patiently. *"Dinna ye ken that a world would die with no sun? Tha crops would perish an' the people would starve. An' dinna ye see here where it says someone will bring back tha sun and lead our kind in a war?"*

"Exactly! We must find this so-called savior and stop them! Else we will be their puppet in a horrific war rather than living in peace in a nocturnal paradise."

To her dismay, Silas held firm in his conviction. Even worse, he did not experience any visions of their promised kingdom. Not even when she'd drugged him. Selena had watched eagerly as Silas collapsed on the chaise, thrashing and moaning. She fetched scribes with orders to document his ravings.

The scribes had written furiously as Silas convulsed and roared. *"Och! Ma bonny lass of raven curls... what is this? A carriage without horses? ...Such music! ...The angels are raging..."*

Disappointment had threatened to crush her where she stood. He'd said nothing about the other world or the prophecy, only garbled nonsense.

The next night he was gone.

After hours of raging and destroying everything in her room, Selena was convinced that Silas saw something of the prophecy and was going to seek it without her. She summoned her spies and set them to find Silas and report his doings to her.

For centuries, her suspicions bore no fruit. It appeared that McNaught truly was on a foolish quest for redemption. He traveled all over Europe and made fortunes just to give them away to pitiful humans. He stopped killing long before it was outlawed by the Elders, only taking enough blood to survive. Silas even used his feedings as a way to help humans. These days, he fed off of drunks and gave them money for taxis so they wouldn't endanger themselves and others by driving their automobiles. It was sickening. Still, Selena did not relax her surveillance...

"Your Holiness!" Michael, her favorite apostle, jolted her back into the present. "Your envoy has returned from America with momentous news."

"Send him in," she commanded.

Crushing the heart in her hand like a dried tomato, she dropped it on the stone floor.

The youngling rushed in and bowed so low his head touched the floor. "My lady, McNaught was visited by none other than Delgarias himself!"

Selena gasped. "I knew it! I knew he was involved with the prophecy all along! What else have you learned?"

"McNaught has done the strangest thing. He has Marked a mortal woman and taken her to live in his house."

Selena was ready to dismiss the news as another pathetic attempt by Silas to be a Good Samaritan. Then a memory gave her pause. "What does the girl look like?"

"Oh, her beauty cannot compare with yours," the youngling breathed.

"That is not what I asked." She waved an impatient hand. "What does she look like?"

"She is quite small, with curly black hair and purple eyes. She dresses like a boy so it was hard to discern her figure." The messenger looked at his feet. "She looks to be between seventeen and twenty."

Selena frowned. Silas had raved about a girl with dark curls... perhaps she had something to do with the prophecy. But how was she going to find out? Tugging a lock of her hair, she willed herself to concentrate. Suddenly, a wicked smile curved her lips. The youngling cringed.

The answer was surprisingly simple. Get him in trouble with the Elders. McNaught was a relatively new Lord, only having held the status for a century. If he lost his status, then a Lord as old as she could petition for his land and property and gain it with ease. It was time to renew good relations with Marcus, the Lord of Rome. Aside from the Thirteenth, Marcus was among the most powerful of the Elders.

"Return to the States and watch Silas closely." She commanded the spy. "As soon as he does something that could implicate him, let me know."

The youngling bowed again and scurried away. Selena licked the blood from her hands and cackled. Finally she would have her revenge.

Chapter Six

Akasha woke late. The funeral was due to start in less than two hours and she had no idea how she was going to get there. Xochitl likely assumed Silas would take her. She could kick herself for not asking for a ride yesterday.

"Fuck!"

She changed into her new outfit and struggled with the makeup as her mind raced. She could call a cab. Silas had given her money. That decided, she fumbled with the eyeliner —and poked herself in the eye.

"Fuck," she repeated, reaching for a wad of toilet paper to dab at her watering eyes.

A half hour later, Akasha looked dubiously at the mirror. At least after this first attempt she didn't look like a whore or a B-movie reject. It took another half hour to find a phone book and another ten minutes to figure out how her phone worked.

By the time she got hold of the cab company, she was told that it would be a forty-five minute wait because everyone was getting out of church. All the others she called said the same.

"Fuck, fuck, fuck!" she roared at the empty house.

She *had* to go to this funeral. She had to do it for Xochitl.

A glint of metal caught the corner of her eye.

A set of car keys hung from a hook on the wall next to the door to the garage. Furtively, she opened the door and sucked in a breath at the sight of Silas's glorious Barracuda crouching in the garage like a beautiful slumbering predator.

Akasha blinked in disbelief. Why did he leave his car behind? Did he carpool with a coworker or was he such a big-shot that he took a limo or something?

Unbidden, her fingers crept towards the keys.

Do I dare?

Desire and trepidation warred within her until she slumped against the wall and covered her eyes with a hand, blocking the distracting luxury surrounding her.

Well, it would serve McNaught right if she borrowed his car. She didn't ask him to take her out of the group home and throw her into an environment in which she had no idea what to do. Besides, he wasn't supposed to be back until evening. She could have the car back and he'd never know. The man didn't strike her as the type to obsessively check his odometer. But if Silas did find out, maybe he'd be so pissed that he'd relinquish his guardianship.

Akasha grasped the keys to the 'Cuda, her hands trembling with excitement. It seemed to whisper to her, beckoning her closer until she was powerless to resist its siren's call. A faint, tantalizing scent wafted out when she opened the door. Her cheeks heated. It was Silas's cologne. The leather creaked deliciously as she slid into the driver's seat. After she adjusted the seat so she could reach the pedals, she noticed the garage door opener clipped to the sun visor. It must be providence.

As the garage door opened, she pushed in the clutch pedal and turned the key. A soft moan of ecstasy escaped her lips at the sound of the roaring engine. It had been too long since she'd had the pleasure of being behind the wheel of such a beauty. The only thing better would be getting under its hood with a wrench in her hand.

The 'Cuda handled like the dream it was. It was agony to keep to the speed limit and not send the baby full-throttle across town. Instead, she slowly crawled down back roads, eyes flicking to the rear-view mirror for cops. Damn, she really needed to approach Silas about getting her license.

Too soon she arrived at the gates of Forest Cemetery, where Kerainne Leonine would at last be laid to rest. The burial had been delayed for nearly a month due to Xochitl's situation being dealt with. Akasha cursed the authorities for being so cruel.

As soon as she parked behind the long line of other cars, Akasha could see the wide stares of the funeral party. Her flesh prickled as she got out of the 'Cuda, feeling like an imposter in her chic black suit and shining pumps.

Shifting her attention to the coffin blanketed in flowers, a pang of sadness pierced her chest. Her parents had not received this honor. It was almost hard not to be jealous of Xochitl. At least she had a place to lay flowers in her mother's memory. Akasha would never know what the uniformed men did with the bodies of her parents. Guilt curled in her belly for such uncharitable thoughts and she turned to see how her friend was holding up.

Xochitl looked numb with grief. Tendrils of black and purple hair blew in her face and a raindrop dangled precariously from her silver eyebrow ring, but she did not brush either away. Xochitl's best friend, Sylvis, clung to her hand and gave Akasha a sad smile of greeting.

Aurora and Beau, Xochitl's other friends, stepped aside to make room for Akasha. Aurora placed a warm brown hand on Akasha's shoulder. Again she felt that strange, yet blissful feeling of *rightness.*

"I'm glad you could make it," Aurora whispered and shifted her umbrella to cover them both. "My parents want to take us out to an early supper afterwards. Can you come too?"

Akasha nodded and managed a small smile when Beau kissed her on the cheek. Unlike with other males, his touch didn't alarm her and not only because he was gay. His friendliness made her feel safe.

Xochitl and her group were practically joined at the hip. They had even formed a metal band with the bitchin' name, *Rage of Angels*. For the last three years, Akasha had watched them in the halls of school, envious longing filling her at the sight of their closeness. Watching Xochitl and Sylvis on the college campus bonding over their guitars had been even worse.

But once she befriended Xochitl, Akasha was welcomed into their inner circle. Never having friends before, she was terrified of doing something to destroy the band's regard.

When the service ended, Akasha stepped aside to allow the other mourners to console Xochitl. Bill and Susan, Xochitl's new foster parents, didn't appear to recognize Akasha from the group home. Bill kept darting hostile looks at the only black couple in attendance, which could only be Aurora's parents, while Susan's orange drawn-on eyebrows knit together as she sneered at everything with pious disapproval. Akasha shuddered as she saw the zealot's pyre burning in the woman's eyes. Only Mrs. Steele had been more frightening.

Beau sidled next to her, hazel eyes bright under burgundy bangs. "So where'd you get the new threads… and that hot ride?"

"I was assigned a legal guardian." Akasha looked down at her boots and shrugged. "Well, sort of."

A sassy voice cut in. "I hope he or she is a damn sight better than the pair Xochitl ended up with." Aurora's mom smiled at Akasha and continued in a warm Southern accent. "I'm Loretta Lee, Aurora's mama. You must be Akasha. Xochitl said she met you in that hell hole of a group home."

Akasha nodded in assent to both of Loretta's remarks. Silas may be the most confusing and frustrating man she'd ever met, but she was definitely better off with him rather than people like Bill and Susan. Loretta was returning Bill's sneer with a glare of her own when her husband, Daniel Lee introduced himself.

"We're taking Xochitl and the others out to Denny's. I hope you'll join us." Mr. Lee smiled in approval at Akasha's firm handshake.

Bill and Susan attempted to protest Xochitl's accompanying the Lees, but Loretta's firm insistence would tolerate no refusal. And when Sylvis's parents stepped in, the game was lost.

During dinner, everyone discussed Xochitl's mom. From the stories and descriptions, the late Kerainne Leonine must have been an angel. Akasha couldn't help but think it odd that a sweet preschool teacher had reared a hell-raiser like Xochitl alone. When Akasha had asked about her father, a guarded look crossed Xoch's face. *"Mom said he was a very bad man,"* she'd said quickly before dropping the subject.

Akasha picked at her food as she struggled to recall her own mother's face. Afterwards, the parents left them to drink coffee and talk amongst themselves with the admonition to be home by eight since it was a school night.

When they left, Beau set down his cup and fixed his gaze on Akasha. "Okay, I've had enough of this grief for now. Let's talk about you. So spill. Xoch' told us about your millionaire guardian."

Akasha nodded. "He's more like a glorified roommate. And he's hardly ever around." Looking down at her coffee and trying not to squirm in the booth, she told them about Silas and his confusing generosity.

"Still," Aurora said as she drummed her silverware, "that's fucked up, since you're nineteen. You should be on your own... and buying us cigarettes."

"Yeah, well..." Akasha trailed off, warmed that Xochitl apparently told her friends the truth about her age and they actually believed her.

Beau leaned forward, his tousled hair gleaming under the table lamp. "Is he hot? When do we get to meet him and see this fancy castle?"

"I don't know." Akasha's breath caught as another result of her new situation struck her.

In the group home she had to sneak out to see her friends, but no more. Silas had made that clear. Now she could see them whenever she wanted, in fact, she now had a bitchin' place where they could all hang out. She smiled as she pictured the polished and sophisticated Silas McNaught's reaction to *Rage of Angels*. Doubtless he would turn his nose up in disapproval.

Sylvis glanced up from the dessert menu, the blue lettering matching the shade of her spiky hair. "Did he buy you that car too?"

Akasha laughed. "I wish. I'm just borrowing it from him." A pang of shame at the lie surprised her as she prattled on. "I wish I could get under the hood. It's in dire need of a tune up and a new clutch."

Aurora's ebony eyes widened. "No shit, you can fix cars?"

Akasha nodded and smiled at her impressed tone.

"She totally can! That's what she's gonna major in at the college next year." Xochitl exclaimed. "Maybe sometime you can finally look at Little Beast. You heard her. She literally goes, 'put-put-put.' That can't be good, right?"

"No, probably not. I'd be happy to look at her any time," Akasha replied, eager to help.

For the next hour, the band listened raptly as Akasha related diagnostic theories on Xochitl's Datsun. Their admiring gazes were a revelation and she didn't want the day to end.

As if the thought invoked a bad omen, she realized that dusk had fallen and Silas would likely be on his way home any minute.

"Oh shit, I gotta go!" Ignoring her friends' raised brows, she fled from the diner, heart hammering.

All of her bravado fled like autumn leaves. She did *not* want Silas to catch her borrowing his car.

Chapter Seven

Silas stared at his empty garage in disbelief. After only two days, Akasha was gone. To add insult to injury, she took his car. He frowned. Nothing in her file indicated she knew how to drive. Pulling his phone out of his pocket, he called her number with little hope that she'd answer. Its ring blared from the kitchen. He picked it up and scrolled through the recent calls before dialing the numbers in the memory. All three were cab companies. He was slightly mollified that her theft had been a last resort. But why hadn't she taken a taxi? He'd given her plenty of money.

Hoping she hadn't gotten far, Silas opened his mind to the Mark between them. It flared to life, strong and close. She was near. Although he wanted to go after her right away, the blood thirst roared within him. He couldn't face her until after he fed.

His phone bleeped the announcement of an incoming text message. Silas read it and cursed. He'd forgotten all about tonight's appointment with one of his subordinates. Being that it was the beginning of a new financial quarter, he couldn't afford to cancel it, especially at a half hour's notice. The hunger made its presence known again, surging at him with a vengeance. Fortunately, the trotting footsteps of a nearby jogger pricked his sensitive ears. He went outside, salivating as he could hear the jogger's laboring breath. A person had to be insane to use this steep hill for exercise and in the dark, at that.

In a flash of preternatural speed, he was on his victim. The man's sweat was bitter on his tongue and the high amount of protein and vitamins in his blood, though no doubt nutritious, had a faint medicinal taste unlike the sweetness of the drunks he usually fed from.

"Are you all right?" he asked the man once he'd healed the wound and cleared the jogger's memory.

"Yeah, I just got a little dizzy," the man panted.

"This hill is awfully steep for jogging," Silas admonished. His mind reached out to touch Akasha's Mark.

She hadn't moved. *Had the car broken down?* He tried to remember how much gas was left in the tank.

By the time McNaught returned to his house, his subordinate was on the porch waiting for him.

"Good evening, Jonas," Silas struggled to be polite, though he was gnashing his teeth in impatience. *Where is Akasha? Why did she leave me?*

Jonas shrank at his tone, clutching his briefcase as if he wanted to use it as a shield. "I'm sorry I'm late, my lord."

Silas shook his head. "It's not you. I am vexed with another matter. Please, come inside." He forced a smile. "I think you'll be pleased with your third quarter earnings and I have some suggestions for future investments."

As Jonas sat at the dining room table and opened his briefcase, Silas headed up to his office to fetch his laptop. No doubt Akasha would be infuriated when he came to collect her. And just how he would go about bringing her back, he did not know.

Ten minutes into his meeting, the unmistakable sound of his car came to his ears. Moments later, he heard the garage door opening. Relief flooded him along with a twinge of annoyance at her for taking his car.

"My lord?" Jonas inquired, darting a curious glance towards the door.

Silas waved a dismissive hand and turned his attention back to the figures, resuming his report. He hid a smile as he heard Akasha curse as she shut the car door. No doubt she'd hoped her temporary theft had gone undetected.

***

"Fuck," Akasha muttered again as she got out of the car. It was long past dark and Silas was bound to be waiting for her. Still, maybe he wasn't. Maybe he'd gone on a long business trip and hadn't yet returned.

Her meager hope died the second she got in the house. Silas's glittering emerald eyes met hers with a look that said he knew everything. But she couldn't tell if he was pissed or not. A movement in the corner of her eye caught her attention. Silas had company. A man in a business suit froze with one hand on his briefcase, staring at her. She glared at him until he flushed and dropped his gaze. A measure of gratitude for his presence brought a smile to her lips. It would put off the confrontation. She turned to head up to her room, but Silas stopped her with a gesture.

"Akasha, would you please remain here for a few minutes? I would like to speak with you when I am finished with this meeting." His tone was bland, professional, and infuriatingly impossible to decipher.

She shrugged helplessly and hung the keys back on their hook. "Okay." If she refused, she'd look like a bitch in front of the other guy. Now his presence was irritating.

Both men watched her as she passed them and went to the kitchen to get a beer. As she twisted the cap off the bottle on her way to the living room, Silas resumed his conversation with his guest.

He pointed at his laptop screen. "If you look at these figures, you will see that these management companies have averaged a fifteen percent return on their accounts, with the highest earning thirty percent."

"Well, why don't you put my money with one of them?" the man asked.

"It is better to diversify your investments, if you can." Silas leaned forward, grabbing a piece of paper and sliding it between them. "Now, if you move about thirty thousand from here and put it with this company, the risk would be relatively low and the chance of profit would be at reasonable levels."

Akasha was fascinated despite herself. *If I could invest something at fifteen percent I'd make a fortune!* She lit a cigarette and struggled to hide her rapt attention. Silas's client kept darting curious looks at her until she felt like standing up and screaming, *"What the fuck are you looking at?"*

Silas had ignored her presence up until then. "All right, Jonas, I think we have everything covered until next quarter."

"Yes, M—"

Silas gave him a sharp look and slightly inclined his head towards Akasha.

"Yes, Mr. McNaught," Jonas flinched and gave her another nervous glance.

Akasha frowned. *What the hell was that?* It sounded as if Jonas was about to call Silas "master" or "my lord" or some other subservient term.

With narrowed eyes, she watched Jonas scoop up his papers and stuff them quickly into the briefcase, cringing at Silas as if he expected a reprimand. The guy actually bowed when he left.

Now she was alone with Silas. The air suddenly charged with tension. Akasha tried to hide her shiver of trepidation with a swig of beer.

Her new guardian closed his laptop and met her gaze, his eyes still unreadable. "What were you doing with my car?" he asked softly.

Akasha knew she should apologize, but she had a perverse desire to see this calm, unshakeable businessman get angry. She wanted to see that cool façade shaken up.

"I told you, I had to go to a funeral," she snapped. Unbidden, her voice softened. "I was running too late to hire a cab because I couldn't figure out that damn phone you bought for me."

Silas stood up and stalked over to her. "Ye should have told me that ye were needing a ride to the funeral." A husky brogue crept into his voice. "I would ha' arranged transportation for ye." His green eyes seemed to glow, but then an odd shadow passed over his gaze, sending heat through her belly. "I had thought ye ran away."

"You're from Scotland!" she exclaimed, finally placing the accent.

"Doon change tha' subject, lass." He sounded like Scrooge McDuck on a 'roid rage. "An' last time I checked, ye needed a license to be driving a car. Why, if ye'd been stopped by the police, no doot I would ha' been nearly beggared paying for your bail and the impound fees."

The sudden pang of guilt that struck Akasha was infuriating. "That's what you get for taking me here and fucking up my plans. And by the way," she retorted, "you should take better care of your car. The 'Cuda needs a new clutch and it's badly in need of a tune up. It's practically sacrilege for you to neglect such a beauty."

Silas's eyes narrowed, ignoring her words. "What do ye mean I upset your plans? Had ye planned tae run away from the group home?"

Sucking in a breath at his intent gaze, she murmured, "No."

His face was a study of confusion. "Well then what did I ruin for ye? Ye cannot tell me ye were happy in that place." His voice grew hard and cold. "I willna' tolerate lies."

Akasha hid a shiver and rolled her eyes at his stupidity. "No, it sucked there, but as a ward of the state I qualified for financial assistance with the dual enrollment program and would have gotten grants for college next year. Now they'll go off of your income and I won't get shit. Hell, I'll probably get kicked out of the program and have to finish my diploma at the high school with the rest of the jerks there."

To her fury, Silas laughed. "Oh, is that all? Your dual enrollment is already paid for. And, I will pay for your college if that's where you're wanting to go." His accent faded. "Now what do you plan to study?"

"Automotive and Business Management. I want to own my own shop," Akasha blurted without thinking. Her fists clenched in annoyance that he got her off the subject. "But that's not the point. At least at the group home I knew what to expect." Her voice rose against her will. "Now, I'm living under the roof of a complete stranger in a place where I don't belong, and—"

"You don't think you're worthy of nice things?" Silas asked softly.

Akasha nearly growled, continuing her rant. "If you think you can buy my approval, or make me *like* you, or whatever, you got another thing coming. I—"

Silas held up a hand. "I think, as things stand, I am indulging you at my own pleasure. Now what is it you were saying about my car? It needs a..." His hand dropped and he shrugged helplessly.

"Clutch," Akasha finished. "And when's the last time you changed the oil?" Her eyes narrowed in accusation as she continued. "Or the plugs, the wires, the filters, and all that stuff?"

"I had it looked over when I bought it two years ago."

She nearly choked in outrage. "Two *years*? I would never let it go that long! Why did you buy such a valuable car if you won't take care of it?"

He shrugged. "I thought it looked nice."

"*Nice?*" Akasha's mind swam with baffled outrage at his nonchalance. "Do you know how many people would give their right arm for a car like that? Damn, you think you can just buy anything you want without even understanding it, don't you?"

Silas's drowning green gaze met hers as he studied her long and intently. "I think you may be right."

Somehow she got the feeling he wasn't only referring to the car. An odd shiver ran through her body. "I am?"

He ran a hand through his silken black hair, suddenly looking tired and pensive. "Yes, so how about we see to the car now?"

Akasha's heart ached with desire to get under the hood of the Barracuda and get it into its best running condition. Timidly, she offered, "I could take care of it for you, if you'd like."

Silas gave her another long considering look that made her squirm. "I thought that was a man's profession."

Akasha glared at him. "You turn a wrench with your hand, not your dick." Before he could recover from her words, she asked, "So are you going to let me fix it, or not? Because if I'm going to do this, I need tools."

He laughed, walked to the door, and grabbed his keys. "Very well. I suppose we may as well go fetch what is needed now. I trust you know where such wares are sold?"

Two hours later they were back in Silas's garage with over two thousand dollars worth of tools and car parts. Akasha had no idea what the hell happened. Who had won the argument? But then the 'Cuda's hood was open and she had a wrench in her hand at last, so she was too happy to give a shit.

Chapter Eight

Silas watched in awe as Akasha operated on his car like a master surgeon. Where had she learned such a skill? *Certainly not at the group home.* He longed to ask her but held back, not wanting to see her eyes darken again with pain and hostility. For once she seemed at ease with him, alternating between lecturing him on his neglect of vehicle maintenance and commanding him where to point the flashlight. She'd even smiled when the tools had been placed in her hands. The curve of her lips and the dimples in her cheeks took his breath away. It seemed he found the key to her happiness.

"I don't like the look of this fuel filter," Akasha said, so close to him, he could feel her breath on his ear. "Could you step back a little and shine the light a bit more to the left?"

Silas pointed the beam where she directed. Now her curved backside was turned enticingly toward him, awakening his loins with a torturous vengeance. Her feminine scent, mingled with the smell of oil and tobacco tormented his senses. Silas ran his tongue along his fangs and took a deep shuddering breath. After centuries of experiencing her embrace in his visions, it was maddening not to touch her.

Akasha held one end of the filter to her nose and sniffed. Her nose wrinkled at the rancid odor. "It might just be old gas that made this orange residue. I was afraid your tank was rusted." She tapped her wrench against her hip, oblivious to the mess accumulating on her new slacks. "Still, I'm going to double check after you go through two full tanks. Could you grab the new filter?"

Silas straightened up to see to her request. Akasha's hand came down on his back so hard and fast that it knocked his breath out and he almost dropped the flashlight.

"Be careful! You almost clocked your head on the hood." Her eyes were wide and dark purple with obvious concern.

"Thank you," he gasped, slack-jawed in astonishment. The strength she had imparted in holding him down was immense, impossible.

Akasha snatched her hand back as if it had been burned. "Um... the filter is in that small box with the blue logo." The longing on her face, begging for him to ignore what had just happened was as apparent as the crimson blush on her cheeks from their brief physical contact.

Silas decided to honor her unspoken request and fetched the fuel filter. It seemed Akasha had yet another secret for him to unlock, but he would leave her be for the time being. For now it was enough to watch that becoming blush and revel in her nearness as she worked. Unbidden, his gaze traveled over her exquisite form bent over the car and his cock stirred once more. *Ah, but this was sweet torment.* He thanked the fates above that his jacket covered the bulge in his trousers.

As he handed her the filter, holding back a sigh as his hand brushed her skin, Akasha's eyes met his tentatively. "I didn't... hurt you, did I?" she asked carefully.

"No," Silas said. "You startled me. That's all. Now where shall I point the light?"

Her sigh of relief was nearly inaudible. "Over here."

They worked together in silence until Akasha had installed every new part they were able to acquire. The clutch would have to wait until it was shipped from another store back east. By the time they finished, Silas was in a state of painful arousal. When Akasha wrapped her lips around the opening of a beer bottle, he nearly groaned in agony.

"I am going to go for a walk." His voice shook with need. Perhaps if he fed again, it would abate a fraction of his lust. "Thank you so much for the work you've done on my car. I shall have to get you one of your own when you get your license."

He left before she could reply. The chilly October air did little to cool his ardor. With shock, he realized that it hadn't been that much warmer in the garage with Akasha. The heat between them had been too great for either to notice.

Silas let out a growl of frustration. He longed to cover Akasha's lips in devouring kisses and hold that delectable rear of hers as he plunged his shaft deep inside her sweetness. But for now it was not to be.

He had no idea what made her eyes narrow in suspicion every time he offered her a kindness. Her past must be terrible enough to have damaged her spirit. And he knew that if he made the slightest advance towards her, she would be gone and he would be lucky to escape without a knife wound... or crushed by her unnatural strength. He'd have to be very careful around her.

When he arrived at the nearest tavern, Silas wasted no time in selecting his victim. But the bar fly's blood and the cloying odor of her perfume did nothing to banish the memory of Akasha's sweet scent. Nor did his brisk walk home. Thankfully, the house was dark when he returned and a quick check on his Mark told him Akasha was upstairs getting ready for bed.

Silas stalked up to his office and grabbed his sword from the wall. The ancient Claymore gleamed at him in the moonlight from the windows. Perhaps some exercise would do him good.

***

Akasha tossed and turned in bed as her mind raced. She couldn't stop thinking about the enigma that was Silas McNaught. Why did he bring her here? He'd kept to his word and not made any unwelcome advances towards her and he was truly gone from dawn to dusk. She borrowed his car without permission and was rewarded rather than punished. More confusing was that he spoke to her like an equal, yet he'd treated his client like a subordinate.

She sighed and tried to push the thoughts away. *What do I care as long as I get to work on that beautiful car!*

A reluctant smile tugged at her lips. For a businessman, Silas knew how to aim a flashlight well. Maybe he could assist her in adjusting the clutch linkage when the time came. At least then he wouldn't be in danger of hitting his head.

Her smile vanished and her heart jumped a moment as she remembered stopping him earlier. Had he realized her abnormal strength? At first, from his gaping expression, it seemed like it. But then he hadn't said anything and they'd gone back to work as if everything were normal. Her pulse eased. He must not have noticed.

As her trepidation faded, Akasha couldn't stop remembering the feel of hard muscle under the fabric of Silas's jacket and the faint scent of his cologne when he stood next to her. When his silken hair had brushed her cheek, she'd shivered, but not in fear. Strangely, she hadn't noticed that it was cold in the garage until he left for his walk... She forced the thought away.

It seemed Silas went on a lot of walks. Maybe he had OCD or something.

Akasha shifted around on the bed a while longer before she gave up and kicked the blankets aside. Maybe a cigarette would help her relax. She pulled on her robe, grabbed her smokes, and went out on her balcony.

Before she struck her lighter, a movement from below made her freeze. Silas was in the backyard, shirtless and wielding a sword. Her breath caught. She felt as if she was struck in the chest by a ball peen hammer. His body was not the typical soft form carried by most businessmen. No, this was hard steel masculinity displayed in the bright moonlight.

Though it was so cold that the ground was crunchy with frost and Silas's breath came out in puffy clouds, a fine sheen of sweat glistened on his smooth muscular chest. He thrust the massive weapon with such controlled strength she could tell he was an expert. What the hell was a finance guy doing with a sword? The thought ceased as she watched the sweat trail down one hardened nipple to run down his flat stomach. She gasped as warmth flooded between her legs.

Was this what Xochitl called "lady wood?" Akasha's cheeks heated. Because of her traumatic past, she'd never been sexually aroused before. But now, at the sight of this Scottish wet dream, her core throbbed and pulsed with its own inner life.

Silas looked up, and their eyes met for one eternal moment. The breath fled from Akasha's body as electric heat flared between them. The world tilted as she stumbled backward. At the last second, she caught herself on the balcony's support beam and fled back to her room with her face flaming.

Chapter Nine
Phoenix, Arizona

Agent Holmes listened with rapt fascination as Francis Milbury related the story behind the missing mutant woman.

In 1979, a cell mutating serum was invented. When injected into chimpanzees, it gave them quicker reflexes, greater endurance, resistance to disease and extreme temperatures... and incredible strength. The U.S. military was elated. They could create the perfect soldier. Eager to see the effects of the serum in action, a squad of troops bound for the Gulf War was injected. At first the results were optimistic. The squad had the highest kill count, succeeded in the most difficult ambushes, and arrived fast to rendezvous points.

Unfortunately, another side effect evinced itself. The injected soldiers also developed heightened intelligence and became too independent. They refused to follow orders, preferring to do things their own way. Many refused to kill civilians when necessary. It was decided that the project would be terminated. The soldiers were sent on suicide missions and those that survived met with "accidents." But, to the military's chagrin, one soldier went AWOL and could not be found.

Private Jamison Lindsey remained missing long after the war, despite fervent attempts to locate him. It was discovered he'd been in Ireland and married a local girl by the name of O'Reilly, but they'd left the country several years prior.

Finally Lindsey was found in the Colorado National Forest, using his wife's last name. They had a daughter, which was a shock because the injected men were supposed to be sterile. This child needed to be studied.

Orders went out to terminate the couple and secure the child. The first part of the mission was a success. The second: a failure. Somehow, an eight year old girl had escaped four of the government's top assassins.

Holmes let out a low whistle. "And you say they never found any leads?"

"Inquiries were made at every orphanage and convent in the surrounding areas. No children by the name O'Reilly or Lindsey was found. The man in charge at the time quit looking then. He'd assumed she died in the woods, either killed by an animal or dead from exposure, though a body was never recovered, only a scrap of bloody fabric from her coat." Milbury leaned back in his chair and ran a hand through his silver buzz cut. "But when I took over the case and read through the file, I had a hunch that she was still alive and at large."

Holmes nodded. Hunches were his bread and butter. "Did they try looking for her by her first name?"

Milbury shook his head. "We don't know it. If there'd been a birth certificate, we would have caught Lindsey right away and avoided this whole mess. The only way we knew his daughter's age was because we found eight candles next to the remainder of the birthday cake."

"What about the forest rangers," Joe asked. "Did any of them see anything?"

From the Major's startled look, it was obvious no one in the department had considered the option. Typical military arrogance, Holmes thought with a wry grin.

"Damn it!" Francis pounded his fist on the arm of the chair. "I'll bet they didn't think to ask since the perimeter was secured. But if the girl had gotten far enough and a ranger had picked her up..." he trailed off and pulled out his phone. "I need to make some calls."

***

Dread filled Akasha as Coeur d'Alene High School came into view. When she got into the dual enrollment program, she thought she'd escaped its blue and white halls for good. But Xochitl and Sylvis insisted they pick up Beau and Aurora every day for lunch.

So once more she found herself walking through the clique-filled cafeteria, feeling more like a fraud than before in her new clothes.

The cheerleaders tossed their blonde hair and tittered as Akasha willed herself not to knock their teeth in. Then Xochitl approached them, resplendent in black lipstick and a spiked collar.

She fixed the head cheerleader with a potent stare and began to chant in an eerie melodic language.

The girl turned a ghastly shade of grayish white and fled with her followers.

"Thanks, Xoch'." Akasha smiled gratefully. "Did you just try and cast a spell on that cheerleader?" She didn't believe in magic, but wanted to see if her friend was gullible enough to.

Xochitl laughed and tossed back her waist length black and purple hair. Her silver eyebrow ring seemed to glint mischievously "No. I told her in Chinese that her tits look lopsided and maybe she should ask her daddy to buy her better implants next time. It's what she believes that matters. That's how voodoo works n' stuff."

Akasha gasped. "No shit, you speak Chinese?" Every new facet Xochitl displayed was astounding.

Beau plopped down next to Akasha and began to play with her hair. "And Spanish, German and Latin. Her mom could speak even more languages."

Xochitl's eyes darkened with pain at the mention of her mother before she changed the subject. "So, what were the bimbos worked up about this time?"

Akasha gently extracted her curls from Beau's grasp. "My new jeans, if you can believe it. I don't get it."

"I can't believe those assholes are fucking with you 'cuz you got a new guardian." Aurora shook her head, making the silver beads in her braids clink like tiny wind chimes.

"I can." Sylvis rolled her eyes. "People aren't supposed to get out of their assigned roles. First, I know they hate it that we get to go to college early and they don't. Also, it probably makes the rich kids sick that a poor orphan is suddenly on 'their level.'"

Beau nodded, hazel eyes twinkling. "That, and they're jealous."

"Jealous?" Akasha spluttered. "Where the fuck do you get that idea?"

He laughed. "Oh, honey, you're so precious. Do you ever look in the mirror? Those bitches could overlook it when you were poor, but now..." he grinned. "We so need to take you shopping and get some sexy outfits to throw in their faces."

Akasha's cheeks heated. Did Silas think she was beautiful? She thrust the thought away. "I just got a shit-load of new clothes."

Beau waved a dismissive hand. "I said 'sexy clothes,' not stuff like you wear all the time. Granted, those jeans are fabulous."

Xochitl nodded. "They are, and you're short enough that I could totally steal 'em. Anyway, come smoke with us, 'Kash."

Akasha pasted on a wan smile and followed the Goths. Shouts of, *"Freaks" "Satan worshippers"* and *"Fag!"* accompanied the five on their way outside. Akasha saw Beau's shoulders tense at the last insult. *Why the hell do kids have to be so cruel?*

They piled into Xochitl's battered blue 1980 Datsun 210. Xoch' hadn't been kidding. The engine really did putter. It probably only ran on three cylinders. Akasha frowned and dug out her pack of Camels. *I gotta run a compression test on this poor baby, ASAP.*

Everyone but Sylvis lit up the second the car pulled out of the school parking lot. Sylvis had a newspaper with the classified section open on her lap and was skimming the ads, highlighter in one hand, and a bag of Skittles in the other.

"How about this one?" she mumbled through a mouthful of candy. "Commercial building on Northwest Boulevard: $600 a month. That's a nice deal!"

Xochitl sighed. "You forget. I'm between jobs now. Burger Hut fired me because they didn't want to give me time off for Mom's funeral. 'Right to Work state' my ass."

"Those assholes!" Akasha roared, carefully flicking her cigarette ashes into an empty Red Bull can. "Why do you want to rent a building?"

Aurora turned to her and flicked her cigarette in the can. "We need to find a new place to practice our music. Our lease ran out on our old place, but the building was condemned anyway... and haunted."

"Yeah, but that part was fun!" Xochitl grinned at her in the rearview mirror. "You shouldda been there 'Kash! It was this creepy old church and there was a freezing cold place in the bell tower that kept our drinks cold even in the summer and..."

As Xochitl chattered away, Akasha took a deep drag of her cigarette as an idea occurred to her. The band needed a place to practice and Silas had a huge garage... and he wasn't even around most of the time. If they could use it, they'd be so happy.

"Hey guys," she said, eager to repay the kindness her friends had shown her. "Don't sign any leases until tomorrow. I may have an idea."

***

When Akasha approached Silas in his office to ask if her friends could use his garage to practice their music, it was all he could do not to grin in triumph. The opportunity to begin fulfilling Delgarias's request had literally fallen into his lap. He'd been agonizing on how to broach the subject of Akasha's friends without the lass getting suspicious and defensive.

He leaned back in his chair and fixed his expression into one of mild interest as she stumbled awkwardly over her request, obviously unused to wheedling a man. With those delicious lips and sparkling eyes, God help him if she ever learned feminine wiles.

"It's not like they'd be in the way, since you're not around much," Akasha finished, shifting back and forth on her toes, barely meeting his gaze.

Silas couldn't hide his pleased smile any longer. "How noble you are to ask for something for others rather than yourself."

A bright blush tinged her cheeks, like dawn's light on freshly fallen snow. "Well, I just thought…" she trailed off.

"But the garage will likely be too cold soon, even with the space heater," he began. Akasha's face fell in disappointment. Her succulent lower lip thrust out and he longed to take it in his mouth like a ripe cherry. Silas took a deep breath and forced his focus back on the subject. "I think it would be better if they used the basement."

Akasha blinked as she digested his words. "Really? Thank you. What made you decide to get such a huge place anyway?"

Silas chuckled and looked around at the elaborate setting he had provided just for this woman who'd haunted his visions for centuries. "You wouldn't believe me if I told you."

"Well, okay." She shrugged. "I'll invite them over tomorrow, after the Halloween kegger." Her gaze leveled on him. "They're kinda weird, but really nice."

"And who will be driving you home from this kegger?" Silas asked with a dangerous note to his voice that promised ill if her answer was unsatisfactory.

"Xochitl's driving Aurora's van. She doesn't like beer, so she'll be sober," she said, undaunted. "Chill, we're not stupid."

Silas frowned. That may be, but it wouldn't stop him from checking on her all the same.

Chapter Ten

"Lord McNaught, do I have your permission to start a business in your territory?" the vampire repeated.

Silas had to fight to keep his attention on the petitioner, anxious to get his first glimpse of Akasha's friends before they arrived here for the evening. He regretted setting this appointment, but his responsibilities as Lord of the City couldn't be ignored without dire consequences. Every vampire wanting to reside in his territory must be completely checked out and Silas had to make his rules clear at the offset. Punishments must be doled out immediately to those who disobeyed, for if he lost control there were plenty of other powerful vampires who wouldn't hesitate to swoop down and snatch this city for themselves.

"I do think a doctor would be useful here. Greenbriar, was it?" Silas finally replied.

The doctor nodded. "Yes, my lord. Please, call me Jonathon."

"And your former Lord is fine with your leaving?"

"Not only do I have her writ of permission," the vampire reached into his breast pocket, "but she also included a letter of recommendation."

Silas read both impatiently. "Very well, Jonathon." He handed him a packet of papers. "Here's your contract of residence with the laws of my territory, my listings of properties for rent and my loan information if you need funds to get a start. I'll see you tomorrow when you've read and signed everything. I apologize, but I must conclude this interview. I have another pressing matter to see to."

The minute Jonathon was out the door Silas went outside and opened his mind to the Mark between him and Akasha. As he got into the car, he felt her a few miles southeast.

He was on a dirt road past the lake and near the Fernan Saddle when he saw the light of the bonfire and heard the music. Silas pulled over and walked the rest of the way, not wanting to be seen. As he drew closer to the party, he sensed the presence of something not human... and not vampire either. It could be none other than the daughter of Mephistopheles. McNaught peered through the trees and saw a mass of young people indulging in drunken debauchery that he hadn't enjoyed for five centuries. Two boys held the legs of another as he drank from a keg upside down. Silas chuckled, remembering doing just that from a barrel of ale.

His heart gave a pang of longing as he spotted Akasha, standing near a crudely erected stage, drinking beer and watching a group of musicians perform. Drums sounded and a demonic scream rent the air.

Goose bumps rose up on the vampire's skin as a power prickled the air. The creature on the stage with the black and purple hair was the inhuman presence: Xochitl, the daughter of the creator of vampires. She stood before the microphone, playing a guitar with expert fingers and singing with the most beautiful voice he'd ever heard, punctuating the song with screams of rage. Power thrummed through her, the likes of which he'd never felt.

As Silas's gaze traveled over her and the other musicians, a premonition hit him.

This is supposed to be, an inner voice announced. *They and their music will shape your destiny and those of many worlds.* That insistent voice unnerved him far worse than his visions, for it came so rarely.

The vampire's breath caught at the sounds of the music. He'd never before cared for heavy metal music, but the way these four combined rhythms and melodies could have made Mozart weep. They had great talent at such tender ages. *How much is learned, and how much is the destiny that binds them?* Silas could almost see the lines of power linking the group. Xochitl looked ethereally beautiful up on stage; her jet black and purple hair flowed in the wind, her eyes molten amber in the firelight. The other three were an impressive sight with all the passion they displayed.

Silas watched the performance, periodically looking at Akasha who appeared to be just as amazed. The other revelers danced with abandon, oblivious that powerful magic was at work here. The song ended and he had to fight to keep from applauding with the rest of the audience.

A boy stumbled near his hiding spot to urinate, so he had to back away.

When he found another vantage point the band had exited the stage, put away their instruments and joined Akasha.

"You guys were fucking incredible!" Her amethyst eyes sparkled.

The bass player had his arm around Akasha as other girls began to swarm him. Silas bared his fangs. How dare that messy-haired brat touch her! It was all he could do not to leap forward and pull her into his arms.

"Hey! You lookin' at me fag?" A Goliath of a boy in a letterman jacket approached the bass player.

The bassist rolled his eyes. "No, I don't do jocks, jackass."

"What'd you call me?" The jock grabbed the boy, towering over him and emanating menace.

Akasha grabbed the assailant, lifted him in the air and threw him. He crashed into a group of other boys in matching jackets.

How in God's name did she do that? The lad outweighs her by at least a hundred pounds! Silas froze, remembering her unnatural strength the night they tuned up his car. *So I didn't imagine it then.*

"You fuck with Beau, you fuck with me," Akasha growled, turning Silas's attention back to the fight.

A crowd gathered, cheering at the entertainment. Xochitl and the other two girls leapt into the fray. Beau didn't need Akasha's help. Though he was small and wiry, the lad held his own just fine, fists flying into the faces of his attackers and jumping back up when he took a blow. To the vampire's further astonishment, Xochitl and the blue-haired guitar player both appeared to be skilled in hand to hand combat. After a few lightning-quick hits and roundhouse kicks their enemies avoided them completely. Their opponents tried to help their comrade fight Beau, but Xochitl and her friend wouldn't let them near.

Akasha and the drummer were at the far end of the circle of spectators. The drummer straddled her opponent, bashing his head on the ground until he begged for mercy. Akasha was being careful with her enemy, only shoving him away and dodging his blows. She didn't deliver a single punch, obviously careful not to display her inhuman strength again.

Finally, the attackers gave up and left the party with a parting shot from the leader.

"You'll pay for this, freaks. I'll get you all!"

"I just don't understand why that asshole thinks I want his body," Beau said with a dramatic sigh. "He's totally not my type. I like my boys with a little more brains."

"He's probably hung like a squirrel," Xochitl replied with a dismissive shrug.

Silas nearly choked, holding back his laughter as he headed back to his car. Xochitl may be a powerful creature, but that made her no less a rambunctious youth.

***

Three weeks later

They were loud. Silas looked at the clock and buried his face in his hands in a futile effort to dim the sound of Aurora's drums. The sun would not set for another hour, but Akasha's friends had yet again awakened him early with their raucous music.

His efforts to charm the four had worked too well. For the past few weeks, it seemed *Rage of Angels*, as they called themselves, had practically moved in. The basement—

inconveniently above his hidden sleeping quarters— was now a veritable haven for the group, when they weren't working as his new cleaning service.

Silas smiled. It had been so easy to get them under his thumb. One would think Delgarias had planned it that way.

Despite their unruly music and morbid taste in clothing, Akasha's eccentric friends were better mannered than the average adolescents. Also, they were far more dedicated to their goals than most mortals. Silas closed his eyes and thought of the four musicians.

To his relief, the bass player, Beau, had no interest in Akasha. From the way the boy looked at Silas when they were first introduced, it was apparent Beau's interests lay in his own gender.

The guitarist, Sylvis, seemed to be a shy thing at first, but he quickly learned she was something of a comedienne. The girl had been Xochitl's best friend since early childhood and it seemed they had a language of their own, often punctuated with bouts of hysterical laughter. Both were finishing their high school diplomas at the college with Akasha. Aurora and Beau hadn't qualified. After scenting marijuana on the two, Silas was not surprised.

However, despite her taste for illegal herbs, Aurora, the drummer, was definitely not lacking in intelligence. As the unspoken leader of the band, when she tapped on her drums like a judge with a gavel, looking like a queen as she declared it was time to practice, or that some melody should be cut, her word was law.

Silas yawned. Then there was Xochitl, the walking, singing conundrum. Although she was supposed to be the offspring of an evil being, she did not seem to be malevolent in the slightest. Her mother had been a preschool teacher, of all things.

Xochitl's bubbly cheer and impulsiveness hid a frightening intellect, which made its appearance at the most surprising times. Just last night, she had sat across from him at the dining room table decked out in leather and fishnet as she sipped wine like a duchess and discussed the battle of Flodden Field with him— in German. According to Akasha, Xochitl could speak six languages. Silas had only mastered four. The next time he saw her, she was scampering about the house wearing a ragged baby blanket about her shoulders like an ill-fitting cape.

Together, the four filled his castle with chaos, amusement, and music. After centuries of solitude, having a full house was unnerving, yet invigorating. It seemed the musicians never slept. When they weren't practicing their music, they were talking, laughing, and often watching movies.

Silas shuddered. They had horrible taste in movies. Thanks to them, he could likely recite every line from *Monty Python and the Holy Grail* as well as everything done by Mel Brooks. They loved horror movies equally well. Practically every vampire movie, from the silliest to the most grotesque, had been paraded before his eyes. Silas lived in increasing fear of what would happen if the group found out *he* was a vampire. Would they attempt to stake him or kiss him? He took more care than ever when entering and leaving his lair, ensuring they never discovered the secret entrance.

On weekends, they laid out sleeping bags and camped on the floor while Akasha gleefully joined them. Silas sighed. Since Halloween, he'd barely had a moment alone with her.

On a happier note, Akasha smiled far more frequently since Xochitl and her group started practicing at his house. And her laugh... *Oh God, her laugh.* Silas shivered the first time the deep, throaty sound poured from her lips. Smooth and strong as single malt Scotch, it was a sound made for closed bedroom doors, for nights of pleasure under silk sheets.

The incessant drums finally stopped and Silas allowed sleep to carry him off in an erotic dream.

Chapter Eleven

Akasha crept out of the shed. Under the cover of darkness, she made her way to the garbage cans, careful not to let the slight finger of light from the windows touch her. Her breath made clouds and her teeth chattered, but she ignored the bitter cold, focusing on her goal.

With utmost care, she lifted the lid of the first can without a sound. Her eyes widened at the bounty. A half sandwich and a can with a few mouthfuls of beans! Gently, she set down the lid. Her hand stuck to the icy handle. She bit her lip to hold in a cry of pain when she freed it.

The unmistakable sound of a gun being cocked pierced the frigid air.

"Hold it right there," a gravelly voice commanded. "Turn around."

Akasha obeyed, clinging to the sandwich and beans like a lifeline. The man was tall and built like an ex football player. Her eyes rested on meaty hands that held the rifle on her. They could just as easily snap her neck like a toothpick.

"So, you've been eating out of my garbage, eh?" His tone was unreadable. "And I'll bet you've been living in my shed too?" Her throat was too dry to speak, but he was merciless. He pointed the gun at her again. "Answer me!"

She cringed like a kicked dog, praying he wouldn't shoot. "Y-yes. I'm sorry."

"How old are you, kid?"

"Tw-twelve."

"Shit." He stared at her for a long time before lowering the gun. *"Get your ass in here."*

On quaking legs, she followed the man into the house. He led her into a dirty kitchen and had her sit at the table. *"Don't move 'till I get back."*

He soon returned with a frayed blanket and wrapped it around her. *"Damn, girl, your hands are purple! Wrap em' up and let's get some food in ya."* She stared at him in mute awe as he opened the fridge and pulled out two pieces of pizza. He put them in the microwave and poured her a glass of water. *"What's your name, kid?"*

"Akasha."

"I'm Max."

They stared at each other, silently assessing until the microwave beeped. Max put the steaming plate in front of her. *"Not another word 'till this plate is clean. Got it?"*

Her hands tingled from the warmth of the crust. The first bite burned her mouth, but it tasted like heaven itself and she nearly moaned in pleasure of the experience. It had been over two years since she had a hot meal. The first piece of pizza seemed too good to be true. Akasha savored every nibble, chewing slowly, concentrating wholly on the flavor. The second, she devoured like a ravenous beast. The water felt like the elixir of the gods as it slid down her throat.

Max sat across from her and folded his work-worn hands. *"Did you run away from home or something? Where are your parents?"*

"They died when I was eight. Then I lived in a foster home. The woman was crazy, so I left." She crossed her arms.

He scratched his beard. *"I see. So you've been on the streets ever since."*

He was quiet until Akasha finally built up the nerve to speak. "You gonna call the cops?"

"Hell no! I hate cops!"

She was relieved, but only a little. "What are you going to do?"

"Hell if I know. But one thing's for sure. You're not gonna freeze your ass off in my shed, so you'll sleep on the couch. Maybe I'll figure something out in the morning."

He provided her with a pillow and blanket. Compared to the frigid wood floor of the shed, the couch was a warm paradise. Exhausted and with a full stomach for the first time in months, she was blissfully comatose until late the next morning. When she awoke, Max cooked her breakfast and again refused to speak to her until she finished every bite.

"All right, kid, here's what I figured out." Max grabbed two cans of Coors from the fridge, opening one and setting it before her. "I can't let you be out on the streets, starvin' and freezin'. That just don't settle well with me. Y'hear?"

She nodded, sipping her beer, trying not to make a face as she tried to decide whether she liked it or not.

"So here's the deal. Either you live here and earn your board cleanin' this place and maybe earn some money helpin' me in my garage, or I'll call the welfare department and they can deal with you."

***

Akasha slid out from under Xochitl's Datsun, eyes burning from the memory, heart aching from missing Max. *Where is he now?*

The door opened, pulling her from her thoughts.

Beau poked his head in the doorway, grinning at her. "We're taking off, okay, babe?"

"Sure," she replied distractedly and pushed out with her feet to get the creeper rolling. *These sway bar bushings look like they'll be a pain in the ass.* Still, it was easier to spot obvious problems in a parallelogram steering system rather than rack and pinion.

"Hey, 'Kash!" Xochitl's voice echoed in the garage. "Thanks again for fixing Little Beast. Is there anything I can do to repay you?"

Akasha smiled and rolled the creeper back out. "Just keep playing your music. When you're famous you can send me backstage passes for every concert."

Xochitl grinned. "Speaking of concerts... have you asked Silas about taking us?"

Although Akasha couldn't remember the name of the performing band, she remembered camping out with Xochitl, Sylvis, Aurora and Beau to get the tickets. She also remembered all four sets of parents saying they couldn't go without an adult.

Naturally, none volunteered and she'd been putting off asking Silas because she didn't like asking him for favors. His pleased reactions made her feel strange... something about the gleam in those emerald eyes, the curve of his lips... that obscenely sexy accent.

"I'll ask him tonight," Akasha promised, struggling to get her mind back on her work.

"Awesome. I'll see you tomorrow." Xochitl skipped off, her hair bouncing like a black and purple cloud.

Akasha looked at the clock to see if she had enough time to call the machinist and see if the Datsun's cylinder head had been finished.

Nope, it was after five.

She cursed and turned back to the engine block then stopped. Silas would be home soon. Then at least she could ask him about the concert. She looked down at her hands. They were black with grease and oil. For some reason she didn't want him to see her covered with grime. After giving

Xochitl's car one last longing glance, she left the garage and dashed upstairs to clean up.

When she had fixed her appearance, Akasha went downstairs to wait for Silas. She paced back and forth through the hallway, eyes darting every few seconds to the front door. *No, I must not look too eager. He'll think I missed him or something.*

She forced her attention to a painting of a beautiful oil landscape of the Scottish highlands with a mighty castle in the background. It was crooked. She tried to adjust it, but her hands were still shaking from excitement and it came off the wall, clattering to the floor. *Oh, great. The damn thing probably cost a fortune.*

Cursing under her breath, she scooped it up and quickly checked for damage. It was fine. She lifted it back to the wall and froze when she saw something strange.

There was a knob on the wall where the painting would have hung. At least it *looked* like a knob... She set the painting down and peered at it. The silver gleamed dimly, making it look like a tarnished bauble. It was cool to her fingertips. Slowly, she twisted the knob, shuddering as it moved.

Creak!

The sound made her jerk in surprise. Her eyes snapped open, and she looked around for the source. There it was. A hidden door had opened in the wall beside her.

"Holy shit!" Her whisper echoed in the corridor. "A secret passageway! I knew he was hiding something."

For some reason, being right all along didn't feel as good as she'd thought. Her stomach pitched as the opening gaped at her, a pitch-dark abyss. Akasha fished inside her pocket for her Bic. The feeble light revealed a set of stairs going downwards. Slowly, she made her way down, noting that the air wasn't musty as one would expect. *What is he hiding down here?* She hoped it wasn't dead bodies. She glanced over her shoulder, watching for Silas's approach until her neck cramped.

Just when the lighter was getting too hot and burning her fingers, the stairs turned sharply, and she could see a bit of light below. She licked her stinging fingers and pocketed the lighter. As she neared the light, an eerie feeling crept over her and the hairs at the nape of her neck stood up. The feeling intensified, and by the time she reached the bottom her body was covered in goose bumps.

A long shadowy hallway stretched across five doors. Akasha shook her head. *Another basement? Does this fucking house ever end?* With a trembling hand, she reached for the knob on the first door, one fist held up and ready to beat something to a bloody pulp if it startled her. The door moved soundlessly open. There was a faint light in the room. Taking a deep breath, she stepped inside.

Akasha stood awestruck in a candlelit chamber. It was too dim for her to see how large the room was, but in the center she could make out a large bed. All of her instincts screamed at her to go back, to run out of there as fast as she could, but her curiosity was relentless and pushed her legs forward. As she approached the bed she saw that someone was in it. Yes, there was definitely a body tucked under the covers, lying as still as a corpse. The realization terrified her, but her treacherous legs brought her yet closer. She could almost make out a face.

Then she saw him.

Silas lay on the bed, still as death. Then his chest moved up and down almost imperceptibly. Unbidden, a relieved sigh escaped her lips. As she drew closer, his beauty hit her full force. His chiseled features and sensuous mouth looked so inviting, making her stomach clench. She drew in a breath as her hand reached out of its own volition to touch him.

Silas's eyes snapped open, and he saw her. Akasha gasped when she saw his green eyes glowing with demonic radiance. Time seemed to go in slow motion as his mouth opened to reveal sharp fangs.

Vampire.

The word hit her mind like a bucket of ice water. Silas sat up and threw off the covers, fangs bared, blazing gaze fixed on her like a target.

"Oh shit!" Akasha turned and fled the room, darting up the stairs as fast as her legs would carry her.

Her heart pounded louder than Aurora's drums, drowning out all sound, but she didn't need to hear his footsteps to know he was behind her. She could feel him. Not daring to look back, she continued running, stumbling up the dark stairs, terror gripping her mercilessly.

Finally, she made it out of the passageway and ran down the hall, lungs heaving. If he caught her... no, she wasn't going to think about that. She got to the living room and almost cried out in relief when the front door was in sight.

But then Silas appeared, blocking her escape. She tried to turn around, but with obscene speed, he caught her, imprisoning her in his arms. Cold seeped over her as she raised her eyes to look up at him. His eyes still glowed like green fire. She shivered. *I'm going to die now. I might as well do it on my feet.*

Gazing up at him resolutely, Akasha took in the sight of his tall, dark form looming over her. His bare chest was surprisingly warm against her palms. *He has muscles like iron*, a part of her mused distractedly.

She flinched as his lips curled upward, revealing the glistening fangs. Time seemed suspended as she stared at him, spellbound by his dark beauty. His grip tightened on her and she held her breath, waiting to feel his teeth sink into her neck.

Will it hurt? … Or will I like it?

The slow motion movie sensation continued as Silas lowered his head. His hair tumbled forward to caress his face. Akasha's fists clenched, resisting an insane urge to tangle her fingers in those silken tresses.

His lips came down on hers.

The heat of the kiss encompassed her body like the fire in a combustion chamber. She closed her eyes and gave herself over to the mind-bending pleasure. Unconsciously, she reached up to put her arms around him, but suddenly it was over.

She opened her eyes. He was gone.

Akasha sank to the floor and hugged her knees, unable to stop trembling.

Chapter Twelve

"Silas is a vampire." Akasha surprised herself at the glib way in which the words rolled off her tongue.

It made sense given his nocturnal schedule. *Financial advisor, my ass!* A bubble of laughter escaped her lips.

A vampire... she lived with a vampire. She couldn't help but wonder why he took her from the group home. There were never any odd marks on her neck in the morning, or anything. Furthermore, why did he let her live?

He'd had ample opportunities to kill her, especially just now, but he didn't. Instead, he'd kissed her. She pressed two shaky fingers to lips that still tingled. A rush of heat flooded her body at the memory of the kiss. Akasha shook her head in a futile attempt to clear it.

Well, at least I'm not the only abnormal being on the planet. Sighing, she dragged herself up from the floor and hurried to the kitchen for a beer.

Akasha pounded down the beer so fast it made her dizzy— or maybe she was in shock. The walls seemed to be closing in on her, heightening her confusion. *I gotta get out of here for awhile. I need to think.* That decided, she paused at the door, debating on whether to leave a note.

"Dear Silas, finding out that you're a vampire kinda unnerved me, so I went for a walk to think about it, be back later. Love, Akasha." Again came the helpless giggle.

"Yeah, right," she muttered, grabbing her coat and heading out the door.

Akasha walked aimlessly for nearly an hour. She could see families through the windows of the houses on 15th street, eating dinner, watching TV, laughing and talking. Normal people... *If any of them knew a vampire lived up on Cherry Hill, they'd shit a brick.* She walked further, trying to quell her racing thoughts, until she reached Xochitl's neighborhood. It would be nice to have someone to talk to. *Should I tell her?* A chord of foreboding leveled the thought. *No!* Silas might kill anyone who knew his secret.

Bill, Xochitl's foster father answered the door and called for Xochitl in a voice thick with irritation.

"What's wrong, 'Kash?" Xochitl asked when Bill went back to watching football.

"Uh, nothing," she lied. *Damn, is it that obvious?*

Her friend rolled her eyes. "Yeah, right. C'mon, let's go to my room."

Akasha followed Xochitl down the stairs to the basement. *Maybe I shouldn't have come. Xochitl's too fucking perceptive.*

"So, what happened?" she demanded once they were settled on the bed.

Akasha sighed. The best way to lie was to tell as much truth as possible. Besides, she did want to tell Xochitl part of what happened. "He kissed me."

"Who?" Xochitl began, then her eyes widened. *"Silas!"*

"Yeah." The room felt warmer.

Still gasping, Xochitl seized Akasha's shoulders. "Well, what happened? Why'd he do it? Did you like it?"

"I don't know why he did it." Akasha stared at the floor. "I, um… was going to ask him about the concert… and uh… he just kissed me and left."

"Hmm…" Xochitl opened the window and turned on the fan, lighting a cigarette. "That's odd."

"Yeah, odd. I know," Akasha murmured as she lit up.

It was obvious Xochitl didn't completely buy the story. Yet her brown eyes gleamed in impish fascination. "Well, did you like it?"

"Yes." The word was torn from her.

"I *knew* it!" Xochitl smirked. "I knew you liked him. That's why you hate it when anyone calls him your dad."

"Uh… Yeah." Akasha wanted to die from embarrassment, though she was relieved that Xochitl hadn't guessed the truth.

Xochitl wasn't finished. "Well, he *is* hot. And he can't be that old. Do you even know how old he is yet?"

"No." *He could be centuries old!*

"Well, what are you going to do about it?" Xochitl leaned forward, fascination written all over her face.

Images of a shirtless Silas holding and kissing her… of running her fingers across those hard muscles haunted Akasha's mind, making her knees weak as her lower half tingled.

"I have no idea," she said finally. After an endless uncomfortable silence, Akasha asked, "What is sex like?"

It was an odd question since she was technically not a virgin, but Akasha was becoming certain that sex between two willing parties was completely different.

Xochitl blinked. "I don't know. I've never done it."

"But you talk about hot guys a lot," Akasha protested, "And the way you sing certain songs... I thought..." she trailed off in embarrassment.

Her friend giggled. "I would if I had the chance, but no hot guys seem willing to oblige me." Her gaze turned serious for a moment. "They're all too scared of me."

Akasha nodded. At school, the kids parted like the Red Sea in the halls for Xochitl. It was strange that a five foot tall girl could incite such fear.

"So, what are you going to do about Silas?" Xochitl repeated.

Akasha shook her head and took a deep drag of her cigarette, mind racing as she watched the smoke get sucked into the fan. "I don't know. I need some time to digest this. Why don't you play me that song you just wrote?"

***

Silas paced the house, cursing in regret for how badly he handled the situation. If only he hadn't been so hungry, he could have stopped Akasha from leaving. Now she knew what he was and he had frightened her away. He could only imagine how monstrous he must have looked to her with his eyes glowing and his fangs bared.

If only he'd hidden the entrance to his lair better. Silas shook his head in self recrimination. He'd underestimated Akasha's intelligence badly. Had she suspected what he was and went looking for the secret passageway on purpose? Or did she find it by accident? Either situation was entirely possible. One thing was certain: she was lucky.

When Silas awoke that night, the hunger was at its strongest. To have a warm, fresh source of blood right at his fingertips... It was amazing that he didn't crush her to him and feast upon her right away. He almost did, but when he caught her, the strangest thing happened.

Akasha didn't scream or struggle. She didn't try to fight him. She stood proud, staring up at him, practically daring him to take her. She looked so beautiful then, so tender, and so brave. His eyes drank in her sweetness. She roused his hunger even as she stirred his heart.

Her glittering eyes had darkened to a purple so deep that he could drown in it. Her lush cupid's-bow lips looked soft as rose petals. How many times had he looked at those lips and been nearly driven to madness? Yet he'd never been as mad as he was then. Unable to stop himself any more than he could stop the sun from rising, he gripped her shoulders tighter, drew her to him and captured those lips with his own. They were softer than his richest imagining, and warm... so warm.

He'd held her tighter, feeling the delicious heat wash over him. He could hear her heart beating; a tantalizing melody that reawakened the hunger within him, but for now it was his passion that was more aroused. He relished the pleasure of this kiss, wrong as it was, with the rapture of a man who'd been starved for centuries.

The scent of her blood rose up, growing more tempting by the second. When he became torn between the desire to either take her to bed or sink his teeth in her neck, some semblance of sanity struck him like a whiplash, making him realize what he was doing.

Suddenly he was back in England, ravaging the countryside on his bloody quest for vengeance against the people who'd savaged his clan. A comely lass had fled from him, and with preternatural speed, he'd caught her. Silas tore her gown, ready to do what the English soldiers had done to good Scots women.

But when he heard the maiden scream and saw the terror in her eyes, bile rose in his throat. Silas had released her and vomited immediately.

Returned to the present, Silas had felt Akasha tremble in his arms. The old self-disgust rose up within at the thought of those amethyst eyes filling with terror. Despite the protests of his body, he tore away from her, knowing that until he fed, the farther he was from her, the safer she would be.

After his hunger for blood had been slaked on a hapless pedestrian, the desire to hold Akasha, kiss her, to merely be in her company rose up stronger than ever. Silas headed back to the house, his mind tormenting him with vile images of what he would find there.

Would she be on the floor, sobbing in a pitiful ball of misery and terror? Or would she be swathed in garlic, a cross around her neck and armed with a wooden stake? Not that these things would cause him any physical harm, but the gesture would hurt all the same.

A thought struck him, chilling him worse than the November air. What if his vision was about to come true? *What if I am the one to make Akasha cry?*

When Silas returned home, his worst fears were realized. Akasha was gone. The realization beat at him, relentless. She knew what he was... she *knew*. Things would change irrevocably for them now. The Elders would be furious. It was frowned upon for a mortal to know of his kind and leave, but he couldn't kill her, and thanks to Delgarias's command, he couldn't Change her. The thought of letting her go refused to cross his mind. Akasha was his and would remain his forever. No, he wouldn't let her go, couldn't let her go. He... loved her.

The vampire leaned against the wall and slowly sank down to the floor, overcome with the realization. The Akasha from his visions had been a phantom, sweet and biddable in his imagination, yet distant and safe.

Akasha the woman, however, was gruff and coarse with limitless courage and a will of steel. Stoically, she bore the humiliation of being treated like a child by the authorities and the indignity of going to school with younger peers. She'd even put up with Silas ripping her from all that was familiar and thrusting her into his world. Throughout all this, she held to her goals for a stable future with a tenacity that was beyond admirable.

Silas closed his eyes, pride rushing through him at her strength. He must get her back. And somehow, some way, he would ensure that Akasha succeeded in whatever she desired. Somehow, he would make her happy.

Once he got hold of himself, Silas checked the garage and was relieved to see that his Barracuda was still there. She had gone on foot. Not only would that make her easier to find, he didn't like the idea of her driving in the tumultuous emotional state she had to be in.

He got in his car and drove slowly down the road with the windows down, tracing her presence through the Mark. He caught it to the west, towards Xochitl's house. His hands gripped the steering wheel so tightly that he had to fight not to damage it. In moments he would learn how Akasha felt about living with a monster.

Chapter Thirteen

"Xochitl, Mr. McNaught is here to pick up your friend," Bill yelled down the stairs.

A ball of panic dropped into Akasha's stomach. *He came after me! What is he going to do?*

"'Kash, you gonna be okay?" Xochitl compassionate gaze was like warm honey.

She nodded. "I'm sure he just wants to talk." *Does he?*

Her legs were as heavy as lead, but she managed to get to her feet. As if she could sense Akasha's foreboding, Xochitl put a comforting hand on her shoulder before leading the way up the stairs as if she would protect her.

When they got to the kitchen, they glanced at each other, wide-eyed in confusion. Bill, Susan and Silas were sitting at the table, talking as if they were the best of friends.

"Ever since Xochitl's been around, I've seen vast improvement in Akasha's schoolwork... and her behavior, for the most part anyway. But you know teenagers." Silas sounded like a character from an old sitcom. "I look forward to having her over again soon."

Bill and Susan nodded vigorously in agreement.

"I thought they didn't like Silas," Akasha whispered even as she wondered if she'd put her friend in danger.

Xochitl frowned. "They don't. This looks really fucked up."

Had he hypnotized them? Silas's eyes fell upon her and Akasha's breath left her body. Those emerald irises were no longer glowing, but the intensity of his gaze was no less fiery. *Vampire... Undead.* She tried to feel fear and revulsion, but all that came was apprehension coupled with a morbid sense of exhilaration. She wasn't the only freak in this house. She wasn't alone.

"Hello Mr. McNaught." Xochitl broke the silence tentatively.

"Xochitl, hello." Silas inclined his head, but studied her inquisitively. "Did Akasha tell you she is grounded?"

Grounded? What the hell is he pulling? Does he even know what the word means? Akasha's mind darted around.

"Um... no." Xochitl gave her a questioning look.

Play along, Akasha, if you know what's good for you. Akasha heard the vampire's voice in her head, but his lips weren't moving. She suppressed a shudder at the intimacy of Silas speaking in her mind alone and did what she was told.

"Uh, sorry. I guess I forgot." She hung her head in what she hoped was a gesture of shame.

Silas stood. His voice rang with universal authority. "Come along, Akasha."

Bill and Susan beamed their approval of his "parental" skills and Akasha choked on bitter laughter. If only they knew.

"See ya later, Xoch'." She bit her lip. *At least I hope so.*

Once they were outside, tension charged the air between them. Silas turned to her, eyes inquisitive yet still rife with command. "You didn't tell her about me, did you?"

She shook her head vigorously as her boots crunched on frosty leaves. "Hell, no! Do you think I'm a moron?"

His expression was one of such profound relief that a stab of fear struck her. What would have happened if she had told Xochitl his secret?

The vampire gave a curt nod and opened the passenger door of the Barracuda. He avoided her gaze as she got in. Her heart pounded with trepidation. As the car roared down the road, crackling on newly installed studded tires, Akasha studied his profile, trying to figure out what he was feeling. Silas's face remained blank as a statue as he watched the road. She hoped he wasn't angry with her. At least he probably wouldn't kill her. After all, he hadn't when he caught her.

As she wondered what he *was* going to do, a thousand other questions swam in her mind. Akasha couldn't bring herself to voice a single one. All she could think was: *Silas is a vampire... I'm riding in a car with a vampire... I'm going home with a vampire... I live with a vampire... I was kissed by a vampire!* On the heels of the thought was: *holy shit! That was my first kiss!*

They got to the house and she wordlessly followed him in. She shot a glance at Xochitl's Datsun in the garage and bit her lip. *Will I get to finish working on it?*

When they entered the living room, the vampire bade her to sit down.

"I'm going to get you a beer." His voice was just as cordial... and cautious as it had the night before. Akasha's hands shook as she struggled to unzip her jacket. A low, impatient sound escaped from her throat. Silas returned from the kitchen, set down the can of Coors and reached for her. His long, elegant fingers grasped the zipper of her jacket and pulled it down. Gently, he gripped the leather by the lapels and pulled as she shrugged it off her shoulders. Goose bumps rose up all over at his light touch.

Before Silas hung up her jacket, he reached into the pocket, retrieved her cigarettes and lit one for her. The cigarette looked weird between his lips. She wondered if he could read her mind. She also wondered why he was still being so nice. Surely the gloves were off now.

Silas turned on the gas fireplace, then sat down on the couch next to her, folding his hands in a steeple under his chin. His gaze deepened in intensity as he stared at the fire. Akasha tried not to squirm. He'd never sat next to her before. He always sat in his recliner.

Finally, he spoke. "Now Akasha, we must talk."

Her throat went painfully dry as her eyes met his. Silas's close proximity made her shiver, though it had little to do with what he was. She took a deep drink of her beer, for once wishing for something harder.

"Well," he began. "Now you know what I am. Before I decide what to do with you, I wish to know your thoughts on the situation."

Akasha blinked in surprise at his inquiry. She chugged the rest of the beer for courage, grateful for the warm tingle it sent to her head. He handed her another from the mini-fridge.

"Well... actually... um... I guess it's okay." She froze, shocked at her own boldness and the strange yet irrefutable logic in her statement.

Silas gave her a bemused look, brow arched. "It's *okay*?"

Something about his expression made her belly flutter. Maybe it was because he seemed so solemn most of the time. Akasha struggled to regain her thoughts. "Well, yeah. I mean, all my friends have fantasized about encountering vampires. And to think, I've been living with one for the past month." Akasha choked back nervous laughter. "What I want to know is why."

"Why?" the vampire inquired.

He looks just as tense as I am. Akasha shook her head at the thought. "Yeah, what does an immortal, all-powerful being like you want with me? What the hell possessed you to bring me here?"

She sucked in a breath as the obvious again occurred to her. *Just because there were no marks...* Unconsciously, her hand crept up to the side of her neck.

"Not that, Akasha," Silas said with aching gentleness. "I have never fed from you."

Her eyes narrowed. "Why should I believe you?"

He sighed. "I do not blame you for your suspicion. However, I beg you to consider this: Have I ever done anything to harm you? And, more importantly, have I ever lied to you?"

"You told me you were a financial advisor," she accused.

Silas laughed, and for once didn't cover his mouth. She saw his fangs glisten in the firelight. *That's why he covered his mouth.* "Oh, but I am, Akasha. It's just that most of my clients are other vampires."

Vampires in finance... Akasha shook her head to clear the muddled thought away and guzzled her second beer. "If you didn't take me to be a snack, why did you bring me here?"

"As I told you in the first place, I was lonely and desired a companion." His voice was level, yet it still seemed he was hiding something.

"But why *me?*" She couldn't prevent the hysterical note creeping into her voice. The empty beer can was crushed in her grip. "How did you find me in the first place, and what did you know about me?"

Silas's expression turned so serious that she had an urge to scoot away from him. "Fine, I'll tell you. I have had visions of you for centuries. When I found you at last, I wasn't about to let you stay in that miserable group home."

"Visions?" A chill skittered across her flesh as she remembered his words the first night they met. *"Would you believe me if I told you I was psychic?"* Then the next day he'd said, *"You better wear a coat tomorrow. It's going to rain."*

Masking her unease, she grabbed a third beer from the mini fridge.

"Yes," Silas answered the unspoken thought with a slight nod. "I am something of a clairvoyant. I was in my mortal years and my powers have multiplied since I was Changed."

Akasha frowned as she struggled to digest this new phenomenon. "You had visions of me... what were they like?" The chill intensified. *Had he seen my past? Does he know what I have done?*

Silas shifted on the couch, his discomfort apparent. "I really did not see much besides your face." He paused and looked away. "You were crying."

"I never cry." She loathed the defensive tone of her voice.

Silas nodded. "I know that now."

She studied his face, willing him to say more. It was obvious he was still hiding things. But nothing in his attitude showed disgust so she was willing to let it go... for now. Whatever it was, he didn't know her worst secret.

"So, what are you going to do with me?" She sipped her beer, feigning nonchalance.

Silas studied her. "You *will* agree to stay here with me, won't you?"

"Of course," Akasha replied, not having to think about it. After all, he treated her better than anyone had in her entire life. She wasn't about to walk out on him just because he was a nocturnal bloodsucker.

"That is good." He nodded with satisfaction, then looked away. "I really did not want to force you. I'm not about to let you go. I cannot, in fact, because you know what I am and also because I Marked you. It would not bode well for my reputation as a Lord of this city."

"What is a Lord, and what do you mean, you 'Marked' me?" Another tremor of fear trickled down her spine. The word could not mean anything good.

Silas avoided her gaze again. "The mini-fridge is empty. Why don't you go get another beer from the kitchen and I will explain."

When Akasha returned, she sat back down next to him on the couch to show him she wasn't afraid. If only her hands would stop shaking.

"A Lord is a vampire who is older and more powerful than others," Silas began. "We usually take charge of a territory and either bar it from all other vampires or keep some in our employ to secure the power base."

Her eyes widened in fascination. "So it's a political thing?"

Silas nodded. "For the most part. I myself have no interest in politics or power struggles. That is why I chose Coeur d' Alene as my city. Very few vampires live here."

"And what about this 'Marking' thing you mentioned?" It was hard to keep her voice steady. "What does that mean?"

"I have given you a few drops of my blood." Again, he looked away. "All of my kind will detect it. To them, it means you are my property and to harm you is to incur my wrath."

Anger flared at his explanation. "So what, you fucking own me now?" she growled.

Silas continued to avoid her gaze. "According to the laws of my kind, yes."

Akasha glared at him. Vampire laws or no, she was pissed. "What gave you the right to do that? This is my fucking life you're talking about. I oughtta kick your ass—"

He held up a hand, cutting off her rant. "I did it for your safety, Akasha." His voice took on a hard edge as his piercing gaze once more locked on her. "Would you rather be a meal to any vampire who encounters you? Or perhaps have another vampire Mark you?" His brow rose in challenge. "One who would not be as kind as I?"

She let out a shuddering sigh as a measure of her pent up rage dissipated. "No," she said sullenly and punched the arm of the couch. He *owned* her. "Fuck."

The vampire sighed and looked at his watch. "Is there anything else you would like to know… about me?"

Grudgingly, Akasha let go of her anger and complied with the subject change. It seemed there was nothing she could do about it anyway. "How long have you been a vampire?"

Silas's gaze turned distant. "Since 1513. I was defending my clan and country from the English. The battle was lost; all of my family and clan were slain. I had taken a mortal wound in the gut. The pain was agonizing. I was still alive come nightfall, when a vampire found me. He offered me immortality and I accepted it eagerly, vowing to avenge my people." A look of tortured shame crossed his beautiful face. "I will tell you the whole story another time."

Akasha digested this all silently as she finished her beer and lit another cigarette. "Do you regret it?"

Silas sighed, long and tired. "Sometimes when dawn is about to come and I am tired and alone. For the most part, I do not regret my choice. This is the path I chose and I shall tread it with as much honor as possible."

With honor... a strange reply. The pain in his voice made her heart twinge in discomfort. She steered her questions to more technical ground. "So, do you have to kill people?"

His shoulders relaxed in obvious relief at the change in topic, though his eyes still swam with guilt. "When I was young I killed at least one English soldier a night, though it is not necessary to kill. In fact, humans have more blood in their bodies than a vampire can drink in one sitting. However, if I happen to encounter a murderer or rapist, I won't hesitate to make a feast out of them, providing I can make the death look like an accident."

Akasha lit another cigarette. "How do you know they're murderers or rapists? Can you read minds like the stories say? Or is it more because you're psychic?"

He nodded. "Not all of us have that ability, though when most of us feed, we see all our victims' secrets."

She shivered. "Then... can you read my mind?"

He gave her an odd look. "No. Your mind moves far too fast for me to read. And strangely, if I touch you, I see no visions. That is why I have been so curious about you. I am unaccustomed to mortals keeping secrets from me."

Keeping secrets... Indeed, that is what she'd been doing for years. Akasha didn't know if she was ready to let them go. She changed the subject again, realizing this conversation was becoming a strange evasive dance. "How can vampires be killed?"

He raised a brow, but his smile was teasing. "Are you planning something?"

Her cheeks heated. "No. I mean… I would like to be able to defend myself, but mostly I just want to know which of the stories are true." Akasha attempted an equally mocking tone, but her voice shook. "Xochitl cooks with a lot of garlic, you know."

Silas smiled. "I rather like garlic. That myth came from the southern Slavic areas hundreds of years ago. The herb was said to combat witches. Mr. Stoker popularized it in the late nineteenth century."

Akasha shook her head, awed by his textbook style recital. "What about stakes?"

He frowned and resumed his former seriousness. "Anything that damages the heart can be fatal, though most survive bullet wounds, even silver, which is another myth, unless perhaps werewolves *do* exist. I, for one, have never seen one. Other myths are the ones about holy items, running water, and iron." He rattled off the list with his fingers. "Fire and sunlight are our bane."

"You won't come in my room unless invited," Akasha said, her curiosity rising with everything she learned.

Silas nodded. "Most of us believe in manners, and it is somewhat of a faux pas to drink from someone in their abode." He turned to her, those emerald eyes seemed to peer into her soul. "I think you know enough about me for now. Let's talk about you."

Akasha hid her trepidation with a big yawn. "It's getting late. I should probably go to bed." She couldn't conceal the trembling of her voice.

She stood up and moved to leave, but Silas's hand locked on her wrist. Electricity flared at the contact. "You think to escape so easily? There are many explanations you still owe me."

"I know." She stared at the floor, hoping he couldn't see her reaction to his touch. "I-I'm just not ready to talk about it yet, okay?"

"Akasha, I know you are stronger than the average mortal..." His thumb caressed her wrist.

Panic clawed at her throat. He *did* know! But he didn't seem to be repulsed, so he couldn't know everything.

"Why did you kiss me, Silas?" Akasha cut him off, seeking any tactic to distract him.

He released her so abruptly that she stumbled, barely catching the arm of the couch. The room swam in her vision. She hadn't been this drunk in a while. Silas reached out and steadied her, his hands on her hips. Warmth pooled in her belly at his touch.

"You may go to bed." His tone was guarded and for once he avoided her gaze.

She stepped closer to him. He was so tall that while she was standing they were nearly eye to eye. "Wait. One more thing."

"Yes?" he asked cautiously.

"Open your mouth." She didn't know if it was curiosity that pushed her request or a desire to punish him for his insistence in knowing about her past... her *abnormality*.

Silas rolled his eyes but did as she asked. Those sensuously sculpted lips parted... and there they were. His fangs gleamed in the firelight, white and sharp and starkly real. She touched one with a shaky finger. Immediately, the lethal point pierced her flesh. Akasha withdrew her finger with a hiss, staring in shock as the digit stung and welled up with blood.

"Fuck! I didn't know they were that sharp!" The room spun again and she swayed.

Silas caught her once more. He took her hand and raised her finger to his lips. His tongue darted out and licked the blood from the tiny wound. Akasha trembled, heat flooding her core as the blood rushed to her head.

"Be more careful next time." His voice was low and husky.

Her knees went weak, and she knew it wasn't from the half-rack she downed. "Okay… uh… goodnight then."

"Promise me you'll be here at sunset tomorrow," he said.

She nodded and stumbled up the stairs, refusing his offer to help.

Chapter Fourteen

Despite the revelation that Silas was an immortal creature of myth who'd decided to take her under his roof because of a mysterious psychic vision, Akasha's routine was surprisingly unaltered. She continued her work on Xochitl's Datsun and *Rage of Angels* continued practicing in the basement. The only thing that had changed was that now Silas seemed to be avoiding her instead of the other way around. She'd barely had time to ask him to take her and her friends to the concert before he left to go bite some unsuspecting person.

Akasha frowned as she bolted the Datsun's engine to the transmission. *Is he avoiding me because of the whole vampire thing...or because of the kiss*? Her knees weakened at the memory of Silas's lips against hers. *Where will we go after that?* She may be crazy, but *that* was a bigger concern than her guardian's dietary habits.

The same questions chased each other in her mind since that fateful night. *Will he kiss me again? And if he did, would things go further?* Common sense told her they would.

Then the most unsettling question arose: *Could I handle such intimacy after what happened?*

Akasha bit her lip and fastened the engine to the cherry picker. Closing her eyes, she pictured Silas's naked chest pressed against her flesh... of him thrusting inside her. No thread of the usual revulsion came. *Maybe....*

"Good evening, Akasha," Silas's voice interrupted her thoughts, making her hand slip on the hydraulic lever of the hoist.

With desperate speed, she caught the lever before the Datsun's power train crashed to the floor. Her cheeks flamed. "Uh... hi."

"I am surprised to see you up so late," he commented, eyes roving over the car. "You have school tomorrow."

Akasha's fists clenched in frustration at his vague tone. A thousand questions leapt to her mind, but all were too embarrassing. Instead, she looked at the Datsun as if it was the most important thing in the world. "I wanted to get the engine and transmission back in the car. I'll be finished sooner if you would care to help." Her lips curved up in a bitter smile. *Let him get his hands dirty for once!*

Silas sighed and she felt a sadistic tremor of pleasure at his discomfort. "Very well. Why did you attach the transmission to it first?"

"It's easier this way with stick shifts." She wheeled the hoist over the car. "Could you help me line the engine up on the mounts when I lower it, then hold it still while I bolt it in?"

Silas looked like he had three thumbs through the entire process as the engine rocked dangerously on the hoist. Akasha stifled a giggle... then dropped her wrench as his proximity made her quiver. It seemed her demand had backfired. She willed her stomach to quit fluttering and her eyes to quit gazing at him like a love struck girl.

Eventually, they got the job done.

"I should have it running in about two days," she said and followed him into the house, heading straight for the kitchen. "If all goes well, Xochitl should be able to drive it to the concert."

117

"About that." Silas grabbed a beer from the fridge and opened it, handing it to her. "Aurora's parents insisted I drive you all. It will be a tight squeeze, but I'm certain it will work. The Barracuda has a large back seat."

Akasha looked away before he could see her reactions to the words, "tight squeeze" and "large back seat." Forcing the naughty images from her mind, she took a swig of beer. "Why didn't you use your vampire mind tricks on them?"

A surprised flicker flashed in his eyes at that. "You are not at all afraid of me, are you?"

"Should I be?" She shook her head. She *was* afraid, just not in the sense he meant. "Besides, you're too nice."

Silas stepped closer to her, his graceful movements full of barely checked power. His knuckles brushed across her cheek, a whisper of a caress.

"I am not always so nice," he whispered. His fangs glistened with dangerous promise and she trembled, leaning forward. Silas released a low growl, his eyes glowing like phosphorus.

Akasha reached for him— and grasped the empty air. He'd vanished again.

"Damn it," she whispered, aching with half-understood longing.

If things kept up like this for long, the tension would be unbearable.

***

This is a big mistake... Silas followed Akasha and her friends, struggling against the mass of sweating mortals. But he could refuse Akasha nothing... especially after the scare he'd given her the other night.

She walked in front of him now, spine straight and confident, so close he could reach out and touch her. Ever since Akasha learned his secret, she behaved as if nothing happened. No doubt she hoped to avoid his questions. Silas sighed. Two could play at this game.

Again, she left his sight as they wove through the crowd. His heart jolted every time he lost her.

When Akasha asked him to take her and her friends to this concert, Silas never imagined it would be like this. He'd shaken his head at the pitying looks that Aurora's and Sylvis's parents gave him. He should have heeded them. This was bedlam, pure and simple. What was worse was that he'd sent a message to the Lord of Spokane informing him that he'd be in the territory on peaceful business and he never received a reply. Silas clenched his jaw, getting a decidedly bad feeling which grew worse every second.

"We're almost there!" Xochitl's exuberant shout pulled him from his thoughts.

They were trying to get to the "mosh pit," whatever that was.

"Are you sure you want to go with us?" Akasha asked, sounding worried. "It gets pretty crazy down there."

"I'm not leaving you alone." Silas fought back an urge to bare his fangs. There was no way he was letting any of them out of his sight. *"Guard them,"* Delgarias had commanded. Had the Elder anticipated the chaos of a heavy metal concert?

Oblivious to his worry, Akasha shrugged and hurried after her friends.

Silas cast another anxious glance at a group of hulking tattooed men that literally tossed people out of their path before he followed Akasha.

Even after listening to the raucous music of *Rage of Angels*, he never imagined a concert to be this chaotic and dangerous. No wonder their parents wouldn't let them go without a supervising adult even as they refused to volunteer.

Finally, they reached "the pit." Akasha and her friends pushed their way to the front as people filed in until they were shoulder to shoulder. The lights went dim as the band came onto the stage. Screaming and cheering erupted. Silas winced as the sound pierced his sensitive ears.

The first notes on the guitar were struck and everyone around the vampire— including his charges— went wild. Silas had to fight to keep his footing as the entire weight of the crowd jostled him. The wild energy of the crowd beat against his psychic shields, threatening to tumble him into maddening visions he'd controlled for centuries. The riot seemed to last an eternity. When the last song ended and the band exited the stage, he heaved a sigh of relief. He reached for Akasha to ask her if she was ready to go.

She laughed. "That was only the opening band."

Sure enough, the next band mounted the stage and cheering erupted before the music even started. He barely heard Xochitl exclaim, "Holy shit, it's really them!"

Chaos ensued. The crowd thrust forward and he stumbled into Akasha. He tried to apologize, but she just grinned and shoved the people next to her. A boot struck him in the head as a man was being passed around atop the crowd. Silas now knew what a mosh pit was. He could have lived content without the knowledge. *Why did I ever agree to this?* He thought. *Why, oh, why?*

Akasha went up then. Silas tried to pull her back down, but it was too late. She sailed over the top of the mob like a twig in a whirlpool. He had to catch her. *She could get hurt!* A low growl built in his throat as he pushed his way through the mass only to get lost in a tide of thrashing bodies. From the corner of his eye, he saw a man being carried away on a stretcher by a team of medics and his worry increased. Thousands of squirming people engulfed him like a hot sea. As his temper and panic rose, so did the scent of blood. A multitude of bleeding cuts tempted him mercilessly to sink his teeth in and feast until he was satiated.

At last, Silas reached the edge of the pit. A blast of fresh air hit him in the face and he needed no other prompt to get out. He stood there for a moment, gasping for breath, trying to get a grip on his blood thirst before it became apparent to all. The mosh pit had been utter madness. He couldn't believe Akasha and her crazy friends wanted to be in it. And now he lost them. Akasha's Mark was obscured amongst the chaos.

His fangs throbbed with the need to punish. These were his charges. *If something happened to them...*

Power prickled his flesh. *Xochitl!* His mind shouted in triumph as he detected her presence. If he found her, perhaps she could find Akasha and the others. Silas circled the pit with renewed determination.

When he'd almost made his way around, he caught Xochitl's essence in the opposite direction. *She must have needed air too.* He followed the sense like a hound on a hunt. As her presence grew stronger, he detected another one of his kind. They both came into sight at the same moment. A male, about a century old followed Xochitl like a wolf on the hunt. Silas could taste his intent to capture her unawares. As she got in line to use the restroom, he thrust the miscreant to a far corner of the arena.

"Stay away from her," Silas commanded, fangs bared.

"Wh-what is she?" the other vampire asked, his blue eyes already glowing with desire.

"She is mine." McNaught didn't need to admit his ignorance to this weakling.

"I don't see your Mark upon her." the other replied with growing insolence. "As far as I see, she's up for grabs."

Silas growled. "You will have to go through me first, youngling."

He prayed the vampire wouldn't take up the offer, not when there were so many mortals around and Xochitl was so close. Unfortunately, the fool appeared as if he was considering it.

"Why do *you* want her anyway?" The intruder sneered. "You already have a pet mortal. I've seen her, tasted your Mark and left her alone. I claim this one, even if she isn't human."

"I am a Lord. I can have as many as I want." He wasn't really sure if that was true, but he doubted the other vampire would know any different.

"Well, you're not *my* Lord."

Silas took a fleeting glance at oblivious bystanders before grabbing the other's fingers and twisting them until he heard the satisfying crunch of bone. He jerked the vampire closer, baring his fangs and allowing his eyes to glow demonically. "Leave now, and you live."

The upstart needed no further encouragement. After he fled, Silas heaved a sigh of relief. This couldn't happen again.

"Oh, hi, Silas." Xochitl emerged from the bathroom. "What's up?"

Silas seized her arm and jerked her towards him, capturing her mind with his as he pulled her into a dark alcove away from prying eyes. Xochitl's mind was slippery and chaotic with thousands of thoughts overlaid with the music of countless songs. After a phenomenal struggle, he held on and managed to put her into a deep sleep. He fed her his blood and recited the Marking ritual.

But when he reached out with his mind to touch the Mark, the strangest thing happened. Xochitl's mind opened into a vortex and he was sucked inside.

Xochitl was walking in a garden of black roses. Her thoughts still buzzed chaotically, but the effect was muted. Two moons glimmered in the starry sky. The sight of those moons— one silver— one gold, struck him forcibly. He'd seen them before.

"Dammit, I really wish you'd quit bringing me here," Xochitl grumbled.

Apparently this was a recurring dream. How interesting.

A rasping noise began to permeate the garden. She shook her head back and forth and moaned. "No! I don't want to see it again!"

All around her the roses were withering; petals browned and fell. Thorny branches turned brittle and cracked. There was something sinister about roses dying so fast that one could hear them.

A shadow fell over Xochitl's slight figure. A man stood before her, cloaked in shadows. He emanated such raw power that Silas could feel it. Xochitl bore the brunt of it and trembled. The man reached for her.

"Don't!" Silas whispered without thinking.

Unbelievably, the man's gaze whipped towards him. Their eyes locked and he snarled, "GET OUT!"

Thunder rumbled.

"SHE IS MINE!" Lightning shot out of the man's hand and struck the vampire in the chest.

Silas slammed back into his body with painful force. He wiped a sheen of sweat from his brow, overcome with the feeling he'd set the wheels in motion for something that couldn't be stopped. *Had Delgarias known this would happen?* The thought gave him chills.

"Xochitl, are you all right?" he asked when she came to.

"Uh, yeah, I just got dizzy." She looked at him with bleary eyes.

The urge to protect her came forth, verifying that despite the odd experience, the Mark was a success.

"Well, let us get some water and find the others." Silas would Mark them all after the concert, just to be safe. He only prayed there'd be no more nasty surprises.

***

"I want us to be big," Xochitl's voice was abnormally firm. The force of her will seemed to fill the confines of the car.

Silas gripped the steering wheel and forced himself to focus on driving. The Marks he'd put upon the four seemed to mold into one large pulsing thing that threatened to blast apart his consciousness in one burst of psychic overload.

"I wouldn't worry about that," Akasha said, glancing back at them from the passenger seat. "You guys are good, really good. You'll get a record deal in no time."

"I'm sure we will," Xochitl said without a trace of ego. "But that's not what I meant. I want us to be big and good enough to tour with the greats. Not one of those bands who's always the opening act, but never gets to be the headliner."

Aurora's voice was quiet but unnaturally grave. "Do you know what you're saying, Xoch'?" Her will surged forward, entwining with that of the others, drawing them towards her.

"Yeah, I know it's gonna be hard," Xochitl replied, unfazed.

"It's gonna be more than hard," Aurora continued, adamant. "It'll be the hardest thing we'll ever do. Like it or not, the world of heavy metal is dominated by heterosexual white men. For three chicks, one of us black, at that— and a gay guy to make it to the top of that world will be damn near impossible."

The guitarist cut in with uncharacteristic passion. "That just means we'll have to do even better than the big guys. Just like every stride women have made. We'll have better guitar solos, faster drums, deeper bass work... and with Xochitl's voice..."

"Yeah!" Beau chimed in, radiating enthusiasm. "I think we can do it. After all, Rob Halford from *Judas Priest* is gay, and he's still one of the big dogs."

"But he didn't officially come out the closet until he already was big," Aurora countered. "And talent alone won't get us to the top. A lot of it will have to be our image."

"You guys going to wear costumes or something?" Akasha teased as she gave Silas a pointed look. Apparently she also sensed that this conversation was of pinnacle importance.

Aurora snorted. "No, I mean we'll have to watch our subject matter for one thing. No girly songs like love ballads and break-up anthems and all that. And once we arrive on the music scene, we cannot, under any circumstances, sleep with our fellow musicians."

"Awwww..." Xochitl and Beau chorused.

Silas could tell their disappointment wasn't completely sincere. The moment Xochitl announced her intentions, the four had been in complete accord. Even Akasha could feel it, if the awed look in her eyes was any indicator.

Did I do this? Silas wondered. *Did I somehow mold these four into a cohesive unit? Or did I strengthen what was already there?* This conversation was serious and just as prophetic as when the Wright brothers spoke of creating their airplane. They *would* do it. They would become the greatest heavy metal band ever known.

"What about groupies?" Beau asked. "Can we sleep with them?"

"Y'know..." Aurora said with a helpless shrug. "I don't know. For now I think we should just focus on what Sylvis said. We need to step it up, do our homework and become the best. Are we all in?"

"Yes!" Even Silas and Akasha found themselves answering.

Dear God, the vampire thought. *What have I done?*

Chapter Fifteen
Colorado State Penitentiary, Psychiatric Ward

The woman resembled a classic fairy tale crone. Milbury took out his notepad as Agent Holmes met her crazed gray eyes.

"Mrs. Steele, may I call you Laura?" Joe said cheerily.

The woman straightened her rail thin spine. "You may not."

"Very well, Mrs. Steele," Holmes was unruffled. "I understand you ran a foster home about seven years ago?"

She nodded and fumbled with the plastic cross around her neck. "I did, until Satan's minions shut me down." As Holmes and Milbury exchanged glances she added, "I blame it on the demon child."

Holmes looked at his notes. "Alex Olson?"

Alex had run away from Mrs. Steele's home and reported her cruelty to the police, causing her to be arrested and her facility to be shut down.

"No!" Mrs. Steele shrieked, causing her guard to step closer. "It was the girl, that demon girl with the purple eyes. No natural child has eyes that color."

Milbury hid a triumphant smile as he scribbled down the eye color. It was the same color the girl's father, Private

Lindsay's, had been. Holmes continued his questioning. "And what was the girl's name?"

The woman's eyes darted around as if she saw things that weren't there. She whispered something, fingering the cross as if it were her last grip on reality. Maybe it was.

"What was that?" Holmes asked politely.

Mrs. Steele's gaze swam back into focus. "I said her name was Akasha."

"Akasha what?"

The woman didn't seem to hear. She clutched the sides of her head and began repeating. "Satan's harlot! Demon spawn!"

The guard stepped forward and looked at Holmes. "I think she's had enough for today. Maybe you could come back tomorrow?"

Milbury ignored him and approached Mrs. Steele. "What did she look like?"

Those wild eyes locked on his. "Messy black hair, the devil's curls. She threw me across the room once. Satan guided her hand with his unholy strength!"

Excitement flared in his chest. It was her, he knew it. He strode forward and demanded. "The last name, give us her last name!"

Mrs. Steele's gaze went out of focus once more and she began mumbling a garbled Bible verse. Just before Milbury was about to shake her, she shouted, "Hope... Akasha Hope!"

Milbury stopped hiding his pleasure. *They had a lead on the mutant.* "Very good. Now what happened to Akasha Hope? Where did she go?"

The woman cackled hysterically. "She's in hell where she belongs." More disjointed Bible quotes followed.

"You killed her?" Holmes asked, blinking in confusion.

Mrs. Steele rounded on him. "Do I look like a priest to you? I can't kill a demon. No, she disappeared one night when she had sown the seeds of evil and the devil's work was done." She hugged herself and began quoting the Bible again.

"Damn it, woman, where is she?" Milbury demanded.

Searing pain exploded in his cheek as Mrs. Steele raked her nails across his face.

The guard pulled the raving woman back before he hit a button on the wall. "I said that's enough! It's time for you to leave. I don't care who you are, I won't have you upsetting her further."

The door opened and more guards poured into the small cell, followed by a nurse armed with a syringe. One of the guards escorted them out.

"We have a name!" Holmes said cheerfully.

Milbury shook his head and growled. "It won't do us much good. The trail's still cold, especially since she's an adult. It could take years to sort through criminal records and vehicle registrations to find her. And if she married..." He stopped at the thought. "Dear God, what if she breeds?"

Holmes scratched his chin. "Yes, what if she does?" His tone was disturbingly speculative. "What if she does?"

"Don't even think about it!" Milbury snarled, concealing a shudder at the thought of a new species of humans who could bench press Volkswagens.

***

Silas whistled a merry tune as he walked, tapping the rhythm on his hip with the latest issue of *Wheel Deals*. Akasha would be returning any minute with her driver's license. She'd been so excited last evening that she forgot her usual reserved demeanor and was downright bubbly. He could hardly wait to help her pick out a car for her Christmas present, to see those amethyst eyes sparkle as she smiled.

Snowflakes began to fall, iridescent in the moonlight. He frowned. Akasha would soon be driving on icy roads. Silas wished he knew more about automobiles so he could be sure she chose a safe one.

As he neared the house he detected Xochitl's powerful presence. She was huddled by the front gate. Silas's breath caught in alarm. Xochitl hated the cold and would go outdoors in winter only if she had no choice. The wind shifted and he heard a soft rumbling in various tones... purring. She was surrounded by cats.

They pressed their sleek bodies against hers and rubbed their faces against Xochitl's as if she was one of them and they were comforting her. Silas drew closer and was able to make out the colored markings on their fur and inhale their musky scent. The felines spotted him, eyes glowing with reflected light. In tandem, they turned to Xochitl. She saw him and waved. Instead of running away from him as most animals did, the cats moved in front of her like an honor guard and growled, fur puffed up and tails swishing.

Xochitl murmured. "It's okay, friends." She made a gesture and they scattered silently into the night.

"I've never seen anything like that before." Silas remarked.

A tremulous smile curved her lips. "Cats love me and I love them... I'm finally going to get a cat!" There was something off about her cheerful tone. *Something that was hurt.* He saw when he got closer.

His fists clenched at his sides and he struggled to suppress a roar of outrage. "My God, what happened, Xochitl?"

Her lip was swollen and split open, dried blood caked on her chin. A nasty purple blossomed on her cheek. Silas ground his teeth, hot with anger. Xochitl was under his protection. *Whoever hurt her would pay.*

She stood and crossed her arms over her chest, teeth chattering. "I had a fight with Bill. But everything's okay now." Her eyes glinted dangerously. "I just need to be away from them for a bit."

He patted her shoulder, fighting through her powerful aura to touch the Mark he'd made on her. The rage within her scalded him. He willed her to calm and answer him truthfully.

"Bill hurt you then?" he prodded gently. *No, everything wasn't okay.* It wouldn't be until Silas dealt with the bastard. Sucking in a deep breath, he grappled with his temper. He must handle this carefully.

"Yeah, but he'll never touch me again." The icy conviction made Silas fear the worst. She hunched over suddenly. "Fuck, my back hurts!"

"What did you do to him?" he demanded, locking on her mind. How would he be able to guard her if she was in prison for murder? Again, there was a vicious struggle that made his skull pound, but then he had her.

Xochitl's eyes glazed over as she answered him. "I made a fire, like this." A ball of flame appeared in her hand, then vanished. "I told them I'd burn them if they ever messed with me again. Scared the shit out of them. Until I'm old enough to move out, things are going to go my way." Her mind broke from his. "Sorry, I spaced out for a minute. What did you say?"

Silas tried to appear calm, but what he'd seen scared the shit out of him too. "I said come on inside. It is freezing out."

As he followed Xochitl into the house he realized she walked like a cat. ... *And she can manifest fire. And is somehow associated with a world that has two moons. What the hell is she?*

He sent her upstairs to clean up and wrap herself in a blanket while he made some cocoa. As the water heated on the stove, Silas poured himself a dram of scotch. He sipped it slowly, wishing he could down it without getting ill. He'd taken guardianship over Akasha and obeyed Delgarias's request to guard Xochitl and the others in order to get more answers. All he was getting were more questions. His destiny was tied with a girl who had the strength of ten men as well as a creature from another world who talked to cats. *What does it mean?*

Akasha returned home just as the water began boiling. Her beautiful smile sent heat through his body.

"I passed! One hundred percent!" She waved her license in the air as she practically skipped over to him.

132

The leather jacket she refused to part with was slung over her shoulder and he could see her nipples poking through her T-shirt. He cursed himself for noticing even as he stirred with arousal.

Silas cleared his throat, forcing his focus to the matter at hand. "Xochitl is upstairs. She had a fight with her foster parents, so she is staying here tonight."

Akasha's eyes widened. "Oh shit, is she okay?"

"Her face is bruised and her lip is split open. And she was out in the cold a wee bit." A measure of rage laced his tone.

"The bastard *hit* her? I'm gonna kick his ass!" She stomped off for the door.

"Akasha, no!" He reached to pull her back. Thankfully, she listened and turned to him, eyes narrowed in fury.

Silas kept his voice level. "Perhaps you should talk to her first. She told me they came to an understanding. I hope she will tell you more. If anything, maybe we can call the police."

"All right." She didn't look happy, but at least she seemed to see his logic. "And maybe you could just bite him or something."

"Used car salesmen usually don't taste good," he said with a wink. When she didn't laugh at his comment, he sighed. "I made some cocoa and an ice pack. Would you please bring them up to her?"

"Sure." Akasha's fists clenched with suppressed violence.

Silas closed his eyes. What kind of abuse had she suffered to make her this way? He wished he had lower scruples. Then he'd just drink from her and find out. His fangs seemed to throb as he imagined her taste.

***

Akasha knocked softly on her bedroom door to avoid smashing the polished mahogany, not trusting her temper.

"'Kash, is that you?" Xochitl's voice was muffled.

"Yeah." It was odd, standing outside her room. *It is mine,* Akasha realized, surprised at the pride that came with the thought.

Behind the door, she heard Xochitl laugh softly. "Dude, it's your room, come in."

Akasha went in, and cursed at her friend's pitiful sight. Xochitl was dwarfed by the huge blanket and still shivering. Her lower lip was huge and purple with a gash in the middle. This was no open handed slap. No, definitely close-fisted.

"Silas said I could crash here. Is that cool?" Xochitl winced when her bruised cheek shifted as she spoke.

Akasha shook her head. "You dumbass. You're my best friend. Of course it's cool. Silas made cocoa, but it probably wouldn't feel good on that cut."

Xochitl took the cup and sighed in pleasure as it warmed her hands.

"So what happened, Xoch'?" Akasha asked quietly, quivering with fury.

"They insulted my mother and I naturally took offense," she explained airily, but her eyes were a dark burgundy, like Beau's hair. They seemed to change color with her moods, and red could not be good. Xochitl rolled her eyes and continued. "I went off on a tangent about what sadistic assholes they are and Bill punched me. His class ring hurt like a bitch."

"That motherfucker!" Akasha growled. "Silas says we could call the cops."

The deep red of Xochitl's eyes was unnerving. "No. They won't touch me again. They're afraid of me now."

"What did you do?" Akasha whispered, not sure she wanted to know as she took a step back. *How the hell were her eyes doing that?*

Xochitl smiled wickedly. "I could ask you how you threw that big jock at the kegger on Halloween."

Akasha gasped, not knowing whether she should be pissed off or scared. She tried to sound casual and leaned against the wall, folding her arms. "It would be dangerous for you to know."

Xochitl nodded. "Don't ask, don't tell. I knew you'd understand. I'm really sorry to be such a bitch about it though. Still friends?" Her eyes bled to puppy-dog brown.

Akasha nodded, shoulders sagging in relief. "As long as you don't 'scare me' like you did them."

Xochitl laughed without malice. "If you don't throw me across the room, I won't need to. Does Silas have any more of that yummy wine?"

"Yeah. He bought a case when he saw how much you liked it." Akasha relaxed slightly at the change of subject.

"Your boyfriend is so awesome. I'd be jealous of you if I didn't know that you've suffered more in life than I have," Xochitl said.

The wisdom and empathy in that statement made her feel uncomfortable.

"Don't call him my boyfriend." Akasha's ears burned as she remembered Silas's kiss. He hadn't made any more moves on her and she couldn't figure out whether she was relieved or disappointed.

Xochitl laughed. "Your boyfriend is hot."

"Dammit Xochitl!" Akasha whacked her friend softly on the shoulder with a pillow, mindful of her injured face.

"Okay!" Xochitl raised her hands in surrender. "So, have you slept with him yet?"

Akasha sighed. "No. Nothing's happened." Things had been awkward since that first and only kiss. Ironically, learning that he was a five hundred year old blood drinker didn't make half the impact on her life as his awakening of her sexuality.

Xochitl seemed to sense her reticence and changed the subject. "Can we get drunk now?"

It was a school night, but... *fuck it.* Her friend had been through hell tonight, despite the fact she was trying to play it cool. She needed to be numb for a bit. Perhaps they both did.

They headed downstairs and saw that Silas was already opening a bottle of Riesling.

Xochitl ran up and hugged him. "My hero!"

Jealously blazed through Akasha until she saw the helpless look Silas gave her. Then it was kind of funny. She was coming to realize that Xochitl could be a runaway freight train when she was emotionally distraught. *This is going to be a long night.*

They sat at the kitchen table as Xochitl went through glass after glass of wine while chain smoking and regaling them with a long monologue about what she was going to do now that she was "free."

"And I'm gonna get a cat, a Siamese, and I'm gonna name her Isis and she'll wear a jewel-studded collar and eat from a crystal dish and go with me everywhere in my car..." Xochitl broke off with a yawn.

"Go to bed, Xoch,'" Akasha ordered when her friend looked ready to fall asleep and Silas returned from another of his walks... Or rather, hunts for blood. It was three in the morning.

She didn't argue. "'Kay."

After Xochitl stumbled up to bed Silas shook his head. "That is the most entertaining drunk woman I've ever seen."

"Yeah." Akasha opened another beer and they shared a somewhat companionable silence punctuated with blips of sexual tension.

She studied him as she sipped her beer. Drops of melted snow gleamed in his silken hair like fairy glitter. One large hand rested on the table and she shivered as she remembered his touch. His other hand was tucked under his firm chin with his thumb near his sensuously chiseled lips. He was so close she could lean over and touch them with hers.

"I should probably go check on Xochitl," Akasha murmured, though for some reason she didn't want to leave. She was enjoying spending time with Silas. After Xochitl's melodrama, the vampire was an oasis of calm.

Silas held up a hand. "If you could spare a few minutes, I brought a *Wheel Deals*. I was hoping we could pick out a car for you."

It was the excuse she needed. "Okay."

Akasha couldn't suppress her excitement. *My own car!*

They flipped through the pages and she nearly squealed with delight as she saw her dream car. "That's it! That's the one!"

"What is it?" His eyes gleamed, reflecting her enthusiasm.

"A '73 Roadrunner." She shrugged in instinctive apology for not choosing something more popular. "I know there were better years, but this one has sentimental value to me. Besides, a 318 is better on gas mileage anyway. Max said it was one of the most bullet-proof v-eights ever built."

"Max?" His voice was silky with inquiry.

"An old friend... He was the one who taught me everything I know about cars," Akasha stammered at the painful memory. "Anyway, that's the car I want."

He frowned dubiously... either at her mention of Max or the advertisement. "It says it needs work."

She nodded, quivering with excitement. "I know. That's great! Then I can restore it from the ground up."

Silas smiled, and she got that melty feeling again. "Christmas is coming soon. Now that you have your license, why don't you borrow my car until you get your own?"

Akasha closed her eyes and pictured the envy in everyone's eyes when she pulled the Barracuda in the student parking lot.

"Really? Thanks! I'll be real careful with it." She nearly hugged him like Xochitl did, but stopped and patted him awkwardly on the shoulder. Who knew what would happen if she was in his arms again?

"And as for the band, I was thinking of getting them new instruments," Silas said, setting aside the *Wheel Deals*. "I wondered if you would be willing to do a little detective work and find out which guitars and such they are pining over."

"Oh... Silas," Akasha gasped at his generosity. "Wouldn't that be too much?"

He shook his head. "Not for me. It's been a long time since I've had anyone to indulge."

His eyes went distant and deep with sadness. Akasha realized he must still miss his family that had been killed five hundred years ago. *Had he really been all alone since then?* A sudden urge to take him into her arms and cradle his head against her breast overcame her. Akasha thrust it away. *What's happening to me?*

"I better check on Xochitl and go to bed," she whispered as their gazes met.

Silas looked deep into her eyes, his gaze seeming to say everything and nothing at all. "Sleep well, Akasha."

Chapter Sixteen
Pisa, Italy

"My lord!" Selena's spy said breathlessly as he burst into her private chambers. "I have returned from the States with momentous news!"

"Do sit down, Charles." Selena feigned scorned boredom though she was quaking with excitement. *Will I finally have ammunition against Silas?*

The vampire obeyed and sat in a chair across from her throne. "Silas McNaught has Marked four more mortals. *Teenagers!*" he finished.

"How very odd." Her brow creased in a frown. Most vampires only Marked one mortal at a time. *What could Silas have been thinking?* And more importantly, how could she use that against him?

"One of the females is not human," Charles added as an afterthought.

Selena jerked upright and narrowed her gaze on the vampire as if he were a fascinating insect. "What do you mean? Is she a vampire then?" *Could one even Mark another vampire?*

Charles shook his head. "No. I don't know what she is, but the creature radiates power, the likes of which I've never felt before." He shuddered.

Licking her lips, Selena leaned forward. Now this was something useful. Perhaps she could claim that Silas was using this creature to build up his power base and overthrow the Elders. It was a far-fetched idea for those who knew McNaught, but entirely believable to those who did not.

But what was this being? She tugged on a lock of her hair as she mused. Then her eyes widened. This must be why Delgarias has paid a visit to Silas. The creature must be the key to the Prophecy! She pulled her hair harder, relishing in the pain. *I must get this inhuman female.* Perhaps she could demand it as her forfeit.

Struggling to keep her patience, Selena forced Charles to recount everything he was able to glean about Silas and the mortals he marked. After the spy departed, she knelt before her altar and lit a candle to honor Mephistopheles as she prayed for guidance.

Searching for the right words, she composed a letter to Marcus, Lord of Rome and the Second Elder. Marcus had shared a few passionate evenings with her and she hoped his fondness for her remained.

A few weeks later, she received her reply. The Elders would send a representative to investigate. A gasp tore from her throat at the name of the representative. It was none other than Razvan Nicolae. A bubble of laughter escaped her lips at the thought of Silas being under investigation by his own maker. And since Silas had failed him before, likely he would not be merciful.

Selena frowned, remembering that she had also failed to find Razvan's missing twin. She grasped another lock of her hair and pulled. The pain forced the disturbing thought away. It was not her powers that failed, she reasoned, it was just that she cared not for his desire.

***

Christmas came and Akasha got her Roadrunner. She hugged Silas then, disregarding her intimacy issues for once. She tried not to dwell on how good his embrace felt, or how bereft she felt when it ended.

"Will you tell me about Max? The man who taught you to work miracles on vehicles?" The gentle plea coupled with his generosity compelled her to give him at least a few words.

"I'd run away from an abusive foster home and he took me in..." Akasha looked away, unwilling to admit Max had caught her eating out of his garbage. "Anyway, in return for room and board, he had me help him in his shop."

Silas frowned. "Why aren't you with him now? He didn't hurt you, did he?"

"No!" Outrage made her shout. Sobering with shame, she explained. "He... well, apparently he had a chop shop or something on the side. The cops came and... I guess he's probably still in prison."

Akasha closed her eyes at the memory.

"Listen!" Max had roared. "If those cops see you they might report you to whoever killed your folks! They're probably still lookin' for ya! Now scat while I distract em'!"

He ruffled her curls one last time and strode back to the house. Akasha heard cars pulling up the driveway. She dashed to the rear door of the shop, opening it carefully. No officers in sight so far. She sprinted to a huge spruce tree and climbed up. She couldn't leave without finding out what happened to Max.

From her new vantage point, she could see him on the front porch. His hands were up and he was speaking calmly to four officers that held their guns trained on him. Max sank to his knees and laced his hands behind his head. Two cops came over and cuffed him. He was escorted to the car.

Soon after, more police arrived and they inspected the garage. Akasha's limbs cramped and screamed from being up in the tree so long. Finally, after the sun had long since set, they departed. She wasn't fooled, though. They would return soon to retrieve the stolen cars and gather up evidence.

She leapt out of the tree and stretched gratefully before rushing to the house. In minutes, she stuffed a backpack full of food, cigarettes, and clothes. She slung her prized leather jacket over her shoulder and chugged a beer on the way out.

On the streets again. She thought with resignation and a touch of remorse. But she was used to this life. Akasha walked a few miles, ate an apple, smoked a cigarette, and fell asleep behind a billboard.

"Where did you go then?" Silas interrupted her thoughts.

A wave of terror and revulsion made the garage swim before her vision. "I don't want to talk about it, okay?"

His brows drew together in a stern frown and he opened his mouth to argue. But then his shoulders slumped and he sighed. "Very well, Akasha. Though I hope someday you can trust me enough to tell me what happened."

Trust... Akasha swallowed a lump in her throat. What an alien concept it was.

As if he sensed her turmoil, Silas leaned down and caressed her cheek, eyes gleaming with sweet compassion. "I will leave you alone and let you return to your project now. But you must promise that if you need anything..."

"I will." She turned away and grabbed her ratchet before he could see the brimming moisture in her eyes.

After two days of working on the Roadrunner almost without pause, Silas suggested she take a break. His worry was obvious, but the real motivation for Akasha to comply was the opportunity to give her friends their presents.

When *Rage of Angels* opened their gifts, tears filled their eyes. Sylvis cradled her Fender Stratocaster like she never wanted to let it go. When Xochitl opened her Dave Mustaine series Jackson King V guitar, her shriek of joy seemed to shake the house. Akasha and Silas were nearly crushed in all the hugs. Isis, Xochitl's bluepoint Siamese kitten wanted nothing to do with Silas, however, and bolted up the stairs as soon as she had the chance.

"You got your 'Isis,' I see." Akasha smiled at the retreating kitten.

Xochitl grinned. "And you got your car, I heard. Come on, let's see it!"

Silas gave them one last smile before he headed off on one of his walks that Akasha now knew were hunts for fresh blood. *Would he bite another woman tonight?* She forced the disturbing thought from her mind and led her friends to the garage.

Aurora and Beau looked doubtful at the now gutted Roadrunner, but Xochitl immediately saw its promise of being a hot rod.

"You should call it the 'Pretty Hate Machine.'" Xochitl thought everyone should name their cars. She'd already named Silas's 'Cuda, "Black Sunshine." Akasha didn't mind. Xochitl picked good names.

Beau and Aurora nodded disinterestedly. Akasha grinned, knowing that Aurora was practically salivating to set up the ten piece Tama drum kit and Beau would have a fit if he didn't get to strum his Lakland bass. She sighed. It looked like her new car would have to wait until tomorrow.

Chapter Seventeen

Silas felt the other vampire before he heard his footsteps approaching in the tavern parking lot. The sinister aura made goose bumps tremble on his flesh and ancient power made his bones ache.

"What do you want, Razvan?" McNaught struggled to keep his voice casual.

"What makes you think that I want anything, Silas?" A deep, heavily accented voice replied before Razvan appeared in front of Silas. "Do I need a reason to pay a visit to my favorite prodigy?" The vampire was shorter than Silas by a few inches, but his dark hair and villainous features would make the devil weep with envy.

Silas's gaze remained fixed upon his maker. "Everything you do, no matter how small, Razvan Nicolae, has a means to an end."

For the longest time, ebony and emerald eyes remained locked on one another as if in combat. Then Razvan's face broke into a wide fanged grin, and he spread his hands in surrender. "All right. I can never fool you, Silas McNaught."

"So…?" Silas prodded, his voice hushed in the falling snow.

Razvan's grin increased. "So, the first reason I am here is so you can congratulate me on becoming Lord of a city."

McNaught's brow rose. "You've ceased your wandering search for your brother? *And* decided to take on a city?"

Razvan nodded, still smiling. Silas couldn't help but grin back. Razvan had been obsessed with nothing but finding his missing twin brother, also a vampire, for centuries. Perhaps there was hope for happiness for his maker after all.

"Somehow I think your ulterior motive for *that* will be a very long story. What is your new city?" Silas asked.

Razvan withdrew his pipe from his coat pocket. "Spokane, Washington."

Silas gaped. "That puts you practically in my backyard! Why Spokane?"

"Why did you take Coeur d'Alene?" Razvan fired back, undaunted.

"It is beautiful, quiet, and there aren't many other vampires around to bother me." He ran a hand through his hair, shaking out a few snowflakes.

A wicked gleam returned to Razvan's eyes as he loaded the pipe. "It is also far from your homeland."

"That is true." Silas stated calmly, unwilling to rise to the jab.

"And you don't think I'd choose this area for similar reasons?" the vampire asked with an arched brow.

Silas sighed. "Perhaps. But it seems more likely a place like this would bore you. Why didn't you answer my message when I entered your territory?"

"I had not moved in yet. And how could I be bored with all these beautiful lakes and mountains? Not to mention the delectable tourists," Razvan's voice was vexingly saccharine.

Silas threw up his hands in exasperation. "All right. What is your other reason for coming here?"

Razvan's expression sobered as he lit his pipe. "The Elders sent me."

An arrow of panic pierced McNaught's heart. "Oh?"

"They have heard some disturbing rumors about you, Silas." His maker's voice was dire with unspoken implications.

Silas kept his face carefully blank. "Have they?"

Razvan nodded and drew deeply on his pipe. Cherry scented tobacco smoke filled the night. "Yes, according to Selena's report you have Marked five mortals... children, even. I know Selena is insane, but the rumors had to have come from somewhere. What have you been doing to merit this kind of talk?"

Silas sighed in defeat. He'd long suspected that Selena would retaliate his leaving her and her cult, but he'd hoped she'd forgotten him over the years. "Actually the rumors are true." *Why didn't Delgarias explain the situation?* The thought struck him suddenly. "The first one I Marked is a young woman I took guardianship over. She belongs to me, so it is within my rights to Mark her. The other four are her friends, which I was instructed by Delgarias himself to guard. There are special circumstances surrounding one of them that cause concern for all their safety. I Marked all of them just to err on the side of caution."

Razvan's jaw gaped. His expression would have made Silas laugh if the situation weren't so grave. "You... you...

became a legal guardian? Have you gone mad? We're *vampires*, not fathers."

"It was not my intention to be her father." Silas protested vehemently.

"Then why did you take her? Do not tell me some of the speculations are correct." Razvan's voice grew harsh with scorn and loathing. "Have you acquired a taste for young flesh?"

Silas shook his head, his mouth filling with a bitter taste at the accusation. "No, nothing like that!"

Razvan nodded, chewing on his pipe stem. "Good. Because I would then feel obligated to warn you that pederasty could bring about your execution, just as it did for the former Lord of Spokane."

"Is that what happened to him?" Silas's stomach roiled with disgust. "I am now glad I did not know him well."

"Never mind that," Razvan said with a dismissive wave. "Now why did you become this girl's legal guardian?"

"Because I have had visions of her for centuries. Somehow, our fates are entwined." The minute the words came out of his mouth he wished he could take them back. He sounded like a fool. "Besides," Silas added quickly. "She's nearly twenty, hardly a child. And she has no one. The poor woman was dressed practically in rags. I have plenty of money and I might as well put it to use."

Razvan stared, dumbfounded. "This is insane. I still don't understand. How can you possibly be legally in charge of a nineteen year old woman? I thought people were considered adults at the age of eighteen in this country. As for the other four, what exactly are the 'special circumstances' surrounding one of them that would motivate you to mark all four?" He took a deep breath and blew out a cloud of smoke. "And I have heard nothing of Delgarias being involved."

Silas regarded him with a humorless smile. "I assume the Elders sent you to see for yourself. Am I correct?"

"You are." Razvan inclined his head in a parody of a bow.

Silas resumed walking and beckoned for him to follow. "Then come along, old friend, I do not have all night."

As they walked back to the house, Silas's mind raced with a thousand questions. *Why didn't Delgarias tell the others of his orders?* Had he forgotten? A disturbing thought struck him and he stopped so suddenly that his foot skidded on the ice and he nearly fell face first into the slushy mess on the road. What if it was a set up?

***

As Razvan followed Silas down the arctic wasteland that passed for a road, he pondered his fledgling's explanations. *Had Delgarias really pressed McNaught to guard a group of silly mortal adolescents?* It did not at all sound like something the ancient would do. But then Silas wasn't the type to lie. A former Scottish warrior, McNaught was still hung up on foolish things like "honor." Razvan sneered. At the least, this investigation should provide him with an amusing diversion.

They turned right and headed up a tortuously steep hill. But when the small castle came into view, he decided the trek was worth the walk.

Razvan whistled his appreciation of Silas's home as they plodded up the driveway. "An American castle... I like it."

Silas bowed. "Thank you. I designed it myself, for Akasha." A strange smile played across his face. "She is not as impressed with it as I had hoped."

As they entered the garage, stomping the clinging snow from their boots, Razvan was startled by a flurry of curses uttered in a feminine voice. The sounds came from a vintage muscle car that was jacked up, hood open on the far side of the garage. Multiple clangs and obscenities came from underneath. Razvan threw Silas a questioning glance. Silas merely grinned and beckoned him to the vehicle.

A pair of dainty feet and shapely denim-encased legs were visible under the car. Silas coughed pointedly.

"Just a minute," a growl echoed through the metal.

More clinking followed. Just when Razvan was about to tap his foot in impatience, a tiny woman who looked like a filthy porcelain doll rolled out from underneath the car.

"I think I got it!" she squealed ecstatically.

"You got what?" Silas asked with a sickening tender smile.

The female's teeth clenched. "That fucking motor mount. Damn, that thing was a bitch!"

The adoration in McNaught's gaze was plain. "That is good. Akasha, I would like for you to meet my friend and associate, Razvan Nicolae."

"Hi. I'd shake your hand, but mine is covered in gunk." The young lady regarded him curiously with startling amethyst eyes.

Razvan blinked at the suspicion in her gaze. *She knows what I am.*

"That is quite all right, Akasha. It is a pleasure to meet you." Razvan struggled to keep a straight face. The Mark on her beat powerfully upon him, informing him that she *definitely* belonged to Silas. He never guessed that his fledgling had that much power.

Another shocking realization came when he looked into Akasha's eyes. He couldn't read her mind! *Unthinkable!* But here it was. It wasn't that her mind was completely shut off to him; her thoughts were just moving in such a rapid buzz that he was unable to discern a single word or image. It made him quite dizzy. Silas had some explaining to do.

"Are your friends still here?" Silas asked her.

"Yeah, they're in the basement practicing." Akasha returned her tools in her royal purple toolbox, her hands shaking nervously. "I think they're staying the night."

Silas nodded and shot Razvan a worried glance. "All right. Why don't you wash up and meet Razvan and me downstairs."

As soon as McNaught's pet mortal departed, Razvan smiled wickedly. Silas *should* be worried. Nonchalantly, he asked what he already suspected. "Does she know what you are?"

McNaught stiffened in apparent unease. "She does, but the others do not. Delgarias forbade it."

"And you trust her not to tell them?" Trust was an alien concept to Razvan.

"Yes," Silas said confidently. "Akasha can keep secrets better than anyone I have met." His lips curved in a humorless smile. "She is keeping plenty from me as it is."

Razvan's eyes widened in disbelief. "Why would you tolerate such a thing? You could feed from her and find out, you know. Or have you forgotten what you are?"

"I *will not* violate her in any way," Silas said firmly.

They remained in the garage for a few more moments as Razvan pondered the great hunk of metal Silas's pet mortal was operating on. "Why do you not buy her a new car?"

McNaught shook his head. "I tried. She wouldn't let me. She wanted this one because it is her 'dream car,' and she's always wanted to restore one from the ground up." Pride infused his voice. "And at least it keeps her from tinkering with mine so much."

"It appears that you have a prodigy on your hands." Razvan couldn't hide his surprise, not only for the woman's unique talent, but also for the warmth in Silas's voice when he spoke of her. To feel that deeply for another was surely dangerous to one's health.

Silas turned back to him, reluctance etched all over his face. "Speaking of prodigies, it's time for you to meet *Rage of Angels*."

"*Rage of Angels*?" Razvan frowned in confusion.

"Yes, the other four I Marked. They are musicians and that is what they call themselves. Their music is most... Interesting."

There was something odd in McNaught's voice, but Razvan could not decipher it, so he shrugged. "I enjoy music. Let's hope these pets of yours can actually manage something resembling a tune."

Razvan followed Silas into the house eager to meet the other "children" Silas had Marked. He wondered if they were as fascinating as Akasha. Of course they really weren't children, not in most vampires' standards. After all, back in his day a sixteen year old girl would already be wed and pregnant with at least a second child and Akasha would be a spinster. He would have to clarify those details to the Elders. Either Selena's spy must have been a youngling, full of modern ideas about the age of adulthood, or Selena was going out of her way to cast a negative light on Silas. Razvan smirked. It was likely the latter.

As they made their way downstairs, he detected a presence... something not human, but not vampire either.

"Silas," he whispered, baring his fangs. "Do you feel that? *Something* is in your home!"

McNaught's lips curved in faint amusement. "I know."

"What?" Razvan began, but Silas cut him off with an impatient gesture.

"Come, you shall see."

Grinding his teeth, Razvan continued to follow him. He had little patience for games.

As they entered the hallway, loud thumping and screeching noises followed by a blood-curdling scream assaulted his ears. "What is that racket?"

Silas opened a door and pointed. "Music."

At the far end of the room, three girls and a boy stood on a small stage. The girl in the back was pounding ferociously on a set of drums while the other three danced their fingers across the strings of their guitars.

Razvan's perusal halted when his eyes rested upon the girl in front. *She* was the inhuman presence! He could throttle Silas for not preparing him for this. *What is she?* There certainly didn't seem to be anything alien in her appearance besides the fact that she was startlingly beautiful and had two bright streaks of purple in her black hair. She could pass for human more easily than a vampire.

His thoughts broke off as she opened her mouth to sing, and he was struck senseless by the power of her song.

No human could sing like that. Her voice was so potent, so passionate, that it was like a tangible thing reaching into his chest and squeezing his heart. The words of the song were lost to Razvan as he could only focus on the sound of her voice, but the emotions behind it were so clear he felt like a blind man finally able to see. The girl struck an angry chord on her guitar and let loose a scream of rage that sent a rush of exhilaration through his body. So this was why they were called "Rage of Angels." Certainly that was the sound of wrathful seraphim.

Too soon, it was over. The silence was palpable, making him ache to hear the melody just once more. Silas placed his hand on his shoulder and he jumped, snapping out of the trance. "What... What?"

"Razvan Nicolae, it is my pleasure to introduce you to Xochitl Leonine." *The daughter of Mephistopheles,* Silas's mind silently whispered.

Silas went on to introduce the others, but Razvan didn't catch their names. Numb with shock, he stared into Xochitl's eyes of dark honey, trying to figure out what sort of creature his protégé' held under his roof. *The daughter of Mephistopheles? Surely that is impossible!*

Almost more startling was the music. Dear God, the music. Silas watched him with a knowing smirk that was decidedly vexing. Razvan composed himself as his mind raced, latching onto the best way to twist this situation to his advantage.

Chapter Eighteen

"You are very skilled," Razvan said to *Rage of Angels*, idly stroking his goatee. "But you still have much to learn."

Silas felt a stab of outrage at the vampire's scornful tone. *How dare he insult them!*

Aurora fixed Razvan with a regal stare. "We know," she replied with a determined lift of her chin. "That's why we're practicing now. We want to become the best."

Razvan's eyes widened at her unflinching, practical reaction to his criticism. But he quickly recovered himself. "I see. Now who are your influences?"

With a grin, Xochitl rattled off over a dozen names. The ancient Lord vampire smiled and rattled off some names of his own. Silas recognized about half.

"Um... could you write those down?" Sylvis asked shyly.

"With pleasure," Razvan nodded, removing a pen from his coat pocket.

"You wouldn't happen to be in the music business, would you?" Beau asked, admiring Razvan's physique in such a way that Silas had to choke back his laughter despite his growing discomfort with the situation.

"No," Razvan replied. "I am merely a long-time music aficionado."

When he finished writing, he turned to Xochitl. "You have quite a voice, young lady, but it lacks a certain richness." He pointed at a few names on his list. "These bands all had the same singer at one time or another. Study him," he commanded. "Emulate him, if you can."

"Okay," Xochitl replied, seemingly overwhelmed with his insistence.

Silas fought to keep his expression composed as he searched his maker's face for any sign of insincerity. He noticed Akasha eyeing Razvan with suspicion as well. He cleared his throat. "I believe we should get started with our meeting now, Mr. Nicolae."

Razvan smirked, but acceded. "Very well, McNaught."

Once they were ensconced in his office, Silas rounded on his maker. "What game are you playing at? Surely you cannot care that much about rock music."

Razvan's eyes narrowed a moment before he laughed coldly. "*That* was not rock; that was a hybridized version of thrash metal which has wandered too far from its classic roots. All that aside, perhaps I do care." He once more removed his pipe and loaded it. "There is much you don't know about me, McNaught. Either way, you'd do best to remember that it's my job to investigate them. And keep in mind that if things do not work out for you, there will be a transfer of ownership. With prodigies of the likes of those four... five if we count the lovely Akasha, well, we would not want them to fall into the wrong hands, would we?" He grinned wickedly as he struck his lighter. "I shall endeavor for them to think well of me. It will be easier that way."

Silas bared his fangs as he met the other vampire's mocking gaze. "You bastard," he hissed, bitter with the knowledge that there was nothing he could do to stop him.

***

Akasha frowned as Silas and Razvan headed up to the office. Razvan was another vampire, she was positive. And from his air of command and the insolent way he looked at everything as if it belonged to him, he wasn't one of Silas's subordinates. Her fists clenched as she remembered the mocking way he'd bowed when Silas introduced him. She didn't like Razvan, not at all.

"So who is that guy?" Xochitl asked after she put her guitar back in its case.

"I dunno." Akasha yawned and stroked Xochitl's kitten. Isis sounded like a mini diesel engine. "Silas said he was an associate, so I guess he's another financial advisor, or maybe a stockbroker."

"Weird financial guy, he sounded like Dracula!"

Akasha shivered. Dracula was too close to the mark. She forced herself to sound casual. "Well, you heard his name; he's probably from Russia or something." *Hell, maybe he's the Lord of Kiev.*

Xochitl couldn't let it go, though. "Y'know, 'Kash, I don't think either of them are financial guys." Her voice was low and speculative. "They didn't seem to talk any business, and Silas is hardly ever on a cell phone. In fact, that Razvan guy seemed more interested in *us.*"

"The band, Xochitl." Akasha avoided her friend's gaze. "You guys are really good. It's not every day people your age have so much musical talent. Besides, I've seen Silas's stock portfolio. *And* I've seen him meet with a few clients."

"Maybe..." Xochitl murmured, unconvinced.

Akasha didn't think that was all either, but she was too disconcerted about this new visitor and Xochitl's voiced suspicions to say anything else. She didn't like the way Razvan had looked at her friend. *What if he's planning to Mark Xochitl?* A surge of protective rage stole her breath. *Silas won't let him... will he?*

Beau plopped down on the couch next to them. "I think he's pretty damn fine. Though Silas has a hotter body."

"How do you know?" Aurora glanced at him as she and Sylvis unrolled their sleeping bags near the TV. "You spying on them in the shower?"

Beau laughed. "Now that's an idea. I'm jealous, 'Kash. Why is your place full of eye candy?"

Sylvis, who seemed oblivious to masculine beauty most of the time, interrupted. "Are we going to start this *Evil Dead* marathon or not?" She held up the DVDs with a grin.

When they were settled around the TV, Akasha went back upstairs to grab some beer and hopefully ask Silas about his new visitor. For a moment she was tempted to go up to the office and eavesdrop, but she discarded the thought. Likely Silas would sense her with his vampire powers. And if he didn't, she suspected that Razvan would.

After she grabbed the case of beer as well as a bottle of wine for Xochitl, she heard Razvan and Silas coming down the stairs. Akasha felt a thread of hope. Maybe he was leaving. She put the drinks back in the fridge and headed out to the living room.

The two vampires seemed not to notice her as they talked in low voices she couldn't discern. When Razvan reached the foyer, he shook Silas's hand and turned to face Akasha. His malevolent black eyes focused on her with unnerving intensity. She stood straight, refusing to tremble, and matched his stare with her own.

Whatever he saw seemed to amuse him and he chuckled and made another mocking bow in her direction. "It was a pleasure to make your acquaintance, Akasha. I bid you both a good evening."

Yup, definitely a vampire, Akasha thought. With that old-school speech, what else could he be? As the door closed, she turned to Silas. "Who the hell was that?"

Silas sighed. "My new neighbor, it seems. Razvan has taken charge of Spokane." But there was more to it. Akasha could see that in every line of strain on his beautiful face.

"And?" she prodded, her stomach tightening with worry.

He gave her a half smile that made her heart turn over before his ominous frown returned. "The Elders have sent him to investigate me."

Akasha frowned and stepped closer to him, a chill crawling over her flesh. "Investigate you for what?"

"Remember that concert I took you and your friends to?" At her nod, he continued. "One of the Spokane vampires took an interest in Xochitl and I had to Mark her to keep her safe. Just to be cautious I also Marked the other three. My intentions seem to have backfired. An old... er... acquaintance of mine caught wind of the incident and has concocted a tale to the Elders, making it appear as if I am building a power base in an attempt to go rogue." He seemed about to say more, but then his shoulders slumped and he sighed.

Akasha frowned. This vampire stuff just kept getting deeper. "Who are the Elders and what exactly is going rogue?"

"The Elders are the thirteen most powerful vampires in the world. They make the rules for our kind and punish all who disobey."

Nodding in understanding, she answered her own question. "And they now suspect you're trying to set up your own government?" At Silas's nod, her heart tore between sympathy for him and dread of what was to come. "That's total bullshit... So does Razvan believe you?"

Silas shrugged and ran a hand through his hair. "It doesn't matter what he believes. Razvan will do whatever is of most benefit to him. He's been that way ever since I met him."

Curiosity sparked her as she slowly drew closer. "How did you meet him?"

"He made me."

Akasha brightened with a measure of relief. "Well, that should be a good thing. He'd be more likely to side with you, right?"

The vampire shook his head. "Not necessarily. We have not spoken in over four hundred years."

"What happens if his report is negative?" She spoke past the knot of worry in her throat.

Silas sighed and stepped even closer to her. "Then I could face a trial, though I have high hopes that it will be avoided."

Now they were almost in kissing distance. "And what if it does and you *are* found guilty?" she whispered with growing fear. After all he'd done for her she couldn't bear the thought of anything bad happening to him.

His hand settled on her shoulder, sending pleasant tingles down her spine. "I would rather not talk about that." Slowly, he bent down to meet her gaze. Glittering green eyes engulfed her vision. "No matter what happens, I promise I will keep you safe," he whispered against her lips.

Akasha trembled and reached for him, but he pulled away. Silas looked down at her, eyes glowing and fangs partially revealed through his parted lips. His gaze roved over body as if she were what he desired most in the world. Her knees weakened.

"Silas…" she began, not knowing what she was going to say next, only that her emotions were in such turmoil that she longed for succor.

"Oh, Akasha," he groaned. "How you try my control sometimes." He straightened his shoulders and walked past her. "I must feed now." When he reached the door, he added, "Razvan could return at any time. Don't *ever* show him any fear. By law, he cannot hurt you, but it would amuse him greatly to make you think he could."

"Uh-huh," she murmured, still dazed at his almost kiss. When the door closed behind him, she slumped against the wall and tried to clear her thoughts.

By the time her legs stopped feeling like they were made of electrified rubber, Akasha was certain of two things. One: Razvan was an asshole. Two: she had an obscenely large crush on her so-called guardian, Silas McNaught, Lord Vampire of Coeur d'Alene. Not only that, but he had come to mean a lot to her.

Akasha clenched her fists. If Razvan or any of those Elders tried to hurt Silas, she would hurt them first.

***

Razvan's low, mocking laughter assaulted Silas's ears the moment he stepped outside. "I knew you wanted the woman badly, but I cannot believe you haven't taken her yet. I usually do not advocate fucking one's food, but if it would relieve your obvious agony..."

"Is there a point to your words?" Silas asked through clenched teeth as he kept walking.

"I am merely making an observation," Razvan said as he lit his pipe and followed. "I do not understand why you deprive yourself when you likely have your pick of the female vampires in this city as well as four delectable women under your roof... and even a male, if such a proclivity is to your taste these days."

"I do not mix business with pleasure," Silas replied, stepping carefully on the icy asphalt. "Besides, you should know why. You should know exactly who Akasha is to me from the time you fed from my dying body and saw all that I knew. Or have you grown so old you cannot remember five centuries back?"

Razvan turned away from him to look up at the moon, but not before the other vampire caught a strange look on his face. "I close my mind to that noise." His voice dripped with derision.

Silas struggled to hide his shock. Seeing and experiencing another's life was one of the main pleasures of feeding. Why would Razvan cut himself off from it? *Unless...*

"You cannot stand feeling empathy!" Silas faced his maker, his gaze challenging him to deny it. "After losing your twin—"

"Enough!" Razvan hissed, walking faster. "It is you who are under investigation, not me." His voice returned to its usual malevolence. "Now what exactly is Akasha to you?"

They stopped at the bottom of the hill. Snowflakes began to fall once more, turning the town into a dream of winter beauty.

"As I told you earlier, I have had visions of Akasha since my mortal days," Silas said slowly. "I believe she may be my one true love."

Razvan laughed and rolled his eyes. "You still believe in that foolish romantic prattle?"

Without warning, Silas seized Razvan's arm and focused his clairvoyant powers. What he saw brought laughter to his lips as the other vampire jerked away from his grip.

"Your time will come, my friend," Silas cheerfully informed him and began walking south on 15th Street before the other vampire could retort. "You will contact Delgarias to confirm his command to me, won't you?" he called over his shoulder.

Razvan glared and nodded stiffly before he rose in the air and flew north, following the 1-90 onramp.

Chapter Nineteen

The rest of Christmas vacation wasn't much of a break for Akasha. Razvan had practically moved in. Silas didn't say anything to confirm or deny it, but she was pretty sure the other vampire was sleeping in one of the spare rooms in the secret lair under the house.

Her nerves screamed in exhausted frustration. She barely had a moment to herself, much less a moment alone with Silas to ask him how the so-called "investigation" was going. It was bullshit. Akasha had to change her schedule to work on the car during the day, because it never failed that when night fell, Razvan would be in the garage, watching her and pestering her with probing questions. *Asshole.*

"Where are you from?" he would ask, circling the car and the engine stand like a restless cat. "What do you remember about your parents?"

"I don't know," she'd repeat until irritation had her on the verge of snapping her wrench.

Razvan would then stare at her as if he were trying to read her mind. Akasha would break out into chills at his scrutiny, careful to only move the engine block when he wasn't looking, so he wouldn't see her unusual strength, though she longed to demonstrate it right in his fucking teeth.

To make matters worse, Xochitl and the band were completely under Razvan's spell. Their earlier misgivings were completely forgotten as he gathered with them in the basement to watch and critique their practice sessions.

Akasha asked Silas if he was doing any vampire mind control on them.

Silas was confident that Razvan wasn't. Which somehow made it more frightening… and irritating.

Razvan was right about what *Rage of Angels* needed to work on. Akasha realized it when she saw the list of bands he'd made out for the group to research in surprisingly elegant handwriting. A lot of them she recognized as Max's old favorites.

Xochitl, Sylvis, Aurora and Beau spent hours on the computer downloading classic songs and watching old concert footage, growing more inspired by the minute.

"What have you learned from your research?" Razvan asked them one evening in the tone of a renowned professor.

Sylvis approached him with a solemn expression and said, "I am deeply ashamed of my generation."

Akasha rolled her eyes and lit a cigarette. *Were all teenagers this easily influenced?*

Sylvis finished her statement with a melodramatic sweep of her hand before she grabbed her guitar and began playing a classic riff. The rest of the band followed suit, playing *Rainbow's* "Man on the Silver Mountain." A reluctant smile pulled at Akasha's lips. She hadn't heard that one since her days in Max's garage.

Akasha was torn between awe at their skill and near-fury with Razvan. Yet again, the son of a bitch had been right. This was exactly what *Rage of Angels* needed. And the influence of Ronnie James Dio made Xochitl's singing even more phenomenal. Razvan had been right about that too. Her voice now held more richness… and more power.

When the song finished, Akasha and Silas couldn't help but stand and applaud.

"That was very good," Razvan pronounced and the band beamed with triumph. "But next time, be a little more loose."

"Loose?" Xochitl asked. "What do you mean? Should we play it slower?"

The vampire shook his head. "I do not know how to explain it. You are just a bit too tight. Relax your fingers and shoulders more and..." his face twisted in a scowl of frustration. "Just be a little looser."

As the band tried to figure out the cryptic advice, Akasha gave Silas another pointed look. He shrugged his shoulders and narrowed his eyes in the typical "keep quiet" look she had quickly grown to recognize. She glared at him and ground her teeth.

Silas didn't like Razvan's attention on the band either, she could tell, but neither of them could do anything about it... and yet again there was the added frustration that the vampire seemed to genuinely be helping them. Their skill was growing at a frightening rate.

Sylvis's face suddenly lit up with comprehension. "I know! He means *Moderato con poco Adagio*."

Xochitl frowned. "Moderate with a little at ease?" she translated.

"Huh?" the other two chorused.

To Akasha's delight Razvan looked even more perplexed. It seemed he didn't know everything.

The guitarist smiled and picked up her guitar, relaxing her shoulders. "Like this."

Sylvis played the beginning riff again, and although it didn't really sound all that different, she and the song seemed to be transformed into something as exquisitely beautiful as it was natural. The others followed suit and the results were astounding, bringing goose bumps to Akasha's flesh and making Silas visibly shiver.

And Xochitl's singing, holy shit, this was a Xochitl to be reckoned with. This was a Xochitl to bow down to. All of Akasha's instincts told her she should be afraid, but as she met Silas's eyes and saw his fear, all she could feel was exhilaration. Whatever game Razvan was playing, it seemed he had found *Rage of Angels'* key to greatness. But that didn't mean she'd like him, and from the look on Silas's face, it didn't mean he'd leave Razvan alone with the band either.

When the song ended, Razvan stood up and applauded again. "Yes! Yes, exactly like that. Have you learned any more from that band yet?"

Beau nodded. "Yes, but Xochitl and Sylvis both don't feel comfortable performing them in front of an audience yet."

Razvan nodded solemnly. "Very well, I can understand that. Perhaps next week? For now, why don't you play me a little more *Megadeth*? I quite like your rendition of them."

Xochitl's smile was impossibly brilliant as she approached the microphone and met Akasha's eyes. "This one's for you, 'Kash. Happy Birthday!"

Silas's gaze whipped over to Akasha, rife with accusation.

They began playing "Sweating Bullets," her favorite song.

"Aw, *fuck*." Akasha groaned under her breath.

She'd forgotten all about her birthday, and if Silas's expression was any indicator, he had too.

***

Silas cursed under his breath at Razvan's infuriating, knowing smirk. The surprise at Xochitl's announcement must have been written all over his face.

Akasha was twenty today… but as far as the state was concerned, she was eighteen. She could now be free of him. His heart clenched as if caught in a vise. Without her, his life and home would be empty.

Oblivious to the impact of their announcement, *Rage of Angels* finished the song and with mischievous expressions they darted over to the closet and pulled out the presents they'd smuggled into the house. Silas watched Akasha's stunned and awkward reactions to her gifts with a lump in his throat. No doubt she never received presents in her years in the group home. If she stayed with him, he would happily shower her with gifts for all eternity... *if she stayed.*

Silas shook his head and stood. He had to know now or he would go mad. Meeting his maker's mocking gaze with a determined stare.

"I would appreciate it if you took yourself off for awhile," he said through gritted teeth, ready to do violence if Razvan dared to be obstinate.

The vampire chuckled. "I see you have something to discuss with your pet. By all means, go. I will be fine here with the prodigies."

"I will not leave you alone with them," Silas hissed, hoping their conversation had not drawn interest. So far, the band was occupied with Akasha, but it wouldn't be long before curious ears perked up in their direction.

Razvan laughed again. "So protective you are. Very well, I shall accede to your wishes... this time." He cleared his throat and turned to the others. "It seems I must go fetch a gift for the birthday girl. What would you like, Akasha?"

Akasha met his sardonic gaze with such cool dignity that Silas swelled with pride. "I don't need anything, thank you."

"Oh, but I insist," he said in a silken voice threaded over steel.

"Fine," she sighed. "A case of Coors, then."

Razvan departed and Silas sighed with relief as a significant amount of tension dissipated. Perhaps it would be a good thing if Akasha left. She and the others may be safer that way. In fact, the investigations might stop if she was out of his life. He gathered his courage and approached the group.

"It seems we should open up a bottle of wine," he said with forced cheer. "And I'm afraid I must borrow Akasha for a moment."

Once they were alone upstairs, Silas fetched the Riesling and a corkscrew, unable to face Akasha's heart-wrenching beauty as the words poured out of him in an uncertain burst.

"You are free now, under state law." The top of the bottle broke off in his hand, spilling wine all over the floor. Numbly, he continued. "You can leave me any time you want now, but... I just want you to know that if you need anything... I'll even buy you a house—"

"Silas," Akasha cut off his tirade with an impatient wave. "Who says I'm leaving now?"

He set down the broken bottle and grabbed a towel to clean up the mess. "Well, since you had all those plans and I ruined them, I had thought..."

She strode after him, snatched the towel from his grip, and tossed it aside. Then she grabbed his shoulders, forcing him to face her. Silas's skin tingled pleasurably at her rare touch. "Do you really think that with all this bullshit going on with the Elders and Razvan sniffing around my friends, I would ditch you? Fuck *that*."

Silas's heart leaped with joy at her words even though his gut clenched in pain that her concern was solely for her friends. "Perhaps it would be better that way." He forced the words out, hating their bitter taste. "Then you might be safe from him... and the Elders as well."

"You want me to go then?" Akasha asked with raised brows... and was that a glimmer of pain in her eyes?

"Good God, no!" Silas grasped her hands, holding her to him. "I've been waiting for you for centuries." The confession tore from his throat. "I built this house and furnished it with only the best for you. But if you would be happier and safer without me, I will let you go."

Akasha looked up at him. A single tear slid down her cheek, gleaming in the lamplight.

"For me?" Her lips parted in awe as she looked about the house as if seeing it for the first time. She shook her head, visibly composing her features. "Well, I'm not going anywhere, just now. Not when you and my friends are in danger, and you're just going to have to deal with it." She smiled, her lips curving and almost within his reach. "That's what you get for messing up my plans." Her heady scent teased his senses, driving him to distraction.

"Oh, Akasha," he whispered. "Forgive me, I can't help myself."

With that Silas dipped his head and captured her lips with his own, reveling in her sweet taste. Since he had fed recently, there was no blood thirst, but his lust for her body was a formidable force of its own. He devoured her lips like one starved, pulling her against him to grind his hardness against her.

"Silas...." Akasha breathed against his lips.

"Dude!" Xochitl coughed behind them. "You guys need to get a room or something."

Akasha pushed Silas away so hard he crashed into the wall. Her face was an alarming shade of crimson.

"Or maybe we could all just leave? Y'know, turn it into a private celebration for two?" Xochitl offered with a teasing grin as she opened the freezer and grabbed two packs of frozen veggies, pressing one to her forehead.

Silas cleared his throat. "That won't be necessary, Miss Leonine. I was just about to order pizza and have Razvan pick up a cake so we may celebrate." He eyed the package of frozen peas. What happened to you?"

Xochitl's cheeks pinkened. "Sylvis and I were head banging too close. Anyway, I gotta bring her an Icepack too. Happy birthday, 'Kash."

Akasha grunted her response, face still flaming as she cleaned up the spilled wine.

Chapter Twenty

The next evening, Akasha hummed and changed into her new outfit while Silas was out hunting for his breakfast. Beau had excellent taste. The black crushed velvet pants made her ass look great and the black and purple corset top made much of her less than impressive rack. She hoped Silas would like it even as she chastised herself for thinking like a girl. One good thing about last night was that she now knew that Silas liked her.

Like. Such a juvenile word for how she was starting to feel about him. The utter pain in his eyes when he thought she would leave him brought a lump in her throat before his declaration of all he'd done for her really got the tears flowing. And his kiss... *damn... his kiss.*

She fastened her bra and reached for the corset top when her door opened. Akasha whipped around, the hair on the back of her neck standing on end.

"Hello, Akasha." Razvan Nicolae sauntered into her bedroom.

Her veins turned to ice at his voice. "W-what the hell are you doing? Can't you see I'm getting dressed? Get the fuck out of here!"

This was the vampire that made Silas, which meant he was older and likely more powerful than her former guardian. Akasha swallowed and crossed her arms over her breasts, her throat dry as sandpaper.

The vampire ignored her outrage and stalked closer. "I have discovered that you know our secrets... All of them."

She nodded, hating the fact that she had to face him wearing only a bra and a pair of flimsy velvet pants. Casting a longing glance at her top, she cursed him.

Razvan smiled, but there was no warmth in it. "So you know why I am here."

"Yeah, as if you didn't make it obvious with your constant hovering around and asking questions." Akasha forced her spine straight. She would *not* let him see any fear. "The Elders want to make sure Silas isn't trying to go against his kind or expand his power base by Marking me and my friends. I just don't understand why they would see it like that. I mean, my friends are just a band and I'm..." She shrugged. *Just a freak.*

Razvan laughed. "Obviously your master hasn't explained our politics to you. Normally, after my first visit I would have left and declared you all harmless. *But*...." He wagged a scolding finger at her. "There is more to you than you let on. You are hiding things. That compels me to investigate further." He took another step closer. "You know I can't read your mind. Why is that?"

She shook her head, not beginning to know how to answer him.

"And there is more, isn't there?" His voice turned low and silken as he grazed her shoulder with his fingertip.

He ran his tongue along his fangs. "You really are a pretty little thing. I can see why Silas fancies you. But tell me, do you fancy him as well?"

"I don't see it as any of your fucking business," Akasha growled, refusing to tremble or step back.

"Oh, but it is." His silken tone carried an edge of a growl. "You see, the things you are hiding are, in fact, things Silas is hiding. And if Silas is hiding things from the Elders, I will have no choice but to tell them. They will not be pleased. Very unpleasant things happen to those who invoke their displeasure."

"You're threatening Silas." Her voice was cool when inside she burned with rage.

Razvan circled around her like a sadistic predator. "Indeed I am, Akasha. Now tell me what I need to know. Why are you different? Why do your thoughts move too fast for me to read? Why won't you tell us where you came from?"

"I don't know!" The words emerged choked and weak with frustration.

The vampire shook his head. "That is not an acceptable answer. I told you, for your stubbornness, Silas will have to pay." Razvan turned to leave the room and perhaps carry out his implied nefarious deeds.

The tentative hold on Akasha's temper snapped.

With speed she didn't know she possessed, she picked Razvan up by his arms and threw him through the sliding-glass door.

He landed hard on the stone balcony in a pile of bloody broken glass.

Akasha strode after him, wincing as a shard of glass sliced her arm. Ignoring the pain, she picked the vampire up by the throat and dangled him over the edge of the balcony.

"Don't ever threaten Silas again," she hissed.

"I knew there was more to you," Razvan's gloating tone, so at odds with his predicament, it only increased her fury.

"I mean it!" She tightened her grip. The blood made her hands slippery.

"You think to kill me this easily, woman?" Though his voice mocked her, she could see the astonishment in his eyes.

Akasha's lips curved in a wicked smile. "The fall wouldn't kill you, but I bet I can get down there fast enough to set you on fire before your bones heal enough for you to move."

Ah, yes. Finally a spark of fear came to his eyes. Razvan tried to laugh, but it was shaky. She debated whether to drop him or let him back up.

"Akasha!" Silas's voice reverberated behind her, holding more wrath than she'd ever heard before. "What are ye doing?"

Tensing at his rage, she struggled to sound casual. "Razvan came in here when I was getting dressed and rudely demanded to know why I'm different. He also threatened you. I thought if I showed him my difference from normal

175

people quickly and bluntly enough, he might quit with the threats and let me put my shirt on."

Silas's eyes blazed emerald flames as he stepped onto the balcony. A ginormous sword was gripped in his hand tight enough to whiten his knuckles. Gone was the white-collar professional. Here stood a formidable warrior. Glass broke beneath his boots in an ominous crunch.

"What is the meanin' of this?" He glared at Razvan; his Scottish brogue thickening his words.

Oh, he's pissed! Akasha bit her lip, praying his ire was only directed at Razvan.

"Ye came intae' her room when she was dressin'? Ye tormented her and threatened me? Och! No wonder yer hangin' off the bloody balcony!" Silas turned to Akasha, still furious. "And as fer ye, lass, do ye ken what ye've done? This is a Lord and a representative of the Elders! Tae treat him like this is an unforgivable insult! Now let him up and get dressed. We three obviously need tae talk."

Akasha sighed in defeat and swung Razvan back over, unceremoniously depositing him on the stone floor in the pile of broken glass. To her surprise, he was still smiling.

"Thank you for your delightful demonstration," he whispered and took her hand and licked a rivulet of his blood off her wrist.

Akasha jerked her hand away and Razvan chuckled at Silas's territorial growl.

The vampire's laughter broke suddenly as he reached into his pocket. His eyes glowed black with deadly menace. "You broke my pipe. I should make you pay for it."

"Fuck you. You're lucky I didn't break your face."

Silas sighed. "May we please get on with this?"

Razvan and Akasha answered in tandem.

"Very well." "*Fine.*"

With a mocking bow, the Lord Vampire of Spokane left the room and she was alone with Silas. His eyes still glowed. Her stomach clenched. Akasha had never seen him this angry before.

"You're hurt." He frowned at the gash on her arm.

She shrugged. "I've had worse."

Silas slowly stepped closer, expression unreadable. Much like Razvan had, he took her hand and bent down. She gasped as his tongue darted out and laved a hot path up her arm. The erotic sensation was so powerful she had to put a hand on his shoulder to remain on her feet. Silas raised a finger to his lips and pierced it with a fang. Gently, he trailed his bleeding finger along the cut. It began to tingle and heal before her eyes.

"Better?" he asked.

"Yes," she whispered, enraptured with his eyes.

He stared down at her for the longest time, seeming to analyze every part of her as if he wanted to devour her. Finally, his gaze rested on her breasts, barely hidden under the black velvet bra. Heat flooded her body.

At last, Silas cleared his throat and met her gaze. "When you are dressed, meet Razvan and me in my chamber... the one I *don't* sleep in."

"'Kay," she managed to squeak.

Her hands shook as she put on her top. For some reason, it didn't make her feel as secure as she'd expected. There was no doubt as to the subject of this impending meeting. Akasha was cornered, no longer allowed to hide her secrets.

Well, after throwing Razvan through a sliding glass door, I suppose it's hardly a secret anymore. A self deprecating smile curved her lips as she headed down the corridor to Silas's fake bedroom. On the heels of that thought sprouted a seed of worry. What would the Elders think about her freakish strength?

When she arrived, Akasha saw that though they were solemn, Silas and Razvan didn't seem to be angry with one another. Instead, their attention was fixated upon *her*. The largest sword of Silas's collection had been taken down from the wall and lay on the floor at their feet.

"Pick up the sword, Akasha," Silas commanded.

A thousand questions darted through her mind, but she obeyed. The sword was heavy, but she lifted it easily and held it above her head.

"Try it with one hand."

She did. Again, it was easy. Razvan smiled triumphantly and it was all she could do not to bring the flat of the blade down upon his head.

Silas spoke again. "The sword you are holding is a Claymore. Only the largest warriors of my clan could wield it. It's a two-handed sword and should be physically impossible for a tiny thing like you to lift, much less handle it like a rapier."

"You have super-human strength, pet mortal," Razvan declared. "Now, how did that happen?"

"I already told you, I don't know." She handed the sword back to Silas. "I was telling the truth."

"But surely you must know something." He stalked towards her, ready to renew his intimidation act.

"I *don't!*" she cried in mournful desperation. "Do you think I don't want to know? To know once and for all why I'm the freak that I am? Fuck, I'd almost kill to know why!"

"Maybe something happened to you in the past and you just have to search your memories." Silas's gentle voice pulled her back from her helpless confusion.

"A lot of things have happened to me," Akasha retorted, then her eyes widened as she grasped his words. *But can I do it?* She straightened her spine. *I have to.* "Silas, I don't think I can tell you all that happened to me... but I can show you." She tilted her head, baring her neck.

She remembered him saying he could see a mortal's entire life as he fed from them. Both vampires regarded her in stunned silence. Then Razvan began to clap slowly as if he had witnessed a really good play. *Smart-ass.*

"All right," Silas whispered, eyes flaming with hunger. "Razvan, you may take your leave. I will tell you everything tomorrow evening."

"Very well. I bid you two *adieu.*" Slowly, he rose up into the air, stopping before his head hit the ceiling.

"You can *fly*?" Akasha's fists clenched in an effort not to yank him down and beat the shit out of him. "You bastard! I thought I actually could have killed you."

"Sorry to disappoint you, little one." He smiled, baring his fangs as his feet returned to the plush carpet.

Akasha bit back another curse. She *was* disappointed, but she wasn't going to rise to his bait and attack him again. Instead, she regarded him with cold eyes.

"Why were you so afraid then?" She'd seen the fear of death in a man's eyes before. It was unforgettable, and Razvan's sinister black gaze had borne a glimmer of it.

He strode over to her and captured her gaze as if he intended to make her his next meal. She stared back, unafraid. Vampire mind control didn't work on her, she'd learned.

"Because, Akasha, you meant it." His black eyes were hard as coal. "You meant to end my existence with every fiber of your being." Then he was gone.

"Are you ready, lass?" Silas's thick Scottish brogue wreaked havoc on her senses.

Slowly, Akasha turned to face him, trembling with a realization.

She was alone with Silas and this time he really was going to bite her.

Chapter Twenty-one

"Can I come back in a few minutes?" Akasha's voice trembled. The air was so thick with tension it was hard to breathe. "I need time to collect myself."

Silas nodded and sat on the bed. His voice still held a husky edge, making her legs weak. "Just be sure that you indeed return. You declared you would let me feed from you before a witness. You cannot go back on it."

Biting her lip at the finality of his words, Akasha walked quickly to her room and threw open her closet door. She had to turn on the light and go to the very back before she found what she was looking for. Minutes later, she smoothed her hands down the black velvet dress that Beau prodded her to buy on their first shopping expedition.

It felt soft and feminine and horribly unfamiliar. Akasha had never before seen the right moment to wear it.

This moment slapped her in the face as the right time. She would let down all her barriers for Silas. To her, wearing a dress for him delivered the message that she was willing to trust him not to do anything awful to her.

After carefully putting on makeup, following Xochitl's and Aurora's hints from memory, she took one last look in the mirror, and left the room.

When she knocked on his "bedroom" door, Silas opened it and the stunned look on his face might have been funny if this wasn't such a cataclysmic time in her life.

His eyes drank her in like she was something delicious and forbidden. "You are so beautiful," he whispered as he took her hand and led her to the bed. "I can't bespell you, as you seem to be immune, but I will do my best to be gentle."

Akasha trembled as she sat, ruining her attempt at nonchalance. "Silas? Promise me you won't hate me for what you see."

He looked at her in surprise before tilting her chin up to meet his gaze. "Akasha, I could never hate you."

The vampire placed a chaste kiss on her cheek before brushing her mass of ebony curls away from her neck. "Are you ready?"

His eyes glowed with hungry fire. For a moment her heart pounded in her throat as she realized what he was and what he was going to do to her. Base instincts told her to flee, but there was no turning back now.

"Yes," she whispered.

Silas lowered his mouth to her neck, and she shivered in delight at the sensation. Then there was a sharp pain as his fangs pierced her flesh before she floated away into oblivion.

***

As Akasha's sweet blood flowed into his mouth, Silas saw her life and emotions flash before his eyes.

He saw her parents murdered by uniformed men.

He saw her recover from her mute shock. He saw her flee from the abusive zealot and take to living on the streets.

He saw her sharing food with other homeless people until a prostitute warned her to leave after the local pimp noticed her.

He saw Max, the grizzled retired biker who became a second father to her. He saw him teach her how to fix cars and give her his late wife's biker jacket.

He felt her heartbreak when Max was arrested.

But the last thing he saw chilled his bones and churned his stomach.

Akasha jumped at the rumble of an approaching car. Her shoulders tensed beneath the straps of her backpack as she was bathed in the glow of the headlights... so exposed.

"Hey Hon, wanna ride?" the driver called.

"No thanks, I'm going home." She cringed but continued walking.

The door opened. Akasha quickened her pace. A gun clicked.

"Drop the bag and come here," the man growled as he stepped out of the car, his pistol trained on her with one hand, the other scratching his sagging gut. "Run, and I'll blow your fuckin' head off."

Oh shit Oh shit Oh shit, *she thought as her backpack thudded to the ground. Her feet dragged her closer to the beast brandishing metallic death.*

"You're a pretty little thing." He scratched his stubbly chin. "Too bad this has to be quick. Pull down your pants."

Oh shit Oh shit OH SHIT! *Max had warned her about this... what men wanted and the lengths some would go to get it.*

"I mean it! Right fuckin' off!" His greasy fingers grabbed her, digging into her flesh as he slammed her against the car.

Akasha bit her lip and with trembling hands, fumbled with the button on her jeans. The barrel of the gun glared at her with its one dark eye. The man ordered her to bend over the hood of the car. Hot metal beneath her palms was a sharp contrast to the cold hard steel of the gun pressing into the back of her skull.

Moments later, something else pressed against her, driving in, splitting her apart. Akasha screamed and he slapped her with his free hand, making her ears ring with the blow. The bastard thrust into her mercilessly; pain exploded throughout her body. She bit her tongue hard, tasting blood as her mind screamed: Not fair!

If it weren't for that pathetic gun, she could overpower him in a heartbeat. Snap his neck with a flick of her wrist. But though she was strong, she doubted she was bulletproof. She bled just as easy as anyone else did.

So Akasha bore the violation with clenched teeth, her fingertips denting the Cadillac's hood, projecting her mind away from the pain, towards anticipation of the end.

With a final grunt, the man removed himself from her. The gun left her head. Akasha waited. When she heard the rustle of his pants being pulled up, she whipped around. Her fist connected with his wrist, snapping the bone in his arm, and the gun sailed off.

Akasha flew at him, howling with rage, punching, kicking, and screaming. She threw him against the car, slamming him repeatedly against the door. He sank to the ground. She buried her hands in his greasy hair and bashed his head against the asphalt.

Over and over again and it still wasn't enough, never enough. She screamed and bashed, screamed and bashed until the man's head came apart in her hands. The sensation jerked her out of her fervor like an M-80 exploding inside her skull.

What she held in her hands felt like goulash mixed with shards of ceramic.

Squelch... A hunk of brain hit the pavement.

Her mother's voice sang in her memory: Humpty Dumpty sat on a wall… Humpty Dumpty had a great fall…

Akasha scrambled to her feet and vomited in the ditch. When she was reduced to dry heaves, she looked at the blood on her hands, back at the corpse, then back at her hands.

"I killed him," she whispered with no remorse. All she felt was terror of being caught and thrown in prison. As she scooped up her dusty backpack her eyes darted to the Cadillac. She had to get out of here.

On the passenger floorboard was a bottle of tequila. Whenever she thought of what she'd done, she took a big slug. The road blurred in her vision, but she kept driving until the car sputtered and died.

She stumbled out of the car and threw up again, drunk and still in shock. Her body screamed for her to lie down, but she changed her bloodstained clothes, burned them, and kept walking. She had to get away.

Hours later, a police officer stopped her. By sunrise, she was still in the interrogation room, clinging to the lie that she'd run away from abusive parents in California. Thankfully, they appeared to believe her.

The officer sighed. "I'm sorry, but we have to track down your parents. It's policy. I'm sure you've been reported missing, so soon I'll have the information I need. I hoped you'd be a good girl and save us both the time." The lady cop smiled smugly and left. What a bitch.

Akasha was sent to a transitional group home. After a few months the police gave up the search for the fictitious parents. She was never connected with the murder. The state assigned her a social security number and after some education tests, Mrs. Kenzie enrolled her as a freshman in high school. All forms said she was fourteen.

"But I told you I'm sixteen," she had protested.

The caseworker's sweet smile was sickening in its falseness. "You look younger. Of course, if you just tell us who your parents are, we could look up your birth certificate and this will all be sorted out."

Akasha didn't budge and eventually she was forgotten by the state authorities, a dirty secret swept under the rug. She endured the loneliness of the group home until Silas swooped into her life like a dark angel and changed everything. And through him she discovered an emotion long forgotten: Love.

Chapter Twenty-two

Silas reverently lowered Akasha to the bed, gazing down at her in wonder. *She loves me!* He could scarcely believe a precious creature like her could love a monster, but he'd experienced the proof through her eyes and thoughts. His brows knit in a frown as he noticed the pallor of her delicate skin, remembering how much blood he'd taken. He bit his wrist and pressed it to her mouth.

"Drink, but only a little or you'll become like me," he commanded.

Slowly, her lashes lifted and she obeyed. Her mouth on his skin was a symphony of pleasure. Too soon, Akasha pulled away, color instantly returned to her cheeks. "Wow. I feel like I just had two of Xochitl's Red Bulls."

He managed a smile. "The effect of our blood never ceases to amaze me."

Unable to hold back any longer, Silas pulled her onto his lap and whispered, "Oh Akasha, you were so brave."

The tears came slowly at first. Akasha tried to blink them back, but they trickled faster down her cheeks, burning her eyes. She gave up the fight and buried her face deeper into his chest, body racked with choking sobs.

Silas held her tight, stroking her hair just as he had in visions. He knew now that she hadn't cried since she was a child, and it was excruciatingly difficult for her.

***

It felt good to cry Akasha realized, and clung to the vampire she loved, warm and safe in his arms. The feeling was surprisingly cleansing and she never wanted to let it go. When the tears finally stopped, she dared to look up at Silas. His eyes shone down on her, so green, like the forest in the springtime. A silken lock of his hair caressed her cheek. He was so beautiful... it almost hurt to look at him.

"Silas," she gasped, remembering his confession the night she learned his secret. *I held you in my arms. You were crying.* "Your vision!"

"Yes," he said simply and kissed the tears from her face. The soft brush of his lips made her flesh sing with awareness. "I'll never let anyone hurt you again. I love you, Akasha," he whispered, and covered her mouth with his before she could reply.

Akasha took a shaky breath as more tears nearly came from his declaration. She'd been so afraid that if he knew the truth about her, the things she'd done, he'd be disgusted. His kiss deepened and she forgot all else as her body filled with heat. A whimper escaped her and she tangled her hands in his hair, returning the kiss with all the passion in her being.

She broke away and raised a hand to his cheek, pleading eyes meeting his. "Please, Silas, make love to me. Show me it isn't all bad."

Silas's eyes widened and his hard form stiffened in her arms. "Are you certain you want me to do this?"

"Yes! I love you, Silas. Now please, make it not hurt anymore, make the shame go away." Akasha met his gaze which was suddenly hard to read. "You want me, don't you?" A kernel of doubt sprouted in her stomach.

The vampire's eyes glowed green fire. His gaze was like a caress, gently touching every inch of her body, making her shiver.

"Oh yes," he said softly. "I want you very much. But after all I've seen I do not wish for you to change your mind later and turn to me with accusing eyes. I have endured your mistrust long enough."

Akasha bit her lip, guilt mingling with her desire. "I won't, I swear."

Silas regarded her seriously. "This is what you want then?" He caressed her cheek as if she were something infinitely precious to him.

She nodded and fought the urge to lower her eyes.

"Then kiss me, Akasha."

Heart pounding, she slowly leaned forward to touch her lips against his. She kissed him, feather light at first, then increasing the pressure as she reached up to stroke his hair. Electric tremors of pleasure reverberated through her being, causing her head to swim with dizziness. But her efforts were rewarded as Silas's arms wrapped around her body, pulling her tight against him. Tentatively, her tongue darted out to taste him.

His embrace grew powerful and deliciously crushing. The kiss became more fervent as he laid her on the soft bed. Akasha tangled her hands in his midnight hair and reveled in the feel of his weight on top of her. Silas kissed her until her lips were swollen and tingly, but still he did not stop.

He rolled with her on the bed until she was on top of him. Akasha sucked in a breath at the feel of his hardness pressing against her core. His hands stroked her hair and caressed her body until she was ready to growl in impatience for him to satisfy her aching need.

Silas pulled her back up to a sitting position. For a moment she thought he'd changed his mind, but then he was grabbing her dress, pulling it off, and a new, gentler fear came. Now he would see her naked. No man had seen her naked, not even her rapist.

After he removed her bra, he stared hungrily at her breasts for an endless moment, eyes aflame. Heat rose to her cheeks.

The spell broke and was replaced with another as he removed his shirt. Her breath caught as her gaze rested on his bare chest. It was broad and magnificent. Tentatively, she touched him. His skin was warm from her blood. She shivered, remembering his mouth on her throat.

Silas took her in his arms again and the heat and softness of his bare skin against hers brought another gasp of excitement.

"Soft," he whispered. "So beautiful."

His hands grazed up and down her back. Goose bumps rose on her arms. Silas buried his face in her neck, kissing and nibbling until she trembled.

He laid her back down and his mouth trailed down to her shoulders, above her heart and finally to her breasts. He cupped them in his hands and covered them with feathery kisses before laving them with his tongue in slow, lazy circles, drawing a moan from her lips before he reached her nipples. These he sucked and nibbled until they were hard, throbbing and her breath came in sharp pants.

Silas shifted on the bed to kiss her belly. It tickled and Akasha bit back a giggle. He removed her panties and gently caressed her legs while kissing her pelvis, then moved his mouth lower.

He isn't! Her mind shouted.

But he was.

Akasha cried out at the electric sensation of his tongue flicking across her core. It seemed to grow and swell until every nerve ending in her body concentrated in that long dormant place. She thrashed and moaned on the bed.

Someone was gasping, "Please... Please!" And she realized it was her.

Silas pulled her back up into a sitting position, only now he was naked and her legs were on either side of him... and his cock pressed against her wet center with no barriers. She'd never been so aware of that part of her before. It was hot and slick and tingly. She arched her hips against him and almost whimpered as ravenous need tore through her. The vampire gripped her shoulders and forced her to meet his burning gaze.

"Akasha," he hissed with barely checked savagery. "If ye want me tae stop, ye had better tell me now."

She could feel him throbbing between her thighs. "Don't you dare stop."

He grabbed her ass and raised her. She looked down at his huge cock and felt a twinge of nervousness. But it was too late. Silas lowered her upon his shaft until, inch by thrilling inch, she was impaled. Devastating pleasure coursed through her until she was overwhelmed by the fullness within.

But it was only the beginning. His lips crushed against hers, his tongue thrusting into her mouth as he slowly moved her hips up and down. Her trepidation receded as her body became a pulsating, writhing thing.

Akasha clung to him and began to rock her hips against him, catching a rhythm as the fire within her roared and built. His hands clenched her body tighter, moving her faster. A strange feeling crept up on her, building up to a hot pressure. The intensity became too much to bear. This must be the climax she had so often read about. The sensation was so potent and wild, it was almost frightening.

Silas seemed to sense her anxiety. "Go with it, my love," he whispered and thrust into her harder, making her cry out.

He nibbled at her neck and held her tight, still keeping the quickening tempo of their locked bodies. The incredible sensations built and built and then… Akasha exploded. The very molecules of her body burst into incandescent electrical pulses.

She started to fall back into her body when Silas gripped her and growled. He quivered inside her and she was filled with a scalding heat that made her dissolve into liquid tremors.

They fell on the bed and remained locked together for what seemed an eternity.

"Holy… shit," Akasha panted, throat raw. "That was… that was…" She floundered for words as her cheeks grew hot.

Silas smiled and kissed her tenderly. "Many people over centuries have called it the 'little death.'"

I can see why, she tried to say, but no words came out. She was still shaking, still feeling the aftershocks of her initiation to carnal pleasure. He seemed to understand and pulled the covers over them and held her until her shivers subsided and her eyelids grew heavy.

Before sleep claimed her, a thought washed over her with drowning impact: *Where do we go from here?*

Chapter Twenty-three

Milbury wrinkled his nose at the stench of the jail. "I swear to God, Holmes, this lead better be more useful than that crazy 'Jesus' lady at that psych ward."

"She *was* useful," the FBI agent argued. "We got a confirmation on the girl's name *and* her inhuman strength."

"Yeah, and a bunch of mumbo jumbo about her being possessed by Satan," Milbury growled. "The bitch clawed me up too. I can't believe they let her run a foster home for twenty years before she was busted."

"Strange world, huh," Holmes replied. "You're healing alright, though. Anyway, Akasha allegedly lived with this guy until he was busted for operating a chop shop within his restoration business. He may be a criminal, but the reports indicate he's sane."

The doors to the visitation room opened. A large man in a standard orange jumpsuit was led in by two guards. Milbury suppressed a shudder. The man's wild gray hair and unkempt beard reminded him of a grizzly bear. Their eyes met, and the Major was unnerved to see an intelligent glint in his eyes. He seemed to know why they were here.

"Max Gunderson," Holmes began when they were seated at the small table. "I am Agent Joe Holmes, FBI. This is Major Francis Milbury. We're here to ask you a few questions."

A hint of fear flickered in his gaze when Max heard their titles. He quickly hid it with a smirk. "The military *and* the Feds workin' together? Now this must be somethin' special. Don't think I'd be any help though. I don't know any terrorists or nothin'."

Milbury opened a briefcase and showed him their most recent photo of Akasha around age ten. "We understand you were living with this girl illegally before you were arrested. Now she was probably a bit older then, but I'm sure you recognize her."

The man opened his mouth, but Holmes cut him off. "Don't bother lying. We have numerous witness reports confirming that Akasha Hope O'Reilly was in your home for approximately four years before your arrest. I hear you have a parole hearing coming up," he added with a glacial smile. "If you cooperate, we can make sure it goes well."

Max drummed his fingers on the table, shoulders straight and defiant. "So, I harbored a runaway. So fucking what? It was nothing perverted like you seem to be implying. The foster home she left was run by a psycho. So I took her in and had her help me out at my shop. Charge me if ya want."

"Do you have any idea where she is?" Milbury asked, grimacing at the horrible taste of the prison coffee.

"I ain't seen that kid since I got busted. She could be anywhere." Max looked down at his plastic sandals as if they were the most fascinating things in the world. Of course in this bland room, perhaps they were.

Milbury could sense the man was hiding something. He leaned over to Holmes and whispered, "Show him the pictures, Joe."

"Are you sure?" Holmes asked. His cheery smile vanished.

"Just do it!" Francis snarled.

Agent Holmes laid out the glossy photos of the murdered rapist. The prisoner looked at them and Milbury felt a little thrill when Max's expression changed from curious confusion to horrified revulsion.

"We have reason to believe 'that kid' did this," Milbury said slowly, relishing the taunt.

Max's face turned ashen. "No. She couldn't have," he gulped. "What proof do you have?"

"The blood, hair, and hymeneal tissue we found indicates a match," Holmes answered in his usual irritating know-it-all tone.

"Shut up!" Milbury snapped. But the damage had been done.

"Hymeneal tissue? You mean he... Oh God!" Max buried his face in his hands. "She's alive, isn't she? You bastards aren't screwing with me, are you?"

"Thanks a lot, Joe," Milbury muttered. The idiot contaminated the witness... and Holmes was *FBI*, for Christ's sake.

"No other bodies have been found, Mr. Gunderson," Holmes assured him in a sickening gentle voice. "We have reason to believe Akasha is alive. We need to question her about this incident. We just want to help. So please, please tell us if you know anything."

"I don't know shit." Max growled, looking sick to his stomach. "How can I? I've been locked up."

A cell phone bleated. Holmes fished it out and answered.

"If you're lying, we *will* find out." Milbury assured him.

Holmes hung up the phone with a happy-ass grin on his face. "That's enough for today, Mr. Gunderson. We'll contact you later." He gave Milbury a triumphant look. They must have received good news at last.

They were almost out of the prison before Holmes whispered, "I may have found her."

Milbury's pulse leapt into his throat. "Where is she?"

"In Coeur d'Alene, Idaho. She was a ward of the state until recently."

"At twenty years old? How the hell is that possible?"

Holmes was still wearing his shit-eating grin. "Well, when we were getting nowhere finding her through police reports and court records, I started thinking. Since Akasha never had a birth certificate, she had no way of proving her age, so maybe the state authorities assumed her to be younger than she was." He shrugged. "Or maybe Akasha herself lied about her age to stay under the radar after she murdered that rapist. So I did some looking around and I found an Akasha Hope, aged seventeen, enrolled in Coeur d'Alene High School and taking part in dual enrollment at the community college. As I said, she'd been a ward of the state, living in a group home until October when she was assigned a legal guardian."

Milbury tried to control his excitement. "We have a location for her?"

Holmes shook his head. "That's the thing, for some reason that information was sealed, but give me some time and I'll get it."

***

Max gazed up at the stained ceiling of his cell as he prayed that Akasha was alive and safe. The knowledge that she had been raped made his heart freeze and his stomach turn to acid. If the son of a bitch weren't already dead, he'd bust out of here and do it himself.

His gut gave another heave. And those damn government spooks were after her, too. If only Akasha was psychic on top of having superhuman strength. He wished he could warn her, but his next parole hearing was three months away. Even then he had no idea where she was.

Max clenched his fists at the thought of the spooks. They said they wanted to "help her." *Bull shit!*

"Please let Akasha be okay, Lord," he prayed fervently. "She's the only daughter I've ever had."

Chapter Twenty-four

Akasha awoke smiling as she inhaled Silas's scent in the sheets. His lovemaking had been a revelation. So much mistrust and pain had been undone with every touch of his lips and body. She was a new woman.

A woman who could trust. A woman in love.

"I'm in love with a vampire," she whispered with a grin. She shook her head. "It's like a dark fairy tale."

Dragging her sated and slightly sore body out of bed, Akasha gasped when she saw what was left on the nightstand.

An open jewelry box revealed an antique silver necklace. A teardrop amethyst the size of her thumb was the pendant. The chain links were simple, elegant Celtic knots. With shaking hands, she picked it up. In her palm, it was more substantial than its meager weight. Akasha had never owned jewelry before. The fact that Silas gave her such a priceless piece made her struggle to hold back tears and giddy squeals all at once.

"Dammit! He's turning me into one of those love-crazed women already!" she grumbled, but couldn't keep the smile off her face as she dashed into the bathroom to try it on.

A gasp of mortification escaped her at the sight of her reflection. Her hair was gnarled and frizzed into a million directions, her lips were swollen from kissing, eyes puffy from crying, and worst of all, her neck was almost completely blue and purple with hickeys. Buried within the darkest one were the puncture wounds from Silas's fangs.

He can't see me like this! Akasha darted back into the bedroom, scooped up her dress and fled to her room. The bedside clock read: 2:09. She had time to undo the damage. She quickly showered, being extra liberal with the conditioner. Still, it took an eternity to get the tangles out of her curls. She donned black corduroy jeans and a turtleneck to hide the mess of her neck.

After yanking on her work boots, she returned to the bathroom to put on makeup. The necklace gleamed next to the sink. With some awkward maneuvering, she fastened it around her neck. Though it clashed with the casual outfit, it was still exquisite.

Akasha went downstairs, grabbed a bagel, and nearly jumped out of her skin when the phone rang. It was the Dodge dealership. The radiator for Silas's 'Cuda, Black Sunshine, was in. She had forgotten all about it.

Two hours later, she was peacefully ensconced in the garage, lifting the old radiator, coolant drained, out of the Barracuda. *Black Sabbath* blared from the radio.

"How is Silas's pet this evening?" Razvan's voice rumbled behind her.

Akasha dropped the radiator on her toe. "Fuck! Don't do that, asshole. You're lucky I wasn't holding a transmission."

"Tsk, Tsk. Such language for such a pretty young thing." The vampire stepped closer and peered under the hood of the car. "What exactly are you doing with your master's conveyance?"

Akasha grabbed a beer from her mini fridge and took a swig, trying to control her irritation. She hated being interrupted when she was working. The fact that it was the obnoxious Razvan goaded her worse. She turned down the radio.

"I was replacing his radiator before you so rudely snuck up on me." She glared at him.

He cocked his head to the side. "Why were you replacing it?"

"It was leaking." Akasha rolled her eyes as she stated the obvious.

Razvan smiled. "Ah. Then you are a very good pet. Perhaps I should get one like you to take care of my vehicle when I procure one."

"I'm no one's pet, jackass," she snarled. Her hand reached across the workbench to grasp her breaker bar.

"Oh, but you are. His Mark beats strongly upon you." Razvan crept closer and tugged down her turtleneck with a fingertip. "I see you obeyed him and revealed your secrets." He leaned in closer to whisper, "And he bedded you as well."

The thought that this dickhead knew about the sacred and intimate moments she'd spent with Silas made her shake with anger and humiliation. She wanted to grab him by the goatee and tear the mocking smile off his face.

She raised the breaker bar, and he backed off.

"Easy, my beauty," he said with uncharacteristic gentleness. "I was only having a little fun. I do think highly of you, Akasha, I swear it on my parents' grave and brother's honor. Silas could not have found a more worthy woman."

Akasha was tempted to call bullshit, but the pain that slashed across his face when he mentioned his family stopped her.

"How do vampires have family?" she asked.

Razvan sighed. "My father was a powerful Lord Vampire. He openly ruled a village in Romania and fell in love with a human woman. She refused to become his Lady because she wanted children. So Father went to the poorest section of the village to bring her a child. In those days if a peasant woman had twins, one was taken outside and left to die, for the couple would be unable to feed both. Father took me from the cold ground, then, for some reason he entered the house and bribed the couple for Radu as well."

"What happened to your parents?" Akasha found herself carried away by his tale, told with feeling in his rich velvet accent. His liquid black eyes were intent with barely suppressed emotion.

"Something happened to make the villagers fear us," Razvan answered distantly. "Radu and I also had a quarrel. I left the area to think and sulk. They burned the castle during the day with our mother and father trapped inside. When I returned, I saw my parents' charred remains, but no sign of Radu. I've searched for him for centuries."

Akasha's eyes widened in comprehension. "Silas told me that's why you Changed him. You wanted him to find Radu."

He nodded. "Yes, but even with his immense powers he failed to find my brother, though he verified that Radu still lives. And for that comfort, I owe Silas everything. That is why I will do anything I can to make sure he is not punished by the Elders. That is why I have to know all your secrets, Akasha. I need to prove to them that nothing is happening which could put our kind at risk." Razvan smiled suddenly, wickedness returning to his gaze. "But… if you could refrain from informing Silas that I am on his side for a little longer, I would much appreciate it."

"You know, Razvan," Akasha eyed him speculatively as she crushed her beer can. "You're not half bad when you're not being an ass."

He offered his hand in a truce and after a moment's hesitation, she took it. "You will turn a man's head with that kind of talk."

"What are ye doon, holdin' hands with ma woman?" Silas demanded as he entered the garage.

"Relax, McNaught. We were coming to an understanding. I don't want her throwing me through any more windows," Razvan assured him with a light chuckle.

Silas embraced Akasha and claimed her lips in a mind-blowing kiss. His eyes searched hers, full of concern. "Are you well, lass?"

"Yeah." She found herself tongue-tied and her stomach wouldn't stop fluttering at the sight of him. *This is love.*

He fingered the necklace, making her skin tingle. "Do you like it?"

"Very much," she whispered, fighting the urge to throw herself in his arms.

He smiled down at her. "It was my mother's. I can't wait to see how it sets off... more pleasant attire."

"With the mess you made of her neck, I think she's 'setting it off' quite nicely," Razvan interjected.

"Shut up!" Akasha hissed, but it was too late. Silas peeled down the neck of her shirt.

His brows knit in dismay. "Oh lass, I am sorry. I forgot to heal the wound, and as for the rest..." The guilt in his eyes made her chest tighten. "Did I hurt you?"

"No! It was..." She looked at Razvan and her face flooded with heat. Even her ears burned. They may have a truce, but that didn't mean she wanted him to know about her sex life.

Razvan laughed at her embarrassment. "Such modesty in these times is refreshing." He turned to Silas. "Now, did you feed well enough to reveal to me what you've learned about her?"

Silas nodded. "Yes, I'm ready whenever you are."

"Wait a minute," Akasha froze as panic washed over her. "Are you actually going to show him... everything?"

"I'm sorry, lass. I have to." Silas's eyes were warm with sympathy. "Razvan will only put what is necessary in his report. Won't you, Nicolae?" He fixed his maker with a glare.

Razvan inclined his head respectfully. "I swear it. I would not have it done this way if it were possible, but the situation with the Elders is so serious that only indisputable truth will be accepted."

"This shouldn't take long, my love." Silas kissed her and the two vampires left the garage.

Fuck. Soon Razvan would know everything about her. It was an uncomfortable thought, to say the least. Akasha opened another beer and went back to work on the car, turned on some AC/DC and did her best to not think about it.

***

Razvan cursed in Romanian as he wiped Silas's blood from his lips. "So much pain for one so young. Now I know why her mind is like iron. Still, the reason for her physical abilities is unclear."

"Yes, and I will die before I allow her to suffer ever again," Silas growled. "Were you able to contact Delgarias?"

Razvan shook his head. "He has seemed to have dropped off the face of the Earth as is his habit." His expression was solemn as he pretended to study the various swords hanging on the walls of Silas's office. "I think you should be prepared for the likelihood that we won't find him in time."

"Damn it!" Silas said as he paced the confines of his office. He rubbed his temples in an effort to subdue a coming headache. "If that ends up being the case, what are you going to tell the Elders?"

"I don't know yet." Razvan sighed and sat down in a chair near the desk. "I still need more information to satisfy them. We need to know more about those uniformed men who killed her parents, why they did it, and if they are still looking for Akasha. Not only that, but we need to know more about Xochitl. Without Delgarias to back us up, it is doubtful the Elders will believe she's the daughter of our mythical creator."

"I'll tell you what I can about her, but I don't know much," Silas said. "As for who is after Akasha, I think I have an idea. But first, I need to feed. Please, guard my love while I am gone?"

Chapter Twenty-five

"So this is pretty serious then," Akasha asked Razvan once they were ensconced in Silas's office awaiting another vampire.

"Yes," the vampire answered without his usual sinister demeanor. "If the Elders decide there is the slightest liability with you or your friends, you will all likely be transferred to a new owner or possibly killed. Silas will either be executed or lose his Lordship status, meaning no Lord would allow him in their territory… so his chances for survival would be slim."

"I don't see how I or my friends could be a 'liability,'" Akasha countered. "Xochitl and the band are just teenagers, and I'm the only one who knows what you are."

"And it's *because* you know about us that makes you a liability." Razvan replied.

"But you were investigating us before you knew I found out about Silas," she argued.

He leaned back in his chair and nodded. "Yes, but that was because of the quantity of mortals that were Marked. Now, your knowledge of our kind, your unique situation, and the possibility of people being after you make things more difficult. To deem you harmless, we need to know why you have such phenomenal strength and who is pursuing you. And as for your friend, Xochitl?"

"What about Xochitl?" she cut in, alarm creeping up her spine. A memory of Xochitl's eyes shifting from brown to red flickered in her mind. *Don't ask, don't tell....*

Razvan's eyes widened. "You mean you don't know?"

Before she could demand more answers, Silas entered the office, escorting the most wimpy-looking vampire she'd ever seen. He had thinning blond hair, watery blue eyes that squinted like he should be wearing glasses, and hunched shoulders. An insipid periwinkle shirt hung on his frail form. His tie was askew, and his eyes kept darting back to Silas as if he expected to be hit.

"Have a seat, Bryan." Silas's tone was curt and brooked no disobedience as he pointed to his seat behind the desk.

Akasha flinched. She had never seen this side of him before. Suddenly he seemed larger than usual.

Bryan cast nervous glances at her and Razvan, before sitting down in Silas's luxurious swiveling seat. "Wh-what can I do for you, Lord McNaught?" he stammered.

Silas fixed him with a commanding stare. "I need your expertise to find out where this woman came from, who killed her parents, and if they are looking for her."

Bryan's face screwed up in a pitiful display of confusion.

"I'm Akasha." She held out her hand. He gave her a trembling, clammy handshake. She squeezed his hand in an attempt of reassurance, but she forgot her strength.

"Ow!" The vampire flinched, eyes comically wide in surprise.

She blushed. "Shit, I'm sorry. I totally didn't mean to hurt you."

"How are you so strong, human?" Bryan's mouth gaped, revealing his fangs.

"That's what you are here to discover, youngling." Razvan told him, smiling in sadistic glee at his discomfort.

Silas grabbed a sharp letter opener from his desk and made a small cut on his wrist. "Drink, Bryan, and I will show you what we know."

Bryan locked his mouth on the wound, sucking greedily. His eyes jittered beneath closed lids like he was in R.E.M. sleep. Akasha realized he was witnessing her parent's murder. She must have done something to indicate her discomfort, for Silas reached over with his free hand and stroked her hair.

"It will be all right, lass," he whispered. "I shall only show him what is necessary."

"How precious." Razvan crooned.

Akasha flipped him off.

Silas worked his wrist free from Bryan's mouth. "That is enough. Can you find out who those men are?"

The nerdy vampire's eyes now gleamed with confidence and intelligence. "I know who they are, Lord McNaught. They're the COAT!"

"COAT?" Razvan, and Akasha asked simultaneously.

Silas slammed his fist on his desk. "Damn it, I shouldha known."

"Covert Operations Assassination Team." Bryan explained. "They're military hit men... er... and women. Since Akasha is still alive, that means that their orders were to take her alive. With her ah... mutation, I assume the COAT wants to study her. My guess is that she's the result of some sort of government experimentation."

"Like people said they did during the Vietnam War?" Akasha asked.

Bryan nodded and approached the computer. "Now I just need to hack into the files. And since they're probably archived by now, it'll be a piece of cake."

"Wait, what are you two talking about?" Razvan interrupted.

Akasha and Bryan began chattering at once. Bryan bowed to Akasha. "Go ahead, my lady, I'll fill in what you leave out."

"The government did a bunch of crazy experiments on the soldiers during 'Nam," she explained. "Haven't you heard of Timothy Leary?"

Silas shook his head. "I was too busy keeping my stocks in order. The economy is precarious during a war, you know."

Akasha shook her head and continued. "Anyway, this guy created a chemical compound for the government in hopes of creating the perfect soldier. What he got was LSD, but he didn't mind, 'cuz he made lots of money off of it, well, until he got busted, that is. The military must have created something that actually worked."

Razvan chuckled. "So you and Bryan think your powers are a result of human experimentation? Fascinating. If you knew so much about this experimenting, why didn't you come to this conclusion sooner?"

Akasha shook her head. "For a long time I lived in denial that I was different. Then, when Max made me face the facts, we didn't talk about it much 'cuz it seemed to make him uncomfortable. And it's not like I've ever been good enough with computers to attempt any research." She shrugged. "Besides, I'm way too young to be a 'Nam baby and my dad didn't seem military at all. We may be wrong anyway."

"One way to find out," Bryan's fingers were already flying across the keyboard of Silas's computer. Gone was the timid unkempt vampire. In his place sat a skilled professional, secure in his abilities. Akasha blinked in amazement.

"His talent is why he was Changed when he approached the Lord of his former home instead of being killed for knowing our secrets," Silas told her as Bryan worked.

"He knew about vampires and actually walked up and asked one to Change him? Damn, I bet that took some balls!" Akasha looked at Bryan with new admiration.

"Yes," Silas agreed and leaned forward. "Bryan was something of a conspiracy theorist in his mortal days and enjoyed breaking into government computers. In the course of his hacking, he discovered a branch of the FBI that is aware of our existence: the AIU, or Abnormal Investigation Unit."

The implication of his words fell like a stone in her stomach. "Holy fuck..."

Silas nodded. "They were targeting the Lord of Topeka, and since the COAT was on his trail for hacking into their files, he decided to warn the Lord in hopes of becoming one of us and getting help with his escape. I bargained to move him into my territory because I find his skills very useful."

"Wait a Sec." Akasha felt a deeper jolt of fear. "Does this AIU know about you?"

"No." Silas shook his head and smiled. "They sent an undercover agent to investigate me about ten years ago. He was posing as a corporate investor, so I took him to dinner and ate a full meal in front of him. They think we can't eat food, you know. Needless to say, I was off the hook with only a bad case of indigestion."

Akasha smiled back. "I wondered about that. I thought you were diabetic with how little you ate and how much water you drink."

"I still love the taste of food, though I can't eat much. As for water, you humans don't drink enough," he admonished.

The rapid clicking of the computer stopped. "I've got it!" Bryan announced.

Akasha, Silas, and Razvan crowded around the computer to read the file. The details of the military's experiments on

American soldiers during the Gulf War were described in vivid, sickening detail.

When they reached the part where the mutated soldiers were killed, Akasha clapped her hand over her mouth, nauseated at the cold way the sequential murder of her father's squad had been narrated, as if they had been commodities rather than human beings.

She held back a silent cheer as she read of her father's escape and success in evading the military for over ten years.

But when they came to the part where her parents were killed, she turned away and rested her head against Silas's chest.

"My father's name was Jamison Lindsey." Akasha murmured, "My mom's name was Kathleen O'Reilly."

Silas laughed softly, "Yer an Irish lass. I should ha' known." His Scottish burr was thick, but Akasha could tell he was doing it on purpose. Her heart warmed at his attempt to cheer her up.

Bryan printed the file and scrolled down to links showing the current status of the case.

"It looks like they're getting close to giving up the search. The case is passed on to an officer named Major Milbury and the Pentagon only gave him a skeleton crew of yeomen and one COAT unit on retainer. The last update to this file was almost a year ago. You're probably not that high of a priority with them anymore." The vampire turned to her with a grin. "So how much can you bench?"

Akasha smiled back, responding to his sudden boyish charm. "I don't know exactly, but I once lifted the back end of a '69 El Camino."

His mouth gaped, fangs gleaming and out of place with his astonishment. "Sweet!"

Razvan approached the desk. "I hate to interrupt, but I need to put this in my report and get it to the Elders as soon as possible, so as they now say, move it!"

Bryan needed no further urging. He darted out of the seat as if Razvan was a demon trying to roast his balls. Akasha couldn't resist yanking Razvan's chain a bit.

She lifted her brows in mock disbelief. "*You* can use a computer? I'm surprised."

He glared at her. "All Lords are required to. We take classes."

The picture of ancient vampires sitting at desks typing under a watchful instructor was too much for her. She started giggling uncontrollably.

"You should go to bed, Akasha." Silas kissed her on the cheek. "You have school tomorrow."

Irritated at being so curtly dismissed, she sighed in resignation and headed to her room. After all, winter break was over and it was time to begin the final half of the school year.

***

Silas stifled a yawn. These past few days had been exhausting. He was still reeling from the knowledge that Akasha was the result of government experimentation. He could believe in magic and miracles, but modern chemistry? It was a new concept. Images of the COAT and their guns flashed in his mind. The thought of Akasha being killed by them was enough to undo him. Bryan seemed to think she was safe, but Silas wasn't convinced.

"Can I leave now, sir?" The youngling asked.

"Soon. I just need one more thing from you." He grasped the vampire and held his gaze, taking over his mind to wipe away the memories of all he'd done tonight. It would be safer for all concerned.

Bryan left, yet Silas's sense of foreboding remained.

Chapter Twenty-six

The minute Akasha entered English 101, Xochitl crooked her finger in a melodramatic "come hither" gesture.

"What happened this weekend?" she whispered, juggling her books. "Were you 'grounded' again?" She made quotation marks in the air. "Or did Silas kiss you again?"

Akasha shook her head as she struggled to decide what to tell her friend. *Oh, let's see. Silas drank my blood and saw everything about my past, We had the greatest sex ever, we found out I'm a government engineered mutant, assassins are after me and a coalition of ancient bloodsuckers may kill us all... yeah.* Even Xochitl with all her strangeness would have trouble buying that. *But I could tell her about the sex.*

"You can't tell anyone. Okay? I swear our friendship is off if you do." Akasha really wanted to talk to another girl, but knew she'd be screwed if it got around.

Xochitl's eyes widened with giddy curiosity. "I swear. After all, I totally owe you for not telling the others about that incident with Bill." She twirled a purple lock of her hair and smiled. "So spill."

Akasha looked down at the floor, trying to hide her burning cheeks. "We, uh... well, kinda slept together."

"Really? What was it like?" Xochitl leaned forward, her lips parted in rapt fascination.

Akasha sighed. This girl talk stuff was harder than she thought. "It was amazing, kinda scary, but amazing."

Her friend giggled and wagged her brows. "How big was it?"

"Xochitl!" Her eyes darted around in embarrassment, looking for eavesdroppers.

Xochitl blinked at her mock innocence. "What? That's what I'm supposed to ask."

"Says who?" Akasha's eyes narrowed.

Xochitl shrugged merrily. "I dunno."

Akasha squirmed in her chair, suddenly uncomfortable with the conversation. "Since it was the first one I've seen, I don't really have anything to compare it to, but I think it was huge."

Xochitl nodded. "I bet he's got a hot body. So is he like your boyfriend for real now?"

A tremor of foreboding sank its claws in her heart. "I don't know. We haven't had a chance to talk about it yet."

The feeling quickly twisted into full-fledged worry. *Did he just make love to me in the heat of the moment? Or does he want me to be his lover for all eternity? Do vampires get married? Am I ready to get married?*

"What do you mean?" Xochitl frowned, picking up on her anxiety. "Has he been avoiding you?"

Akasha shook her head quickly. "No. Razvan was there the whole night. He and Silas had important business to discuss and I had to replace the radiator in Black Sunshine." She paused, remembering something. "Oh, yeah. Razvan wants you and the band to play for him tonight, if you guys can."

Xochitl sighed in a failed attempt to hide her delight. "It's kinda short notice, but I'll ask and see."

"Yeah, sorry about that." Akasha rolled her eyes and rifled through her textbook. "He's kind of a dick."

"Yeah, but he's really helped us a lot. I can't thank him enough for introducing us to all those awesome bands." Suddenly, Xochitl jumped up from her chair and bounced like a giddy schoolgirl. The action was inconsistent with her vinyl pants, chains, and Megadeth baby tee. Everyone stared. "Oh my God, I totally forgot to tell you what happened Friday!"

Akasha couldn't help smiling at her enthusiasm even as she was reminded of their disparity in ages. "What?"

Xochitl sat back down and clapped her hands. "You know how we reserve the high school's auditorium, sometimes to practice on a real stage? Well, we did that Friday and we were practicing those *Rainbow* songs and *first* the art teacher wandered in, and *then* the janitor sat down and it was like we were playing a concert, but then, you'll never guess what happened." She grabbed her pen and waved it like a conductor's baton, drawing out the suspense. "The entire football team came in. They were having a meeting with their coach and when he heard the music he dragged them all in to hear us!"

"No way," Akasha breathed. "The football team? They hate you guys."

Xochitl nodded. "But the coach now loves us. The dude actually had tears in his eyes after we finished and started reminiscing with the art teacher about the concerts they'd been to. But here's the best part: the team started up with their usual bullshit about us being freaks and fags and all that, but the coach whipped around in his seat and told them that if any of them messed with us again, they'd be off the team."

"No *fucking* way," Akasha gaped. "I bet that didn't go over well."

"Nah, and it might make it worse for us," Xochitl said cheerfully. "But the looks on their faces was totally worth it. Too bad we can't make the same happen with the cheerleaders and the Aryan nation wannabes. Anyway, I gotta thank Razvan big time for that. He's a really awesome guy." Her face lit up with adoration.

As class began and the instructor lectured about Mark Twain, Akasha pondered Xochitl's story. Razvan really *was* helping the band; there was no getting around it. Silas thought he was just feigning interest to mess with everyone, but it was beginning to appear genuine. But why? What would a thousand year old vampire do with a metal band? As they reached the Barracuda, she remembered a piece of her conversation with Razvan last night.

"To deem you harmless, we need to know why you have your abilities and who is pursuing you. And as for your friend, Xochitl—"

"What about Xochitl?"

"You mean you don't know?"

Her fist clenched and she had to concentrate on being careful opening the car door. Rage boiled within her. Razvan wasn't the only one being secretive. It seemed Silas was as well, and whatever he was keeping from her had something to do with her best friend.

***

Once the band was settled downstairs with Razvan, Akasha looked up at Silas. "Can we speak in private for a moment?"

He cast a quick glance at Razvan before nodding. He was so beautiful, his eyes so tender. The thought of duplicity from him was all the more agonizing.

Hands shaking, Akasha got a beer and sat in the dining room without turning on the lights. Her heart felt like it was clenched in a vise. If she had to choose between the man she loved and her best friend, it'd kill her.

Silas's dark form entered the room, his tantalizing masculine scent teasing her senses as he sat next to her. "What's wrong, Akasha?"

She took a drink of her beer, trying to wash down the lump in her throat. "What are you hiding from me about Xochitl?" she asked.

His eyes glowed faintly in the darkness. "What do you mean?"

Akasha sighed and avoided his gaze. "Look, Razvan's been dropping all sorts of hints, and you even said something about his interest in her. Are you going to give her to him to be his 'pet mortal'?" She made air quotes, voice dripping with derision at the term. "'Cuz if you think for a minute I'm going to sit quietly and allow her to go to him, you got another thing coming. He may not completely be the monster I thought he was, but I'll still beat the living shit out of you both if you try to fuck with her."

His shoulders were shaking. *Was he crying?* Then Silas threw back his head and laughed. "Oh, you are worried for your friend." He pulled her into his arms. "I thought you were regretting what we did the other night."

"No, I don't regret it." She resisted the urge to rub her cheek on his shoulder and breathe in his scent. "Did you?"

"No, lass. In fact," he whispered against her ear, "I was hoping for more."

Akasha gasped in pleasure as he kissed her neck. Shit, she was getting distracted. She pulled away and grabbed her beer to put distance between them.

"So what's up with Xochitl then?" She fixed him with a glare, determined to get the truth.

Silas sighed. "Xochitl is, well, she's not human."

"What?" Akasha's heart pounded. Really, with her own oddity and the craziness of these last few months, she shouldn't be surprised... yet she still was. "Then what *is* she?"

"I don't know, but she emanates power of the likes I've never felt before." Silas leaned forward. "Delgarias told me she's the daughter of Mephistopheles, the creator of vampires. He commanded me to guard her."

She swallowed as she remembered the odd way Xochitl's eyes changed color. *"Don't ask, don't tell,"* she'd said. Akasha hadn't thought much of the incident until now.

She looked up at him as she toyed with the tablecloth. "So she's part undead?"

"We're not dead." Silas's brows knit in an offended frown.

Her lips parted in surprise. "You're not?"

"No." His voice was firm. "It's a mutation, I suppose. Like yours, only with immortality and other major side effects." He paused, giving her a strange, probing look. "Wait. You thought I was a walking corpse and you still love me?"

Akasha nodded and brushed her lips across his, relieved that Silas didn't intend any harm to Xochitl. "Though it's nice to know you're alive. So, who's Mephisto-whoever and where did vampires come from?"

"Nobody really knows." Now Silas fidgeted with the tablecloth. "The ancient ones speak of a legend of how the first vampires were created by the devil himself and cast out of hell because they refused to feed on innocents. Fallen demons rather than fallen angels. Razvan thinks it is romantic silliness, but Delgarias assures me the legends are true. As Delgarias is the oldest of us, I am inclined to believe him."

"Wow." Akasha lit a cigarette as she digested the information. "So Xochitl is the daughter of Satan?"

Silas shook his head. "I highly doubt Mephistopheles is the actual *devil*, more likely, he's a powerful being who exists in another world."

"You mean like an alternate dimension?" she asked in fascination. "How do you figure?"

Silas took a deep breath. "When I Marked Xochitl at the concert, I was pulled into a vision. Whether it was a dream or a memory, I don't know. She was in a world with two moons, walking in a garden of black roses. The roses were dying. A man approached her and cast me out. Dreams aren't supposed to work that way. They're not supposed to be real." He shuddered and pulled her into his embrace.

He was afraid. That scared the shit out of her. "So she's like an alien? No wonder she's so strange. She has no concept of fear, you know, and she talks to her car. And I swear, sometimes it seems like it answers her."

Silas laughed. "She talks to cats as well. That night her foster father hit her, she was surrounded by the little beasties, communing with them."

"Now I get why Isis listens to her so well." Akasha had a thought. "What do you think she did that night to scare Bill and Susan so bad?"

"She made a ball of flame appear in her hand and threatened to burn them." His tone was rife with awe. "I used my Mark to mesmerize her long enough to get her to tell me. Her mind is strong, so I couldn't hold her long."

Akasha sighed, struggling to digest all this new information. "So Razvan doesn't want her? Are you sure? She's so beautiful."

He caressed her cheek. "As are you, lass. However, neither Razvan nor I feel any lust for her. We feel drawn to her in a strange way, but not sexually, more like..." he frowned, fumbling for the word, "reverence for her. All I know is that she's meant to be here, even if Delgarias hadn't commanded me to guard her and the others. And her music... somehow that is meant to be as well."

Akasha nodded. "They are freakishly good. Is that why Razvan's so interested in them? And what exactly are you supposed to guard them from? Do you think it's that freaky lightning guy in your vision?"

"I certainly hope not." Silas toyed with her hair, making her fight to pay attention to his words. "As for Razvan, I wouldn't worry about him making advances on Xochitl or the other two ladies." He chuckled. "Or Beau, for that matter.

Aside from them being underage, not only is it forbidden without my express permission since I Marked them, but Razvan doesn't dally with humans."

"Why not?" Akasha's curiosity rose up despite her usual irritation with his maker.

Silas shrugged. "Some of the old ones are like that. They prefer to only mate with other vampires. Razvan put it more crudely, though."

She chuckled. "I can imagine. Anyway," she forced herself to focus back on the point of the conversation. "Xochitl and the band are safe from Razvan then?"

"From him, yes," he promised. "As for the Elders, Xochitl is more of an issue. We need to get as much information on her as possible for our report. We need to prove she's not going to be a danger to our kind... but with the way vampires are attracted to her, it will be difficult. Perhaps that's why I'm supposed to guard her. Though, for the record, I honestly believe Razvan is sincere about his admiration with their music." Silas kissed her cheek and stood up as the music stopped downstairs. It was time for her friends to go home.

"Wait, Silas?" Akasha hated the way her voice trembled. "Are you my boyfriend now?" It sounded stupid, but she had to ask.

He chuckled and gave her a smile that made her belly flutter. "Do you want me to be?"

A thrill rushed through her even as she tried to look nonchalant. "Sure. I guess so."

He pulled her into his arms and crushed her lips with his. She moaned and grabbed his ass, wanting him like a starving woman wanted cake. Someone coughed.

They jumped apart to see Xochitl smirking at them from the doorway.

Akasha looked at her friend, really looked at her this time. How could she have assumed Xochitl was human? Her skin was as smooth as airbrushed photos of supermodels... only it was real.

Silas straightened his shirt. "I appreciate your discretion, Miss Leonine."

Xochitl inclined her head regally. Her eyes flickered burgundy and Akasha resisted the urge to step back. "Just know this, Silas. If you hurt her, I'll kick your ass." She did a kung-fu kick in the air and grinned. "So you'd better treat her well."

Silas smiled and gazed down at Akasha. "This is the second time tonight I've been threatened with bodily harm."

Razvan followed came upstairs with the rest of the band. "You four are going to be famous," he was telling them.

After they left, Silas looked at Razvan. "Would you leave us for awhile?"

Razvan raised a brow. "I suppose. I need to feed anyway."

The moment he departed, Silas swept Akasha up in his arms and carried her up the stairs.

Chapter Twenty-seven

The next weeks were happy, but exhausting. Akasha found herself falling asleep in class from staying up late with Silas. They spent their evenings talking like new best friends and making love like newlyweds. He captivated her with his descriptions of life and war in Scotland in the 1500's and nearly moved her to tears with the tale of King James IV.

Hiding her love from her friends was a pain in the ass. She lost count of the times Sylvis and Aurora almost caught her sitting on Silas's lap. And she could swear Beau saw them kissing once. It was a good thing she didn't often wear lipstick.

Eventually, the truth would come out, but Akasha would prefer it to happen after graduation.

After a while, she fixed her routine better so she could spend time with Silas and keep up with school. And best of all, she finished restoring her Roadrunner.

Akasha smiled as she remembered the almost orgasmic feeling when the 318 engine roared to life— and the hilarity of Silas's terror when she broke it in. "Drive it like you stole it" was Max's advice on the process and she had nearly turned the five hundred year-old vampire's hair white as she sent them careening down the streets at breakneck speeds.

Only one problem remained. Though the revelation of Silas's lovemaking seemed to abate the nightmares of her past, the horrific dreams of reliving her rape still came, albeit infrequently. Silas took to accompanying her when she went to bed so that when she awoke screaming, he was there to hold her.

"It's all right, lass," he'd whisper soothingly as he stroked her hair. "It will heal in time."

But Akasha didn't want to wait any longer. It had been nearly four years for fuck's sake! And her passionate nights with Silas proved she wasn't screwed up sexually.

Still, no matter how much beer she drank or how many times Silas brought her to climax in one night, the nightmare would catch her unawares. Suddenly, she would be bent over the Cadillac, pants around her ankles, hot metal burning her hands, cold gun metal pressed to the back of her skull, and the reeking rapist's body tearing her apart.

At a loss for what to do, Akasha decided to confide in Xochitl. Thankfully, her friend didn't bat an eye at her request to talk privately during lunch. Although *Rage of Angels* was generally inseparable, the others didn't seem to mind either and gave her encouraging smiles as they piled in Aurora's van, leaving Xochitl to climb in the Roadrunner's passenger seat.

"You did an awesome job on this car, 'Kash," Xochitl said once they parked in front of a bookstore. "Almost as good as you did with Little Beast."

Akasha lit a cigarette and raised a brow. "The day your Datsun beats my Roadrunner is the day I quit wrenching."

"I dunno," Xochitl grinned impishly. "I'm learning how to airbrush in art class and I'm gonna do some kick-ass flames on her."

"Flames on a station wagon?" Akasha laughed. "Have you been smoking Beau's stash?"

"She's not a station wagon. She's a hatchback hot rod." Xochitl lifted her chin regally and lit her own cigarette. "Now what's going on with you and Silas?" she asked, not missing a beat. "I assume that's why you wanted to talk."

Akasha sighed. "Well, kinda. There's nothing wrong with Silas. It's just... me." She frowned as she struggled for the words. This was harder than she imagined.

"What do you mean?" Xochitl asked patiently.

"Well," Akasha looked down at her lap. "About four years ago... I...," she swallowed before forcing the rest out. "I was raped." The ugliness of the word loomed over her, making her choke.

She closed her eyes to prepare for an embarrassing outpouring of sympathy and empty words of condolence.

Instead, Xochitl's voice was solemn. "I know. We've heard you cry out in your sleep a couple times... and the way you cried when you heard that Tori Amos song. We all wanted to say something, but I figured you'd talk about it when you were ready."

Akasha opened her eyes and cautiously met her friend's gaze. Xochitl's eyes suddenly seemed to belong to someone far older and wiser than those of a seventeen year old aspiring rock star. A strange shame filled her. She'd misjudged her friend yet again. After another awkward silence, the whole story poured out.

"I thought making love with Silas would stop the dreams and it did, for awhile," Akasha said, throat sore from fighting back tears. "But they still come once in awhile. Silas said to give it time, but I don't want to. I just want them to stop!" Her fists clenched impotently.

They sat in silence, smoking cigarettes, watching customers emerge from the store, arms laden with books, smiling in the March sunshine.

Finally, Xochitl spoke. "What if you recreate parts of the dream, but in a good way?"

"What do you mean?" Akasha's eyes narrowed skeptically.

Her friend's honey brown gaze remained intent. "Well, you love Silas, right?"

"Yeah...?"

"And you love cars too." At Akasha's nod, Xochitl continued. "Well, maybe if you have Silas do you on your car, then later when you have the dream, you'll think of him instead of the asshole rapist." She paused and frowned. "Then again, maybe that'd backfire and you'd think of the asshole rapist instead of Silas and it could ruin your sex life."

Akasha imagined bending over the hood of the Roadrunner, feeling Silas's warm breath on the back of her neck instead of a cold steel gun. She shivered as fear and excitement mixed within her body, turning her belly into a whirlpool of contradictory desires.

"I think I'll try it," she said finally, managing a weak smile. "You know, Xoch', for a virgin, you sure seem to know a lot about this kind of thing."

"What can I say? I read a lot of smut. Speaking of..." She nodded towards the bookstore. "Do you think we have time to go in and browse a bit?"

"I killed that asshole rapist," Akasha said quietly, astonished to finally say it aloud.

Xochitl looked at her for a long time. There was no condemnation in her eyes, only fierce conviction. "Good."

***

The COAT agent removed the earpiece and looked at his partner. "We got her."

He flicked off the switches on the audio surveillance equipment. At last this espionage bullshit was over.

Milbury had given them the girl's name, background information and a vague description: "petite, black hair."

That was all.

It took a week to narrow the search down to two possible candidates. The problem was that they were both petite and both had black hair. To make matters worse, they were inseparable.

The agent followed them everywhere in his van, using his low budget equipment to listen in on their conversations — and Murphy's Law seemed to dictate the equipment would fail when the two called each other by name— when he could catch them. Both drove as if they knew they were being tailed.

Finally the curly-haired one told the purple-streaked one about killing a rapist. She must be Akasha. The agent pulled out his phone and sent the news to Milbury. Until his new orders were received, he would follow her.

Chapter Twenty-eight

Hours later, Akasha stood in the garage, wobbling unsteadily on the "fuck me" heels that Xochitl loaned her along with a faux fur coat. Between the space heater and the coat, she was warm enough despite the fact that she wore nothing beneath. For a moment she debated on whether or not to light some candles. *Nah, it wouldn't fit.*

The sound of footsteps outside the garage door made her jump. Silas was back from his first hunt. A panicked voice in the back of her mind urged her to run into the house and take back the note which would lead him in here.

"No," she whispered, clenching her fists. "I can do this. I *want* to do this."

As she waited in tense silence, she closed her eyes and pictured him finding her note on the table. Her pulse quickened.

The door to the garage opened and for a moment she was struck breathless at the vampire's beauty.

"I received your note, Akasha." His voice seemed to caress her under the fur. "What is it you wanted to show me?"

His gaze swept down over her ensemble, eyes widening slightly at the high heels. Akasha felt a pulse of wet warmth between her legs as her trembling fingers undid the buttons on the coat. Forcing her eyes to meet Silas's, she shrugged off the coat and tossed it onto her toolbox. Another tremor pulsed through her core at his harsh indrawn breath.

Naked except for the black stilettos, she slowly walked towards him, reveling in the raw lust in his eyes. Akasha grabbed the lapels of his jacket, pulling him closer.

"I want you to bend me over the car, Silas," she whispered, voice only shaking slightly as she pulled the jacket from his shoulders, "and then I want to feel you inside of me. I want you to chase away my nightmares."

The vampire's mouth opened, then snapped closed. His eyes took on an unholy light, his fangs gleaming as he took a sharp breath and released it with a hiss. "I'm not certain that's a good idea, Akasha," he said finally. "What if—"

His words cut short as she ran her hand down the length of his body, gripping his shaft through the thin fabric of his pants.

"I know you want to," she said softly, unbuttoning his pants and pulling down the zipper. He was hot and rock hard in her hand. A sigh of bliss escaped her lips at the feel of him.

"Akasha..." he began warningly then gasped as she stroked his satiny tip.

"Don't worry, Silas," she said, reaching up with her other hand to unbutton his shirt. "I trust you."

As his arms locked around her waist, Akasha gasped at the sheer truth of her words. Never before had she trusted anyone and it felt strangely liberating. The thought broke off as Silas kissed her, a low growl trickling from his throat.

Frustrated with the slow progress, she let out a growl of her own and tore at his shirt. The silk ripped apart with a sharp sound. Silas raised a brow and shrugged off the remnants of the shirt. With a wicked, sensual smile he slowly slipped off his shoes and pants to stand gloriously naked before her.

Seizing her by the waist, he lifted her in the air. Akasha had a moment to marvel at his strength before his tongue flicked over her breasts, making her cry out in pleasure.

His mouth worshipped her body as he carried her to the car, laying her on the hood with reverent gentleness. However, his savage gaze raking down the line of her body was far from gentle.

When his tongue flicked across her clit, Akasha bit back a scream of ecstasy. The combination of the cool metal against her back and Silas's hot mouth at her core sent her into a delirium of erotic sensation that soon sent her spiraling into an earth-shattering orgasm.

"Are you ready?" Silas's voice was hoarse with desire.

"Yes," she managed to gasp before he carefully pulled her down and helped her turn over.

The bumper was cold against her legs, but the hood was warm from where she'd reclined. Akasha's hands splayed on the Roadrunner's hood scoop for balance as she spread her legs for her lover. The high heels put her at the perfect angle for his entry.

With excruciating slowness, Silas slid into her wet warmth.

Akasha felt a momentary surge of panic as the terrible memory threatened to overtake her... then she realized there was no pain, only pleasure, and the car's hood was cool, not burning hot. It was *her* Roadrunner, not a Cadillac. Instead of a gun pressed to the back of her head, Silas's lips were against her neck, whispering love words in his sexy Scottish brogue as his cock sensuously moved in and out of her wet heat. Her core throbbed with the pleasure and she bucked her hips against him, urging him to go deeper.

***

It took every ounce of Silas's control not to explode from the mind-rending pleasure. After all the times he'd been driven to the brink of insanity at the sight of Akasha bending over her cars, his fantasy was finally being fulfilled.

At first he was afraid of frightening her with his passion, but when her tight wetness pulsed and gripped around him, and her velvet voice gasped "harder," he was lost.

Silas thrust into her like a thing possessed, his hips smacking against her ass in a delicious rhythm. The musky scent of her arousal, coupled with the lingering taste of her womanhood on his tongue awoke his blood thirst, but before he could push it aside, Akasha moaned. "Bite me, now!"

With a low growl, his fangs pierced her delicate throat. As her hot blood flowed across his tongue, his mind melded with hers and he felt her climax tearing through them both. Silas focused the link to greater intensity and when he came, Akasha felt it too. For what seemed an eternity, orgasm after orgasm rolled through them, one feeding the other. Before it ended, Silas sent Akasha a silent command: *No more nightmares.*

And then they collapsed onto the Roadrunner's hood in a sated heap, hearts pounding and gasping for breath.

"Did we dent your car?" He slowly regained his feet and helped her to stand.

Akasha surveyed the gleaming steel. "No, but I may have scratched the paint a bit." She grabbed his arm tightly, wobbling on her heels. "Damn, my legs feel like they're made of neoprene."

Silas gathered her up in his arms and bit his lip, drawing blood before he kissed her neck to heal the puncture wounds. "Do you think your plan worked?"

Akasha smiled up at him as he retrieved the fur coat from her toolbox and wrapped it around her naked body. "If it didn't, we'll just have to try again." She licked her lips. "Maybe we could try the 'Cuda next time?"

His cock stirred at her words, despite the strenuous activity it had been through. Silas nodded and forced his attention to other matters. "Since I took blood from you, it would be good for you to eat something."

"I could go for some ice cream," she murmured as he carried her back in the house. "Maybe some pizza too... and a beer or two and a cigarette, and—Eeeep!" Her words cut short with a girlish scream.

Razvan leaned indolently against the laundry room wall.

"I was going to ask if you'd like to accompany me on tonight's hunt," he drawled, raking them both with an ironic gaze. "But I see you have fed already."

Akasha's face was crimson as Silas adjusted the fur coat to cover them both more fully. Unfortunately, there was nothing he could do about his exposed backside. He cursed himself for forgetting to put his pants back on.

"You could have informed me of your presence," Silas told him with a glare.

Razvan blinked in mock innocence. "And interrupt whatever you two were doing in there? I would never be so rude." His eyes strayed back to Akasha. "Of course I do regret missing the view."

"You didn't miss it entirely," Silas said blandly before he turned and presented Razvan with his bare arse and carried Akasha up the stairs.

Chapter Twenty-nine
Two weeks later

Silas licked the blood from his lips and released his victim from the trance.

"And that'sh how thugh Sheahawks tooks the game," the man slurred. "Hey man, thanksh for the cabs money. Yer alright."

"One less danger on the road." Silas nodded curtly and headed to his car. He loathed drunk drivers. They caused so many senseless deaths, injuries and property damage.

As he drove home, he regretted not being able to be out in daylight for the first time in centuries. The limited time he had with Akasha was not nearly enough. He had to be careful not to keep her up too late; it made her schooling suffer. When she went to college, it would be more vital, since her education would henceforth be dedicated to her career.

Akasha's goals for her auto repair shop had soared. She wanted her business to be open at night so vampires could get their cars fixed.

As Silas reached the top of the hill, he spied Little Beast in his driveway. The second he pulled into the garage and locked onto his Mark with Xochitl, a chord of alarm reverberated through him. Something was wrong.

"Silas!" Akasha ran into the garage, gasping. "Something's wrong with Xochitl. She was attacked and her back's all fucked up!"

"What happened?" His heart leapt with worry while his instincts raged to protect one he Marked.

Akasha's hands shook almost as much as her voice. "She didn't come back from lunch, but after school her car was still in the parking lot. I searched and waited for her, then left a note on her car. She just got here a few minutes ago. She's all scratched up and bruised. They... they tied her up!" she panted.

A roar of outrage built in his throat as he understood her implication. "Did they..."

"I don't know!" Akasha wailed. "She was starting to tell me about it, but her eyes turned red and she started screaming about her back hurting. I don't know what's happening to her. She won't let me call an ambulance and I don't know what to do! I carried her upstairs and put her in bed when I heard your car."

"Well, let's go see." He followed her upstairs, fangs bared in anticipation of slaughtering whoever dared to hurt what was his.

Xochitl lay on her stomach on Akasha's bed, thrashing and groaning in pain. Her wrists were rubbed raw and bleeding from where she was tied.

"Oh, 'Kash, it hurts!" The Mark between her and Silas was fiery with agony and rage.

"Xochitl. I think you need to go to the hospital." He struggled to control the beast within and to stay practical. "If you were raped, it needs to be verified so the bastards who did it can be caught. And your wrists and back need to be attended to."

"They didn't... rape me," she bit out. "I stopped them... Ow... The fuckers!"

A measure of his rage dissipated. Thank God she hadn't been violated.

"Silas, look!" Akasha pointed.

There were lumps under Xochitl's shirt... And they were moving.

"Maybe you should let us look at your back," Silas tried to sound calm, though his flesh crawled at the sight before him.

"O-okay," Xochitl managed to gasp.

Akasha faced him. "Silas, turn around for a minute so I can get her shirt off."

Silas faced the wall, cringing at the pained noises Xochitl made as Akasha removed her shirt. He heard Akasha hiss and his instincts warred between soothing Akasha and protecting Xochitl. Now he knew why vampires were so careful about their Marks.

"Okay, you can look now." Akasha's voice quavered.

He turned around and gasped at the sight of Xochitl's back. The skin was scraped raw all over. The worst part was the moving lumps under the skin at her shoulder blades. Something was pushing and straining under the skin, about to burst out. Xochitl whimpered and shifted on the bed.

"What the fuck?" Akasha breathed. "Xochitl, are you a shapeshifter or something?"

"No. Why? What's going on?" Despite her obvious pain, Xochitl's tone was rife with curiosity.

Akasha cursed. "Shit, Silas, we can't take her to a hospital." Her voice dropped to a whisper. "They'd call those AIU guys or something."

"Never mind that," Silas threw up his hands, at a loss for how to handle this strange situation. "When did it start, Xochitl?"

"When those bastards tied me to a tree," Xochitl growled.

"Who?" Silas demanded, his predatory instincts roiled. "I will make them pay."

"You will not!" the creature on the bed roared with such ferocity that Silas stepped back. "*I'll* take care of it. They'll be lucky if they ever sleep again. They—" The lumps strained on her back harder. "Ow!"

Silas shuddered at the power of her command. Some potent force beneath her words compelled him to obey. Was it because her father had made his kind? The thought was cut short as Xochitl's cries of pain wrenched at him.

If he couldn't punish her enemies, perhaps he could ease her suffering. *But, how?* What was causing this? He had a thought. "Is it worse when you're angry?"

She took a deep breath and appeared to consider the question. "I don't know, maybe."

"You were quite angry when Bill hit you. Did your back hurt then?" He prodded.

She took a deep breath. "I think it did... yeah! I remember now. It hurt like a bitch until..."

"Until the cats came?" he asked, ignoring Akasha's questioning look.

Xochitl nodded. "Uh-huh."

Silas was amazed at how reasonable she was being. Akasha was right. Xochitl really had no fear at all.

Akasha ran a tentative hand across her friend's back. It looked like there were extra bones beneath her skin. Silas watched her struggle not to show her revulsion and knew she was trying to match Xochitl's bravery. At least the movement was slowing.

"Maybe you should try calming down," Akasha said brusquely.

"Okay. Can you get me a smoke?" Xochitl sounded as calm as if she were attending an afternoon tea.

Akasha nodded and pulled her cigarettes out of her pocket. "Sure. Damn, that tree scraped you up bad." Her eyes, pleading amethyst pools, met his. "Silas, can you get a cold cloth and some triple antibiotic ointment?"

Silas went into the bathroom and rummaged through the medicine cabinet as his mind raced. *What the hell was under Xochitl's skin?* He ran a washcloth under cold water and made a decision. He was going to be blunt and ask her. He was tired of all the questions, all of the strange new revelations.

As Akasha cleaned the scrapes on Xochitl's back, she talked to her casually in hopes to calm her down. "Hey Xoch', I was wondering if I could keep the fur coat if I bought you a new one."

Silas gasped. "That was *your* coat?" His cheeks grew hot. "Oh my..."

Akasha and Xochitl looked at him and burst out laughing.

"So you guys desecrated it, did you?" Xochitl asked with a grin, though the skin at the corners of her eyes was tight with pain. "Did the plan work?"

Akasha smiled. "I think so, it's only been a couple weeks, so we'll have to wait and see if we'll have to try again." She grinned at Silas's flaming face.

"I'll buy you a new coat, Miss Leonine." Silas said, hoping his embarrassment wasn't obvious, "Mink, sable..."

"I don't do real fur," Xochitl interrupted. "I only wear leather 'cuz I eat cows."

"Ah, a woman with principles," he said as he tried to think of how to broach the subject of her origins.

By the time Akasha was finished tending Xochitl's wounds, the things in her back had stilled. She was now swaddled in Akasha's purple fuzzy bathrobe, sipping a glass of wine and smoking a cigarette. Silas decided he'd waited long enough.

"Xochitl, what are you?" he asked, praying he wouldn't frighten her by being so direct.

She looked up at him, brown eyes so sad and pitiful, it almost undid him. "I thought I was just different... like

237

Akasha. My mom said we were special. I was never supposed to tell anyone, 'cept Sylvis. But, with what just happened and a couple other things…" Her sigh echoed through the room. "I just don't know anymore."

"You thought you were human?" Silas couldn't hide his sympathy.

Xochitl gave him a droll stare. "I look like a homo sapien, I talk like a homo sapien… the evidence seemed apparent."

"I see. So you have no idea." He struggled to hide his disappointment.

"No," she replied. "I was gonna work up the courage to ask Akasha what she is."

Akasha shook her head and opened a beer. "Just stronger than the average person," she muttered through the cigarette clamped between her teeth.

Xochitl grinned. "C'mon, 'Kash, you're like bionic or something. Now what's your deal?"

"It's a genetic mutation I inherited from my father." She shrugged.

Xochitl nodded. "Well, you're no help. Mom never told me about my father, except to say he was bad news." She finished her wine with an uncharacteristic gulp. "May I please have some more?"

Silas buried his head in his hands. *She doesn't know?*

What a fine mess this is! It seemed he knew more about Xochitl than she did. Another twinge of pity pierced him. He wished he could at least tell her about her father, but there was no way to do that without telling her of his kind and thus breaking Delgarias's decree.

His fists clenched in frustration. If Xochitl didn't know what she was then how was he supposed to figure it out? How would the Elders react?

Akasha refilled her friend's glass and gave Silas a look. *What are we going to do now?*

Silas jolted in surprise at the silent message. It must have taken a great deal of effort for her to slow her rapid thoughts down enough to speak to him telepathically. He sent her a reply. *I'm going to get Razvan. He might have a few ideas in his conniving head.*

Akasha nodded. *Good luck.*

***

"Where'd he go?" Xochitl asked worriedly as soon as Silas left the room. Akasha sighed, not knowing what to tell her. "I think he went to get Razvan."

"Why? I don't want more people knowing about me. 'Kash, you gotta stop him!" She tried to get out of bed, wincing in pain.

"Lay down, Xochitl," Akasha ordered. "I don't want your back acting up again. I won't let Razvan touch you. I promise. I've kicked his ass before and I can do it again."

"You kicked *his* ass?" Xochitl giggled for a moment, then sobered. "But what are they? Why are they so interested in my... my idiosyncrasies?"

Akasha smiled wanly at Xochitl's word for it. Her friend would lapse back into a more scholarly language when her other friends weren't around. She didn't know if Xochitl dumbed down her speech out of embarrassment or consideration for those less well read.

"Why don't you pay Silas back for his bluntness and just ask him?" Akasha suggested, avoiding the question as well as Xochitl's probing gaze. She didn't like where this was going. Silas had been very adamant on the subject of concealing his secrets. Hopefully, he or Razvan could come up with a plausible lie.

Xochitl grinned. "Maybe I will. Was I right, though? Are they mob guys?"

Akasha shook her head and lit a cigarette. "Not exactly." She sat on the bed next to her friend and patted her shoulder awkwardly as she changed the subject. "It's gonna be okay, 'Xoch."

"You don't hate me now because I'm not human, do you?" Xochitl's eyes were soft and pleading. "'Cuz I'd totally understand if you do."

Akasha managed a small, but sincere smile. "No, I don't hate you. Why would you ever think that?"

Xochitl looked away as if she didn't hear her. "I think that's why most people don't like me. It's like they can smell that I'm different, not one of them. People turned away from me in revulsion and called me a freak even before I started dressing Goth. Everyone hated me, except my mom, Sylvis and a few friends... like you. In fact," she said contemplatively. "A lot of people seem to be scared of me."

A wave of sadness washed over Akasha for her friend. How lonely it must have been for her! It had to have been worse than devastating for her when her mom died, the only other one of her kind.

"What's being scared like, 'Kash?" Xochitl asked suddenly.

"It's kind of a sick feeling," Akasha answered automatically. "Like your stomach dropped into your feet and your heart's climbing up your throat while at the same time it's attempting to pound it out of your chest... and all the while you're paralyzed and your nerve endings can't decide whether you're hot or cold."

"Whoa," Xochitl breathed. "That sounds like ultimate suckiness. Do I really affect people that way?"

Akasha shook her head. "I doubt it. If you did, they'd run away at the sight of you. I was talking about complete terror. Maybe you just make people nervous."

Xochitl nodded, digesting the information. "So do people get that way when they see spiders or are up high and stuff?"

"If that's what they're afraid of, I guess." She shrugged. "I'm not bothered by either."

"What are you afraid of?" Xochitl asked quietly, taking a deep drag of her cigarette.

Akasha hesitated before answering quietly, "Guns."

Xochitl's eyes widened. "I kinda figured as much after you freaked at the sight of mine. Is it like Sylvis and Aurora's phobia of clowns? Or did you have a bad experience with them?"

"My parents were shot in front of me when I was little." She shivered and took another sip of beer before giving a brief rundown of the story.

Yet again Xochitl had gotten another secret out of her. *Is this what true friendship is like? Confessing secrets and feeling relieved at sharing the burden?*

Something scratched at Akasha's newly replaced sliding glass door. They both jumped. Xochitl giggled like she always did when her startle reflex was triggered. Akasha wondered if it tickled.

Cautiously, Akasha approached the door, fists clenched in readiness for bad news. She opened the curtains with such force they tore at the edges. Her breath whooshed out in relief. It was Isis.

"Look who's here." Akasha let the kitten in. Isis meowed loudly and bolted into the room and jumped on the bed, purring and rubbing on Xochitl. Xochitl smiled and purred back.

"Maybe you're part cat." Akasha commented.

Xochitl shook her head. "No, my mom wasn't. She *bonded* with children... of all species."

Akasha blinked and lit another cigarette. "Bonded?"

"Yeah. She told me that people like us have a part of nature that we bond with, or have a special relationship with. Cats are mine. They come to me when I need them. Children were drawn to my mom. That's why she was such a good preschool teacher." She stroked Isis's fur softly. "So you're a mutant, huh?"

Akasha smiled and flicked her cigarette in the ashtray. "I guess so."

"So, we're like X-men!" Xochitl grinned. "Only our comic would be so much better."

They laughed a bit over that, but quieted when they heard Silas and Razvan come up the stairs.

"Are you guys Mafia?" Xochitl asked the second the door opened. Razvan and Silas looked at each other and burst out laughing, covering their mouths to hide their fangs. Razvan stalked closer to the bed, still chuckling. He sounded like a bad Dracula.

"Do we really appear to be that nefarious to you, my dear?" he said, stroking his beard like a cartoon villain.

Xochitl eyed him warily. "Sometimes."

Silas put his arm around Akasha and whispered into her mind. *We're going to try to put her in a trance and ask her about that world with the two moons and that man she dreams about.*

The two vampires leaned closer to Xochitl and captured her gaze. Immediately her eyes took on a feverish glint as she focused on them intently.

"Where is that place with the silver and gold moons?" Silas asked.

Xochitl replied in an eerie monotone. "I don't know. I go there in my dreams. The sun died there…"

Akasha and Razvan exchanged looks. *A dying sun?* She mouthed. *What the fuck?*

"Who is the man?" Silas continued; tapping Razvan on the shoulder to keep him focused.

"The dark man… He comes to me almost every night. I don't know what he wants." Xochitl blinked and the glaze left as her mind broke free. "So, really," she said brightly. "What are you guys?"

Razvan laughed. "If we told you, we'd have to kill you."

Silas rolled his eyes. "We're merely eccentrics who dabble in anything interesting. Now, where were you and your friends planning on launching your music career?"

It was a blatant change of subject. Akasha was surprised when Xochitl took it. "Well, I wanted to go to New Orleans, but Sylvis said we'd probably have better luck in Seattle. It's closer anyway."

"Very good." Razvan nodded briskly. "I may have some contacts in that area who could possibly help *Rage of Angels* get a start."

They talked for a while longer about the band and its chances for success before Akasha ordered them out of the room so Xochitl could get some sleep.

"I'll be back in a few to check on you, okay?"

Xochitl gave her a bleary smile and buried her face in her cat's fur.

After Akasha followed the vampires and closed the door behind them, Silas whispered, "I know about that other world… I just didn't think about it until she mentioned the dying sun. It was part of the prophecy Selena stole from Delgarias!"

Razvan looked skeptical. "Even if we were to track down Delgarias, it would be a tough explanation for the Elders to swallow. Still, I'm going to document our discussion with Xochitl and send it immediately with the rest of my report. But now I need to return to Spokane. I've neglected my business for too long." When they reached the bottom of the steps, he embraced Silas and kissed Akasha on both cheeks.

His mustache and goatee tickled her face. "I wish you two the best," he said, and then he was gone.

"Now what?" Akasha asked, suddenly worried.

Silas looked down at her gravely. "Now we pray."

***

The Elders and their advisors skimmed their copies of Razvan's report on Silas McNaught, Lord of Coeur d' Alene, Idaho, United States. They commenced closing arguments moments later.

The Lord of London held the opinion that McNaught was innocent of any conspiracy to overthrow the power balance. He'd known the Scot for a few centuries and pointed out to the others that Silas was wont to act on impulse quite frequently. Marking five teenagers was a foolish thing indeed, but the justification for it was plain in the report. Many nodded in agreement.

"But what of the inhuman girl?" the Lord of Berlin said. "She can make fire on command. It would make her a powerful weapon in anyone's hands. And the fact that she is still an unknown species indicates that many of her powers are probably untapped."

"Are you saying you do not believe this Xochitl is the daughter of Mephistopheles?" the Lord of Bangladesh inquired with a raised brow.

The German vampire laughed derisively. "I think it is complete silliness and fabrication."

There was much muttering in agreement. Others protested that McNaught never showed a hint of ambition or undue violence to his peers. A volatile creature such as Xochitl was probably safest in his peaceable hands.

"You all forget his pet mortal, the mutant," the Lord of Moscow interjected. "Agents of her country's government are looking for her. That is our biggest threat. If they catch her, she could reveal everything about our kind."

"But Nicolae's report states clearly that the government is close to giving up on her," the Lord of London protested. "It seems we should be discussing how to be sure she stays hidden. Damn impetuous Scot, he shouldn't have become involved with such a liability in the first place!" He pounded his fist on his podium.

The debate lasted for hours. Many of the ancient Lords began to glance at the clock gauging the hours they had left to retire to their lairs before daylight hit. They were deadlocked with half of them wanting McNaught punished and the other half wanting him chastised but left alone.

Finally the Lord of Pisa, advisor to the Lord of Rome, swayed enough of them to come to a decision. Many listened to her, for she'd spent a measure of time with Silas after he'd taken his vengeance on the English. It was she who'd stopped him from affecting crucial battles that could have changed history for the worst.

The votes were cast. A runner was sent to America to deliver their decision.

Chapter Thirty

Akasha was so happy she almost skipped down the hall after finishing her meeting with her student advisor. Her application was accepted. She'd gotten into the automotive program at the college. Only about twenty students were taken in every year. She'd been afraid she wouldn't be accepted because she was a woman. Now that worry was over. Her mind raced in eagerness to go through the tool list and see what she had left to get.

She hummed AC/DC's "*Have a Drink on Me*" and headed toward the parking lot. Finals had been a breeze and summer vacation had arrived, at least for her, Xochitl and Sylvis. Poor Aurora and Beau had another month left. But they'd all be together, then for the graduation ceremony.

The sun warmed her immediately. She frowned. Spring was coming and the nights would get even shorter. Silas wouldn't be able to get up for hours yet. But at least she could spend every night in entirety with him during summer vacation until college started. By then the days of hiding her love for Silas would be over.

Of course, there really wouldn't be anyone left to hide it from by that time anyway. Xochitl and the band were moving to Seattle soon after graduation. That is, if the Lord of that city was agreeable. Silas had just sent the request. If it was denied, they were screwed. Akasha had no idea how they could go about changing the band's minds about moving.

"Son of a *bitch*!" she growled when she spotted her car.

Her precious Roadrunner was totally wedged in. On the passenger side was a yuppie-ass BMW and on the driver's side was an ugly yellow cargo truck that was like four inches from touching her door.

"Gonna need a fucking can opener to get out," she grumbled and caressed the Roadrunner's dark green side panels, checking for dents and yellow paint.

A sharp pain erupted in her neck. Akasha reached up and felt a hand. She grabbed it and squeezed, feeling the bones crunch sickeningly under her fingers. Someone cried out in agony and was hushed by his accomplices. *What the fuck!* There was something in her neck. She shivered in revulsion and yanked it out. It was a hypodermic needle.

Oh shit! They shot me up with something! She whipped around to face her attackers, her heart leaping into her throat. Four men in black uniforms faced her, one cradling his hand and glaring. It was the COAT.

Akasha lunged forward to attack the men. But then the drug kicked in. The COAT soldiers disappeared from her vision as asphalt rushed to meet her face. She tried to brace herself for the impact, but her body refused to obey.

Hands grasped her arms. Suddenly, the ground fled from her as she was lifted and pulled through a hole in the side of the yellow truck's cargo box. It was lit up inside like NASA's command center. She found herself strapped to a table with thick steel manacles. They got her. They finally got her. A quote from "The Princess Bride" seemed appropriate at the moment.

My name is Inigo Montoya. You killed my father. Prepare to die.

She had no idea if she said that aloud or not, but it didn't matter. The lights and monitors inside the truck turned into

247

the most captivating starry galaxies and she was sucked inside.

***

Silas awoke with a sense of foreboding so strong he began to hyperventilate the moment he leapt out of bed. He leaned against the wall and tried to steady his racing heart as the hunger blasted within from a dull ache to a roaring inferno. His nerve endings vibrated with dread.

Something is wrong, very wrong.

He reached out with his sixth sense, but the bloodlust was too overpowering to be able to determine anything specific.

He flew up the stairs so fast that his hand cracked the door when he halted to open it. The house was quiet and nearly all the lights were off on the main floor. That wasn't unusual, since Akasha was concerned with saving electricity when she was out. He hoped she would get home soon.

As he flipped on the lights one by one as if the illumination could dispel the unease, he tried again to focus his powers to discover the source of his bad feeling. But no visions came, not even an image that could give him a minute clue. Silas focused on his Mark with Akasha... and felt nothing. He sucked in a breath as his heart froze in his ribcage.

Where is she?

A knock at the door shattered the silence. Muttering a small prayer for good news, Silas smoothed his hair and clothes so he wouldn't resemble a vagrant and opened the door.

"Here you are, my Lord." A century-old British vampire handed him an envelope before bowing and strutting away.

With great effort, Silas suppressed a snarl. This wasn't one of his vampires and the intruder had to have been resting nearby to have gotten here so quickly. It seemed he would be having a talk with his subordinates who were supposed to be keeping an eye out for this sort of thing.

A thought stopped him short. There was only one faction of vampires who would dare insult him by not informing him of a coming visitor. He looked at the missive in his hand and shuddered, his veins filling with ice.

The elaborate black embossed envelope appeared to be an invitation to an exclusive ball, but Silas knew better. Indeed, it was an exclusive invitation, but not a frivolous or desirable one. His bad feeling had been confirmed.

The Elders had responded. With shaky fingers, he removed the ribbon from the missive. A single eye ensconced within two scrolls was their symbol of office. The eye seemed to glare at him balefully. He unfolded the thick parchment and read:

May 11ᵗʰ
Silas McNaught, Lord of Coeur d' Alene, United States:

You are hereby summoned for the purpose of a discussion regarding your case. You are commanded to bring the following mortals: Akasha Hope and Xochitl Leonine.

You will report to our Headquarters in Amsterdam at ten o'clock p.m. on May Fourteenth.

Any attempts to disregard this summons or disobey any part of our instruction will be perceived as an admission of guilt and you will be sentenced accordingly.

We appreciate your cooperation.

The missive was signed by all Elders, but the thirteenth. Delgarias was still gone.

"Fucking son of a *bitch!*" Silas shouted, borrowing from Akasha's vocabulary.

Fury roared through him. Fury, and terror. If the Elders harmed one curly hair on Akasha's head, he would take as many of them down as he could. Hell, he would do his damnedest to persuade Xochitl to burn them all.

Silas strode to the living room and tossed the summons on an end table, wishing he could throw it into the fire and never think of it again. Slumping on the couch, he cradled his head in his hands as the dread washed over him.

What was to become of them? The panic and hunger warred within him, tearing him apart. Perhaps it was best that Akasha wasn't home yet. He didn't want her to see him like this.

Silas clenched his teeth as the bloodlust howled once more within. He needed to feed, needed time to clear his head of the overwhelming sense of foreboding. Afterward, he prayed he could process this situation and come up with a glimmer of hope.

The monster within him roared in triumph at the prospect of satiation as he headed out to the garage and fired up his Barracuda.

Hands gripping the steering wheel, he coasted down the hill in search of a meal. Luckily, he sighted his prey behind a grocery store. A greasy, emaciated man stood in the shadows, waiting to sell corruption and despair in plastic baggies to his hapless victims. Silas fed quickly, relishing the taste of blood, but hating the man's stench.

He gave the miscreant a mental command to flush his wares and seek honest work and added a psychic push to quell the brain's addiction centers before releasing him. Sometimes it worked, sometimes it didn't.

The blood cleared his head some, but the dread remained heavy. He purchased a case of beer for Akasha, hoping with all of his being that she would be around to drink it, and headed home. He wanted to see Akasha, hold her a wee bit before he told her the bad news.

The house was just as quiet as he'd left it. The sense of foreboding grew every minute. Akasha's absence was palpable and he was still unable to feel their Mark. He frowned at the clock which read ten-thirty. She always came home before this time on school nights. He searched the house for a note, nervousness clawing his heart when he didn't find one. He tried her cell phone, praying she remembered to bring it and that it wasn't dead.

Judas Priest's "You Got Another Thing Comin'" rang from the charger upstairs. Silas sighed. She'd forgotten it again. After going upstairs to fetch it, he used her phone and called her friends. Their responses were the same. They hadn't seen her since school let out. Sylvis provided the most help, pointing out that she'd seen her car remaining in the parking lot long after school.

"She had a meeting with her advisor about the automotive program," she added. "I bet she went to talk to the instructors after that. Have her call me when she gets home, 'Kay?"

"All right," he choked out in desolation and hung up.

Silas reached out again with his mind to touch Akasha's Mark. At last, he felt it. The Mark was faint, though, and likely miles away. His fears were confirmed. Either she had abruptly decided to leave him, or more likely she had been taken. For the first time, he wished it had been the former.

Silas growled in frustration at all the time he wasted and dug his phone out of his pocket to call Razvan. If the COAT had her, he'd need help.

"Akasha is gone," he said as soon as his Maker answered.

Razvan cursed. "And you were just summoned to trial by the Elders. I too received a copy. This is the last complication we need. I will be on my way."

"Meet me at the college. Her car was last seen there." Silas thanked the heavens that Razvan could fly fast and grabbed his sword along Akasha's spare keys on his way out the door. No matter what it took, he would get her back.

The sight of the Roadrunner, abandoned and forlorn, gripped his chest with fear and sorrow. The dark green paint looked black in the darkness.

He remembered the unabashed joy on Akasha's face when she opened her eyes to see that car in the garage on Christmas. He remembered her loving work on every detail of its restoration. He remembered her squeal of delight when she first started the engine. But most of all he remembered her constant pacing and anxiety when her prized possession lingered in the paint shop for a week. It must be killing her to know that her most precious possession was stranded here for thieves, vandals, or a tow truck.

Taking a deep breath, Silas placed a palm on the door and focused. He received a quick flash of Akasha examining the car for scratches.

"No... not what I need," he whispered and forced his powers to a finer point.

Suddenly, he caught a faint scent of dried blood... and something else. He crouched down and sniffed. The smell was coming from the asphalt by the fender. He detected only a few drops of blood... and the scent was overpowered by a strong chemical odor.

"What have you found so far?" Razvan landed next to him.

"Shh! I need to concentrate," Silas hissed and put his hand on the asphalt, willing the images to come. *There!*

A needle plunged into Akasha's neck. She fought. Struggled. Collapsed. The men in black uniforms shoved her inside a yellow cargo truck. Two got in back with her. The other two walked to the cab. One cradled a broken finger and whined, "When we get this bitch to Richland, they better get me a doctor."

"They took her to Richland," Silas said, mind racing in impatience. "It's in the Tri-Cities. They drugged her. That's why I couldn't feel the Mark. It's at least a three hour drive."

"Then we had better depart now." Razvan's black eyes were filled with worry as he headed to the Barracuda.

"Hold on." Silas pulled out his phone and called Jonathon Greenbriar, his new doctor. He ordered the doctor to come to the school and pick up his car, bring it to his house, and wait there. "And have your medical supplies ready to treat a human," he added. Hopefully that would be an unnecessary precaution.

"We will be taking Akasha's car." He grabbed his sword from the backseat of the Barracuda. "I know she'll want to see it as soon as we get her back."

"But will they not recognize it?" Razvan asked with a raised brow.

Silas sighed as he unlocked the Roadrunner and placed his sword on the floorboard behind the driver's seat. "I am going to try to avoid it, but my thinking is that if they know where she attends school, they know where she lives. They're more likely going to be looking out for my car more than this one."

"Very well." Razvan opened the door and got into the passenger seat. "I do hope we get her back, McNaught, because if we do not, the Elders will destroy us all."

As they sped down I-90 towards Washington, driving as fast as Akasha had when she broke in the new engine, Silas gritted his teeth and vowed, *I will kill them all.*

Chapter Thirty-one

Akasha awoke to feel something digging into her arm. She tried to raise her hand to slap it away, but couldn't. Steel manacles held her down on a flat surface. Her eyes flew open to see a mad scientist with bushy white hair drawing her blood out of a syringe plunged into her arm. The sight made her skin crawl.

Only Silas had a right to her blood.

The thought broke as the scientist lifted a tape recorder in his other hand and spoke into it. "Subject is now conscious just two hours after her second dose…"

"What the fuck are you doing to me?" Akasha demanded, hating the choking fear in her voice almost as much as her drugged helplessness.

He removed the needle and eyed her calmly. "I'm taking another blood sample to see how you're breaking down the tranquilizer so fast. Your metabolism is amazing. You'd be able to drink a burly Irishman under the table."

Hmm. So that's why I've never had a hangover. Akasha shook off the fascination as her situation hit her clearly. The COAT guy had her strapped to a table and was using her as a fucking lab rat!

She was in a hospital gown. They'd removed her clothes. Disgust at the violation had panic clawing her throat. She struggled and bucked against the restraints in desperation to get loose. The table groaned in protest.

"It's a good thing I calibrated the restraints myself. They were actually planning on using standard handcuffs on you," the scientist commented. For a second Akasha thought she saw a glimmer of pity behind his thick glasses.

He grabbed a rubber ball from his instrument table that was wired up to a gauge of some sort and nudged it toward her right hand. "Would you please squeeze this as hard as you can?"

If she could have moved her wrist enough, she would have thrown it at him. Akasha was tempted to tell him where he could put it, but kept her mouth shut.

Maybe she was curious as to what the gauge reading would be. Maybe it was because he said "please." Maybe it was because she didn't have anything better to do.

She worked her fingers around the ball and squeezed. The dial on the gauge flew to the right, but the glare of the overhead lights prevented her from seeing the actual numbers.

The scientist chuckled as he wrote down the results. "Wonderful!"

"I see she's awake," another voice interrupted.

A man with a graying buzz-cut and built like a brick-house entered the laboratory. His left hand had stubs for fingers. The utter loathing she saw in his hazel eyes made her bite back a retort. This guy was out for her blood. She hoped he wasn't the one in charge.

"What have you got for me so far?" He addressed the scientist with militant command.

"Oh, plenty, sir." The scientist scooped up a stack of notes and his tape recorder. "I'll tell you over coffee."

"Dammit!" Akasha growled when the men left her alone. The big hostile bastard was in charge. She was screwed. Eyes darting around her surroundings, she looked for an escape. It looked like a typical television show laboratory, only much smaller and it had no windows. *No escape.*

Her arms still stung from the IV and assaults from various needles. Akasha raised herself as much as she could, the muscles in her back protesting at the awkward angle. Gritting her teeth against the discomfort, she assessed the damage to her body.

Everything seemed to be where it belonged, except for the damn IV embedded in her forearm where other drugs, nutrients, or both were pumping into her. Also, there were a few little red squares on her legs where patches of skin had been removed. *Shit. How long have I been out?*

Another thought occurred to her. *Shouldn't I have to go to the bathroom?* Akasha spotted the catheter bag hanging from a stand and had her answer. Her skin crawled in revulsion. She hadn't felt this violated, this unclean since...

Uncontrollable tremors wracked her body as she relived her past rape. With the screams of an animal caught in a trap, she thrashed and struggled against her restraints. A red haze obscured her vision, overlaid with black spots as she hyperventilated.

The shrieks dissolved into mournful howls as the restraints held firm. Still, she bucked and fought until her muscles gave up and dizziness forced her head to drop back onto the table.

Gulping in air, she closed her eyes and did her best to replace her panic and the crippling memory with Silas. A measure of warmth returned to her limbs as she remembered the vampire's sweet lovemaking.

Moments later, the shaking died down. Akasha took a deep breath and resumed her observations to try to find out what else had been done to her.

There were little wires attached to her head. She craned her neck to see that they were attached to a monitor that showed what looked like voltage spikes in a constantly changing pattern. They were measuring her brain waves. The table was hard and cold, and the IV and wires poking out of her pinched like insect bites. *What else are they going to do to me? Or are they done and ready to kill me for the sake of national security?*

Akasha growled and struggled uselessly against the steel bands. Escape seemed more impossible every second. Silas must be worried out of his mind. Her throat ached as tears burned her eyes. She would give anything to see him again. Anything to be in his arms… to hear his thick Scots accent whispered in her ear when they made love.

"Oh Silas…" she whispered brokenly.

Silas! That's it! If his powers were as strong as she thought, he just might be able to find her… if the bad guys didn't find him first. They would no doubt salivate at the thought of having a vampire on their examining table. Still, these mere mortals should be no match for an immortal Scottish warrior.

Akasha focused her mind and began shouting his name silently, pausing every few seconds to listen for a reply, or any other sign that he heard her.

Silas had to find her. He just had to. She clung to the gossamer thread of hope like a lifeline.

***

Agent Joseph Holmes tried to keep calm eye contact with Major Milbury as he sipped his coffee and explained the test results. Holmes now knew why he'd allowed him to study the girl so readily, despite his obvious resentment.

Milbury intended to kill him when the testing was over.

Joe Holmes had come upon the information by accident while searching for instructions as to the kind of testing the military wanted done on Akasha. All he'd found were vague orders from over ten years ago. Since Milbury wasn't around to be asked, Joe accessed the Major's personal files to see if he'd received anything current.

To his shock, Holmes discovered Milbury hadn't been corresponding with the military at all.

Milbury was pulling a lone ranger on this project and intended to submit his findings after he'd destroyed the mutant along with everyone involved with the research... which was only Holmes and— though he was pretty sure Milbury didn't know— Holmes's daughter, Lillian.

Holmes had been secretly sending his findings to Lillian through a heavily encrypted server. But if the COAT found out, she would be in danger. He pushed his coffee away, his stomach churning with terror.

How Milbury was planning to get away with the murder of a high ranking FBI agent, Joe didn't know, but he supposed it didn't matter. How to get out of this mess alive was his primary concern. Holmes fixed Milbury with what he hoped was a calm, scholarly gaze.

"To do the most conclusive tests, I'll need her out of restraints. We need to see how much she can lift, how hard a punch she packs, et cetera," Holmes informed him.

Milbury glared. "I'm sure she'd like to demonstrate that to us all personally. I don't want to end up like that corpse you have in your lab." He shook his head. "She's too dangerous. I think we've learned enough."

Joe fought down panic. "Don't be too hasty, Francis. This young lady is one of a kind and I believe we've only hit the tip of the iceberg with her. If I can persuade her to cooperate, we can gain data that will make you a shining star in the eyes of our country."

Holmes hoped he hadn't laid it on too thick. He counted on Francis's pride being wounded enough by being cast off to a low-profile case after losing his fingers. The promise of being valued again might sway him.

"That's a very big 'if.'" Still, Milbury's eyes glimmered with interest. The stubs of his fingers twitched.

Holmes plunged on, struggling to keep a wheedling tone from his voice. "She seemed genuinely interested in my findings. And her school record indicates that she does very well in science classes. I just may be able to nurture that interest enough to get us somewhere."

Francis sighed and waved an irritated hand. "Very well, I'll give you twelve hours. Do what you can, because afterward she will be eliminated. Those are my orders, after all."

"I'll need a little longer than that." Holmes fought against the invisible noose of time, which tightened every second. "It'll take twice that to get the results of half the tests! Give me twenty-four, at least!"

Milbury's lips twisted in a furious scowl. "Sixteen," he countered rising from his seat. "You'll have to do what you can with that. I'll need time to get a flight out of here tomorrow."

"Yes, Sir!" Joe hid his disappointment and gave him a mock salute that he knew would annoy the Major.

Milbury rolled his eyes and slammed the door.

Joe sighed. Sixteen hours to come up with a plan to escape armed guards in an isolated compound on a dry flat prairie. He hoped Akasha would cooperate. He quite liked the girl and decided he would try to save her life as well.

After all, she could be an asset to the AIU, if he played his cards right. He wondered if she was fertile like her father or sterile like the other test soldiers had been. Thankfully, he had the key to find out.

***

"She's in there," Silas whispered, pointing to a drab gray building surrounded by a fourteen-foot high electric fence.

Two armed guards walked the perimeter at a steady march.

They'd hidden the car in an old barn a half mile away when Silas felt Akasha's Mark growing in intensity. He and Razvan covered the city— if you could call it that— on foot. They clouded the minds of mortals so they weren't seen.

"How many humans can you detect in there?" Razvan asked.

"Ten, not counting Akasha," McNaught replied, pacing like a caged lion. "Rather peculiar, don't you think? I would figure with what they know of her, they'd have more people involved."

Razvan chuckled. "Who cares? It's better luck for us. They will be an easy feast."

"Aye. But I dinna want tae rush into this blindly. It could be a trap. And 'tis only an hour before dawn."

Every inch of Silas's flesh crawled with anxiety. He'd tried to contact Akasha mentally and received no response. Had the drugs given to her by the COAT blocked her mind?

"Then let's observe the place a little longer. Perhaps we'll overhear something useful from the guards." Razvan tried to reassure his friend and fight his own growing unease.

Just as the sky began to lighten, the two guards joined each other for a cigarette break. One of them had his hand in a cast.

"The Major gave Holmes another sixteen hours with the freak," the other remarked, kicking a tumbleweed at the fence.

"Dammit!" the wounded one snarled, struggling to light his cigarette. "I want to see the little bitch dead! I may never be able to handle a rifle again thanks to her."

"Chill out, Wetmore," the first guard said impatiently. "It's not like he's gonna let you do the honors. I think it's gonna be me or Orson. But he might let you bag the body. He said he wants you to schedule the transport, anyhow."

"Shouldn't the paper-pushers be handling that?" Wetmore whined.

"He sent them home. The less witnesses the better, y'know."

Wetmore smiled. "Sixteen hours 'til there's a bullet in her brain. I can hardly wait."

Silas choked and tried to move forward, but Razvan held him back and dragged him out of earshot.

"Did you hear something?" the first guard asked.

"Probably a coyote," Wetmore muttered. "This damn hole's infested with 'em."

Silas panted heavily in fear. "Sixteen hours? I dinna think tha sun will be down by then!"

Razvan nodded. "We have no choice. At least it'll be past high noon. We may be able to get in there with only a few burns. Come, McNaught, we had better get to shelter now."

They moved swiftly back to the barn, which thankfully had a cellar. Silas spotted sheets billowing on a clothesline in the distance. They resembled eerie ghosts in the graying desert landscape.

"Stop, Razvan!" he called, "I have an idea."

Chapter Thirty-two

When the scientist who introduced himself as Agent Joe Holmes told Akasha that Major Milbury intended to kill her when the experiments were done, she wasn't surprised. But when Holmes informed her that he was with the FBI and head of the Abnormal Investigation Unit her eyes whipped to his in astonishment.

"But what are you doing working with the COAT?" Her eyes narrowed in accusation. "Isn't the FBI supposed to be protecting American citizens rather than killing them?

Joe coughed uncomfortably and looked at the floor. "Actually, I was the one who led him to you. I didn't know he was going to kill you!" He spread his hands defensively, face flushing in shame. "I just wanted to study you."

Akasha continued to glare as Holmes looked sheepish... and regretful.

"If it's any consolation," he said slowly, "I just discovered that he means to kill me too."

She almost snorted in disbelief, but the utter terror in his eyes gave her pause. The chirps and clicks on the brainwave monitor punctuated the silence.

"What do you mean?" she whispered.

"I came upon it in his reports, but truly, I'm a fool to have not realized it before. There can be no civilian knowledge of what the military does to human beings in times of war. It really would be dangerous to the country." Holmes chuckled bitterly. "And our old University rivalry adds fuel to the fire, I suppose."

Akasha's mind flew through the data and probability of his words. The brainwaves spiked and jogged rapidly across the screen. Lights flashed, machines beeped.

Her body screamed in pain from being locked in the same position. "How do I know you're not feeding me bullshit?" She searched his face for signs of deceit.

Holmes paced nervously, trailing an idle finger across the counter near the beakers and test tubes. "It doesn't matter what you believe. In less than sixteen hours, a soldier will put a bullet in your brain and then mine. We need to come up with a plan of escape before that." He stopped and bent closer to her. "Even if I am lying to you, wouldn't you rather spend your final hours being able to move about?"

She wanted to believe him, but it was too good to be true. But her aching muscles decided it for her. "Okay."

After all, if she was freed, she could tear him limb from limb if he indicated dishonesty in any way.

"By the way," The scientist pulled a pistol from his lab coat. "If you try to get violent with me, I will shoot you and worry about saving my own skin. I don't want to, though. I like your spirit. But I'd like to see my daughter again, and with one murder under your belt, self-defense, though it was, I feel I should be cautious. Do we understand each other?"

Akasha nodded, too stunned that he knew that much about her past to find words.

"Great!" Joe clapped his hands. "Now I'll remove the catheter. Then the IV, and then the probes..."

Minutes later she was taking out her aggression on a punching bag anchored to the floor as well as the ceiling, so it wouldn't bounce back at her. There were impact sensors inside the bag that were much like the ones used in a car's airbag circuit, Joe explained. She'd destroyed them with the first few blows.

"I can't believe I'm going along with this." Akasha grumbled as she beat the living shit out of the punching bag. Her fists were an incredible blur of speed before her eyes.

"I don't blame you for your skepticism, my dear girl." Agent Holmes said as he scribbled notes on his pad. "I find it interesting that Silas McNaught became your guardian," he continued in a blatant and disturbing change of subject. "My department suspected him of being a vampire."

Akasha stopped punching. The bag made a sighing sound as if relieved from its break in punishment.

"I don't suppose he is one, is he?" Joe asked hopefully.

Schooling her features to portray indifference, she avoided the question. "You believe in vampires?" Akasha laced her tone with scorn.

Holmes was undaunted. "Indeed. Would you believe their blood heals wounds and cures all things, even cancer?" He shook his head and smiled. "Fascinating creatures. They're devilishly hard to get hold of, however. Some are even stronger than you, I think."

Akasha was nervous with the subject. She decided to attempt her own subject change. "I want to know how much I can lift. And we should probably plan our escape while we're at it. Is there anything to drink around here? I'm really thirsty."

Hours later, they discovered Akasha could lift five hundred pounds with her arms and twice as much with her legs. She got up to twenty miles an hour on the treadmill and could maintain the speed for about thirty minutes.

But they still had no feasible plan of eluding Milbury and the COAT unit. They couldn't even hope to sneak out because Holmes was locked in with her and they were under camera surveillance, though thankfully there was no audio.

Otherwise, the COAT would have charged in and shot them full of holes for Holmes's betrayal the minute he'd opened his mouth.

Akasha slumped in a hard plastic hair, sore and exhausted, physically and mentally. She chugged her fifth sports drink. The longing for an icy Coors and a cigarette was so bad she was about to scream.

"I've got it!" Joe announced as he was testing her reflexes. "It's a shaky plan at best, but it just might work."

"What?" Her heart raced in anticipation.

He told her.

It *was* a shaky plan, suicidal, in fact. But what choice did they have? Their sixteen hours were almost up and sunset was still far off, so she couldn't expect Silas to come in time.

Still, throwing chemical bombs at armed soldiers who could fire at her any second, while Holmes tried to shoot Major Milbury... So many things could go wrong.

Joe gathered the necessary chemicals and explained each one to Akasha. It was insane that a few innocuous substances could be so deadly when combined. Holmes mixed the compounds in a large beaker and carefully poured the mixture into six test tubes. He then took an eyedropper and a vial of blood and squeezed a few drops into each test tube, turning the fluid pink.

Akasha looked questioningly at this new addition to the formula. Surely her blood wasn't combustible!

"To fool the cameras," Joe said with a wink. "I have to make it look like another of my crazy blood tests."

He arranged the test tubes away from the edge of the counter. "This is a volatile compound. It should explode on impact, so be sure to jump for cover as soon as you throw it."

Akasha chewed her lip. "If they shoot me before I throw the bombs, I could drop them and blow my ass off."

"I trust your reflexes are better than that," Holmes's voice was firm. "But please, *do* be careful and wait for them to get in range."

Footsteps echoed outside, coming closer. Two of the pink test tube bombs were placed in her shaking hands. Holmes put his lab coat over her shoulders and stepped as far from her as he could while avoiding being conspicuous of the effort.

Major Milbury and four COAT soldiers entered. They looked through her like she wasn't there and their rifles weren't drawn, but Akasha wasn't fooled. She knew they saw her and watched her every move. They could have their weapons trained on her in seconds. After all, they made their living by killing people far more dangerous than she.

The split second of clear thinking escaped her. Suddenly, the COAT soldiers superimposed themselves in her vision over those who murdered her parents.

Akasha was a little girl again, shaking, helpless, afraid. The vials wobbled in her quivering hands. Her grip loosened.

***

Silas leapt to his feet as Akasha's Mark cried out to him.

"Razvan," he shouted, shaking the hay from his shoulders. "We must go—" the breath was sucked from his lungs and he fell to his knees as a wave of paralyzing terror crashed over his body.

"What's wrong?" Razvan demanded, voice thick with exhaustion. They hadn't dared to do more than doze this day and risk missing Akasha's rescue.

"She's so afraid!" Silas roared. "She's never been this afraid before."

Razvan pulled bits of hay out of his hair and crossed the small cellar to grab the sheets they'd purloined from the farmhouse. He tossed a few to Silas and began tearing one in wide strips. "We had best hurry then."

Silas tore a sheet of his own and wrapped his hands, fixing his maker with a quizzical stare. "Why are you helping me?" Razvan only cared about his own interests.

The other vampire frowned. "Why are you asking this now?"

"Why not?" he said, manipulating a sheet into a makeshift head covering.

Razvan sighed. "Perhaps I feel guilty. Whatever it is, it is a most uncomfortable sensation."

"Guilty?" Silas couldn't hide the astonishment from his voice. "Guilty for what?"

"Perhaps if I had not abandoned you so soon when you couldn't find my brother, you would not have gone on a killing rampage that left you covered with remorse even to this day." Razvan toyed with his beard and continued. "And perhaps you would not have fallen into Selena's company and thus there would be no trial with the Elders now." He wrapped strips of a sheet around his face like a bandage, leaving only a slit for his eyes. "Since I was not there for you then, the least I can do is to be here for you today."

Silas was glad the fabric hid his expression. No doubt he was gaping like the village idiot. It seemed he did not know Razvan Nicolae as well as he thought.

"Thank you," he said sincerely.

By the time they finished covering themselves, the two vampires resembled desert nomads. They headed up the stairs and into the main floor of the barn, wincing as shafts of sunlight through the cracks pierced their sensitive eyes.

"Besides," Razvan added, his voice muffled under the fabric. "I *like* Akasha."

They huddled together for a moment in the shadows before the barn door. The sun was descending towards the western horizon, but not as far or fast as they'd hoped.

"Are you ready?" Silas asked.

Razvan nodded and thrust the door open without warning. The vampires burst out in a blur of preternatural speed. Even though they were covered, the sunlight burned their flesh, especially their exposed eyes.

Silas gritted his teeth to hold back a shriek of agony and forced his pain-wracked body westward, to the compound. His strength flagged quickly.

If they didn't get to shelter and a source of blood soon, they would burn to death in this desert. He thrust the thought away and pushed his protesting limbs on, not daring to see if Razvan remained at his side.

Please God, he prayed silently, *please let us get there in time.*

Chapter Thirty-three

Akasha caught the explosive vials before they fell. Thankfully the motion was hidden in the long sleeves of the coat. She forced herself to breathe as she fought off the crippling panic and searched the faces of her enemies for signs of suspicion.

"Why is she wearing your lab coat?" Milbury demanded, fixing suspicious eyes on Akasha. The COAT soldiers stopped their approach... just out of range.

"She's cold, obviously," Joe said with impressive nonchalance. "I don't see why you wouldn't allow access to the thermostat in here, Francis. Some of the blood tests require higher temperatures."

Milbury glared at Holmes. The loathing in his chilly stare left no doubt that he meant to kill the scientist. He turned that cold gaze to Akasha. The hatred flared hotter.

"How long did it take you to kill that man in Montana, Akasha?" Milbury sneered as he stalked closer to her. "You look just like a china doll. It's hard to believe you're so deadly."

Akasha shrugged. "Only when I have to defend myself. You and your goons are the deadly ones."

Milbury choked on her words and stepped closer, followed by the guards.

Akasha's palms sweated against the slippery glass test tubes. She stepped back until she reached the operating table, willing them to follow. They moved forward just a half step, but unfortunately remained out of range. She ground her teeth.

Just a little closer...

She decided to aggravate him further.

"Do you really think killing me will bring your prestige back?" she asked coolly. "I'm not a high priority assignment after all. I'm just a freak accident."

"How do you know that?" Milbury hissed.

"Silas hired a hacker." She favored him with a cheerful smile. "We read the entire file. If you get out of this alive, Uncle Sam will only give you a little pat on the back and put you on another petty assignment."

The agent's eyes burned with anguish as she hit her mark. He and the firing squad stepped into her throwing range. He began to lift his mutilated hand to signal the COAT to fire.

Akasha took a deep breath and threw the two bombs in quick succession.

She dove under the table, just as the deafening explosion tore the air. Shards of glass pierced Akasha's arms as she covered her face.

When she dared to look, everything seemed to be happening in slow motion. The closest guard's face ripped apart. His gun went flying. The other three still held their guns. She whipped the steel table on its side to shield her.

Holmes pointed his gun at Milbury, but the Major was faster. He shot Joe in the shoulder, knocking the gun from his grasp. It clattered on the floor, by the computer.

"You slimy, scheming son of a bitch!" Milbury roared and leveled the gun at Holmes's face.

Akasha threw a scalpel.

The tiny blade embedded itself into the Milbury's back. He slumped as if about to fall.

Then he spun around, pointing the gun at her.

***

The vampires heard the explosion just as they were tearing open the jugulars of the two guards. Silas took one last gulp of healing, nourishing blood before dropping his dying victim.

"What in the blazes was that?" Razvan called from the rear of the building.

Silas didn't have time to wonder.

Akasha! His mind roared.

He grabbed the keys off the dead guard, shrieking in agony as the light scorched his hand. His eyes burned and watered in the waning sunlight. He could feel his skin sizzling under its meager covering.

"Razvan! Hurry!" They had to make it in time.

***

Akasha stared down into the black barrel of the gun. The COAT agent seemed to take pleasure in drawing out the moment, taunting her with impending death. She stood there helpless, unable to move or breathe as panic clawed her throat.

Any second, the weapon would spark and smoke as it released the bullet that would pierce her skull, catapulting her into the abyss that was death.

She focused her mind and heart on Silas. She could almost feel the tingling warmth of his presence nearby.

"Now, I'll find out what it's like to kill a mutant," Milbury said, smiling madly. He seemed oblivious to the scalpel embedded in his back like an acupuncturist's pin. "I wonder... will it feel the same as killing a man? Or will I get twice the pleasure from it?"

His finger tightened on the trigger. *Silas I love you,* she cried silently and squeezed her eyes shut.

Instead of a bang, she heard a terrifying battle cry. Rapid gunshots rent the air. Her eyes flew open to witness what looked like Middle-Eastern terrorists attacking Milbury and the COAT. They were dodging bullets and moving so fast that it took her a moment to realize there were only two. One snapped the necks of the remaining soldiers in impossibly rapid succession. The other terrorist had Milbury in his grasp. Akasha noticed his hands were burned. The little bit of his face that showed looked burnt as well. His brilliant green eyes were watery and bloodshot... and achingly familiar.

"Silas!" she cried and scrambled up off the floor.

"Stay put," he commanded, his eyes glowing like phosphorus.

He tore the sheet from his face and bared his fangs. Milbury cringed like a kicked dog and a dark wet stain appeared on the front of his pants, trailing down one leg.

Silas was a horrifying sight. His face was bright red. The burned skin around his eyes was tight and shiny. A nose wrinkling reek of burnt hair permeated the air.

"You shouldna ha' touched ma woman!" he growled and sank his fangs into the Major's neck.

Akasha had never seen him feed before. It was more brutal, more gruesome than any horror movie depiction. Milbury screamed as his neck tore with a wet squelching sound.

Blood dribbled from the corner of the vampire's mouth, turning the collar of the man's shirt a bright crayon red. He jerked and shrieked louder as Razvan bit his wrist, worrying his arm like a rabid dog. The slurping and swallowing sounds were grossly audible in the now silent lab. In her shock she wondered idly when the monitors had quit their droning.

As Milbury's screams died down and the struggling ceased, Akasha realized something. This was not how vampires usually fed. They were being brutal on purpose; they were *making* it hurt. This was a punishment. She would have been terrified and sickened if she didn't know the bastard deserved everything he was getting.

When they were done, Milbury was reduced to a gray, pasty corpse. His body hit the cement floor with a thump. Silas wiped his mouth and took Akasha in his arms. She fought back her fear and returned his embrace.

Gratitude filled her in a glorious fount. She thought she'd never see or feel him again. For a few delirious moments, the lab and all she'd been through this day dissolved into pure bliss as the warmth of his love encompassed her. Then Silas pulled away and ran his hands across her face and down her body.

"Are you all right my love?" The vampire's eyes searched hers frantically.

She tried to laugh off his concern, but choked with tears that threatened to break her. "I think you two are in worse shape..." Her eyes widened and her hand dropped. The burns on the vampires' flesh had faded. All that remained was redness around their eyes and on their hands, as if they'd been out at the beach too long.

"Fascinating..." Holmes breathed behind them.

Silas and Razvan whipped around and had the scientist pinned within seconds. Blood gushed from the wound on his shoulder. Holmes made a small pained sound and Razvan licked his lips, eyes alight with predatory avarice.

"No!" Akasha shoved both vampires back, but they were prepared for her strength and didn't budge. "Don't hurt him!"

Razvan cocked an eyebrow. "Please tell me you are not having tender feelings for your captor?"

Silas looked at her over Holmes's shoulder. His eyes gleamed like lethal emeralds. "Why should we spare him, lass?"

"He helped me," Akasha fixed them both with a glare. "Milbury was going to kill him too. He's not part of the COAT. Please, let him go."

Grudgingly, the vampires released their prey. Holmes shuffled backwards to Akasha's side. His face contorted in pain as he held his bleeding shoulder.

"Thank you for sparing me," he panted. "I'm Joe Holmes, FBI. I'd offer a handshake, but as you can see..." He trailed off as blood dripped all over the floor.

Silas began to laugh. "Head of the AIU department? Oh, this is just precious."

Holmes smiled weakly. "Yes, the irony is not lost on me. Not only did you fool us completely, McNaught, but you know about us?"

"We *all* know about you, and your European counterparts," he replied gruffly.

Holmes fell back into his usual enthusiasm for scientific discovery. "I'd love to ask you some questions."

"Not a chance," Silas shook his head.

"We have not decided whether we will let you live yet, mortal," Razvan added, doing his "dark scary villain" routine, circling the scientist.

"Knock it off, dipshit," Akasha told him. "Can't you see he's been shot? Make yourself useful and either heal him or get me a beer... or at least a cigarette."

Holmes flinched at her words to the vampire, eyes the size of saucers.

Razvan chuckled. "You are quite a mouthy wench today."

She sighed. "It's been a real shitty day."

Sympathy actually glimmered in his onyx eyes. He bowed and dug the bullet out of the scientist's shoulder, oblivious to the cries of pain. Then he bit his finger to apply the healing magic to Holmes's wound.

The man's eyes were huge beneath his glasses as the injury vanished.

"The curative powers of your blood never cease to amaze me," Joe remarked. "I still haven't managed to duplicate it, much less isolate the individual compounds..." He shook his head and tried to smooth his poofy white hair. "I'm sorry for digressing. I suppose you would like to view Milbury's files and destroy them?"

Silas nodded and handed Akasha a cigarette, ignoring Joe's disapproving frown. "I would like to read your findings as well. I want to know everything you have done to her." His piercing gaze made Holmes tremble.

By the time they'd viewed everything it was almost dusk. Akasha convinced the vampires to let Joe go free, but she was still very worried on another account.

"Even if you keep your mouth shut, Joe, and even if we destroy this place and all the data, they'll wonder what happened, and they'll track us down if we don't move." She crushed her cigarette butt on the floor. "I mean, I'm grateful to be alive, but it still looks like we're screwed."

"Not necessarily..." Agent Holmes said, chewing on a pen.

Her eyes narrowed. "What do you mean?"

The scientist grinned. "What is a government good for if not for a cover-up?"

"Explain, mortal," Razvan demanded.

Holmes chuckled. "With the sheets you were wearing, it wouldn't be too hard to adjust the camera footage and leave enough intact to make it look like the work of radical Middle-Eastern terrorists. Especially since Milbury was stationed in Iraq on some secret assignment until he lost his fingers. It's my knowledge of those facts that led to Milbury's ultimate decision to annihilate me, or so I believe."

"Why, that's brilliant!" Silas clapped Holmes on the back. "You can do that for us?"

Holmes smirked. "I can... but for a price."

Silas's eyes glowed and his accent thickened. "Och mon, what game are ye playin'? What price? I should think your life is sufficient tender."

"A vial of your blood." He held up a hand before anyone could object. "I know... you could kill me anytime. I only want the blood to study further... to try to make cures for diseases and such. We already have some, so it wouldn't be a huge betrayal of your kind... I just need more and I would prefer to get it honestly."

There was a long, tangible pause before Silas spoke. "Aye, I could kill you any time. Ye best remember that. If I agree I will have your solemn oath that ye will do as ye said and draw the government's eyes away from Akasha and our kind?"

Holmes nodded emphatically. "I don't want any of you dead!" He attempted to laugh, but it came out dry and rusty. "You people are far more interesting alive."

Silas nodded in impatience. "Get your syringe."

"And hurry up Joe," Akasha added. "I don't mind your company, but still I'd like to get the fuck out of here."

***

Agent Holmes whispered a prayer of thanks for his life when Akasha and the vampires departed.

He'd been terrified that they'd discover his ulterior motives. Not that he didn't want them to be safe, he genuinely admired the love the two so clearly had for each other.

It was only that he had some benefits of his own if the military knew nothing of his involvement with this incident.

He doctored the camera footage and erased all evidence of his presence within a few hours quicker than he expected.

He congratulated himself as he rigged the timed explosives.

Minutes later, he whistled a cheery tune as he carried the cooler containing Akasha's eggs and Silas McNaught's blood out of the building.

***

"You brought my car!" Akasha exclaimed, wiping joyous tears from her eyes. Her Roadrunner glistened before her, racing stripes brilliant in the moonlight.

Silas shrugged. "I thought you would want to see her right away. Do you feel well enough to drive?"

Akasha took a minute to compose herself before she began squealing like a girl. He was so thoughtful. "Maybe for a little while. Where are we, anyway?"

"Richland, Washington," Razvan told her. "It's about a three hour drive home."

"Really?" she said. "That's closer than I thought."

"My guess is they planned it that way." Silas said, a growl of rage still tingeing his voice. "They probably couldn't handle transporting a hellion like you very far. We were very lucky that you were not hurt badly." He took a shuddering breath as if unable to bear the thought. "I have a doctor waiting at home to examine you, in any case."

Akasha slid into the driver's seat, tipping it forward for Razvan to get in the back.

"You want me to ride in the rear?" he asked, outraged. "Surely you jest, woman. I made your master."

Akasha rolled her eyes. "Waaa, fuckin' waaa. The boyfriend always gets shotgun in my car. You can fly home if you like."

Razvan grumbled and got in. "I am too weary to fly all that way."

When they were all settled, Akasha started the engine and honked the horn, smiling as it went "Meep-Meep" just like the roadrunner on "Looney-Tunes." Whoever designed this car was a genius.

"You can hypnotize the cops, right?" she asked as she did a doughnut in the barnyard before pulling onto the road.

Silas grinned, heartbreakingly handsome even in the dark. "I take it you're in a hurry?"

"Yeah. I need a hot shower and a cold beer ASAP... maybe two beers... or six." She lit a cigarette as she got onto I-90, rolling the window down all the way. Akasha didn't like to smoke in her car, but after the hours of captivity and certain death, she didn't give a shit.

They were almost halfway home before her fatigue caught up with her and she was forced to relinquish the wheel to Silas. She was just dozing off when she heard Razvan whisper to Silas. "When are you going to tell her?"

Silas sighed in obvious dread. "I do not know. Soon."

Tell me what? Akasha wanted to ask, but sleep sucked her under.

Chapter Thirty-four

After the doctor departed and Akasha showered, Silas was still whispering prayers of thanks that his love had survived her captivity.

As much as he wished to bask in the joy of their reunion, another threat loomed over them.

He leaned back in his chair at the dining room table and watched Akasha pound her fifth beer as he finished telling her about the summons from the Elders.

She seemed to be taking it quite well.

"You have *got* to be fucking kidding," she growled, crushing her can to a pulp before grabbing another.

Silas sighed and sipped his scotch. "I'm afraid not, lass."

She lit a cigarette and continued pacing like an agitated lioness. "I always wanted to visit Amsterdam, but not to face a possible death sentence. We gotta be there the day after tomorrow you said? How's that gonna work?"

"Razvan scheduled a private jet that will leave tomorrow evening," Silas told her. "It's Xochitl I'm worried about. I can handle her foster parents and I have a man ready to forge passports and identification for you both. I just don't know what to tell her."

Akasha chuckled and flicked her cigarette. "We'll say, 'wanna go to Amsterdam?' She may be an alien or something, but she's still just as nuts about taking a vacation as the rest of us. You and Razvan can bespell her when we get to the courtroom or whatever."

Silas sighed and took another drink. "That's probably the best we can do."

He set down his glass and let his gaze rove over Akasha. Her skin was pink and her sable curls were still damp from her shower. *What a beauty she is.* He longed to nibble on the tiny pink toes peeking under her bathrobe.

"It is only two hours before dawn," Silas said, trying to be discreet.

Akasha's eyes darkened to purple and her rosebud lips parted. "This may be the last time we get to be alone together," she whispered. "Could we... Will you...?" She blushed beautifully, making him hard.

"Come here." His voice was thick with need. She rose and opened her robe, revealing her nakedness.

He sucked in a breath at the sight of her creamy skin, pert breasts and the delicate triangle of dark curls at the juncture of her exquisite thighs. A tiny stitched wound marred her perfection above her pubic bone, off to one side.

"What is that, lass?" He touched the wound; her skin was hot under his fingertips.

Akasha shrugged. "I don't know. I just noticed it in the shower. The doctor missed it 'cuz I wouldn't let him see me naked." She ran a hand through her hair and climbed up onto his lap. "I don't want to think about it right now." Her tongue flicked across his earlobe. "I'd much rather think about you, *all* of you."

The heat of her chased all thoughts away. He captured those sweet lips with his and devoured her mouth as he felt the silk of her skin under his hands. She fumbled with the buttons of his shirt and he groaned when her hands caressed his chest.

Akasha moaned against his lips as she ground herself against the hardness straining against his pants.

"I want you now." She tangled her hands in his hair.

"Hold on lass." He gently lifted her onto the table.

Silas moved his glass out of the way and spread her robe beneath her.

He unzipped his trousers and his eyes drank in the sight of her body spread out on the table before him like a pagan offering. The thought almost undid him.

He slowly slid inside her, gasping at the feel of slick tight heat. She was paradise incarnate. It was all he could do not to ravage her like a thing possessed.

"Harder," she moaned.

It was as if she'd read his mind. "Are you sure?" he asked, feeling sweat gather on his upper lip.

Her hips bucked up to meet his. "Fuck me Silas!"

At her words, the chains of his control snapped. He grabbed her legs and pounded into her with such force the table rocked.

"Yes!" She thrashed beneath him as his thumb rubbed against her clit.

He took her like he wanted to take her the first time he laid eyes on her. *She's finally mine. Mine! Mine!* He felt her clenching on his cock and exploded with a feral roar.

"That was amazing," she panted when they finished.

Her skin flushed pink, strawberries and cream. Silas licked his lips as his cock jerked within her. She trembled, tightening deliciously around his shaft.

A glance at the window told him dawn was on its way. They'd have to move if he wanted to continue.

"I'm not finished with you yet, lass," he whispered.

Akasha's eyes widened. "There's more?"

"Oh yes."

He punctuated his words with another thrust.

***

Akasha gasped in shocked pleasure as Silas lifted her off the table and carried her, still impaled, down the hall. This was a benefit to a vampire's strength she had not imagined. His forearm muscles felt like iron around her waist as he used his other hand to open the secret passage to his lair.

She almost screamed in excitement as he slowly descended the stairs. She could feel him moving inside her with every step. Already on the verge of orgasm when they reached the bottom floor, she came the second they reached the bed.

"Now I want to savor you." Silas's husky whisper promised further pleasure. His skin glistened deliciously in the candlelight.

He made love to her until she was limp with exhaustion. She came so many times she lost count. When they collapsed on the bed sated, he murmured, "Sleep with me awhile. But make sure you're up in time to get Xochitl. The plane leaves at nine."

Akasha nodded slowly and stretched like a contented cat. "If we get out of this alive, promise you'll fuck me in every room of this house."

His chest rumbled as he laughed low. "That is a promise I will gladly keep."

As she snuggled against him, a chill prickled her flesh as her own words haunted her soul.

If we get out of this alive.

Chapter Thirty-five

Getting Xochitl to agree to a trip to Amsterdam was easier than Akasha imagined. It was the fact that they were only going to be there for two days that made her protest.

"But we won't have time to see everything!" she cried for like the fifth time.

Razvan shook his head. "When you are famous, dear girl, you can travel as much and as long as you want. Now take your passport and buckle up. We are about to take off."

"Did you hear that, Isis?" Xochitl said to the complaining cat. "You can get out of that awful carrier soon."

The jet surged as it took off down the runway. Xochitl squealed. "Oh, I've never been on a plane before… or off this continent. This is so awesome!"

Selfish as it was, Akasha was glad Xochitl was going to be there with her. Her childlike enthusiasm for life was just contagious enough to keep Akasha from having a nervous breakdown. She looked over at her friend, caught anew at her stunning beauty. Her pearlescent skin seemed to glow, her hair looked like spun obsidian. The purple streaks appeared simultaneously soft and metallic. If this glorious creature lost her life for being her friend, the guilt would kill her.

Xochitl spent the first couple hours of the flight bouncing around the cabin of the jet, exclaiming over the view and trying to persuade her cat to look out the window. Finally she settled in her seat and slipped her headphones on and relaxed.

The tinny sound of *Iron Maiden* sang in the small compartment.

"Just how are we supposed to explain *her* to the United Nations of vampires?" Akasha muttered.

Silas frowned and ran a hand through his black hair. "I have no idea. What's worse is I don't know what will happen if we do not keep her mind under. If she knows what we are and what is going on…" He grabbed her hand and squeezed. "Do you believe in God, Akasha?"

She shook her head briskly, remembering Mrs. Steele's psychotic religious zeal with a shudder.

"I wish you did," he told her gravely. "We are going to need His help."

***

A vampire flunky met them at the airport. He did some moderately embarrassing bowing and scraping as he promised to take them to their hotel and handle the exchange of their American dollars to Euros.

"They're sure giving us star treatment," Akasha whispered to Silas when they were ensconced in the limo. "Maybe this won't be as bad as we thought."

"It doesn't mean anything, lass," Silas said ruefully. "It's merely an old-world courtesy. We will truly be treated as innocents until proven guilty."

Razvan added, "So you had better make the most of it while you can."

Akasha looked at Xochitl's legs dangling out of the open sunroof of the limo and tried to make light of the fact. "At least we'll be able to have a good last meal. Crab *and* lobster, I think."

Isis meowed loudly. Akasha grinned at the cat hiding under the seat. "Oh, you like the sound of that, do you, precious?"

Xochitl plopped down out of the sunroof. "Who said 'crab?'"

Akasha wondered how they were going to get Xochitl to the trial without her suspecting anything. When they arrived at the hotel, Razvan told her.

Akasha shook her head. "Seriously? You want me to get her stoned?"

Razvan nodded. "Those that are 'smokin' the reefer,' as they say, are ridiculously susceptible to our powers. The sixties were an amusing time for me. I could make those hippies do anything." He chuckled, obviously reliving fond memories.

Silas returned to the sitting room of the suite. He had scratches all over his hands.

"What happened to you?" Akasha asked.

"I was helping Xochitl remove the harness from her wild beast." He looked down at his bloody hands and smiled. "I think it will be your turn next, Razvan."

Razvan shuddered. "I think not. Anyway, it is nearly dawn. We had better go to our quarters." He handed Akasha a briefcase. "Here is all I think you will need. Be back here at sunset. Do not get lost and do not get into trouble."

"Right," Akasha couldn't keep the sarcasm from her voice. *All I have to do is get my friend baked so she can be hypnotized by a dozen ancient bloodsuckers. What's the trouble with that?*

***

A half-hour after sunset, Silas paced the hotel room, cursing under his breath as Isis wove in and out between his legs. "They got lost, I know it. Damn it, Razvan, we should have made them stay here."

Razvan remained in his seat, calmly smoking his pipe. "With life and death on the line? I have more faith in Akasha than that." He cocked his head toward the door as shuffling footsteps and hysterical girlish laughter approached. "There they are now."

Silas opened the door and blinked at the sight of his petite beloved carrying her best friend and a bundle of shopping bags with ease. Her strength would never cease to amaze him.

"Dude, Razvan!" Xochitl exclaimed between giggles. "It was awesome! We bought clothes and souvenirs and sex toys and pipes and pot brownies and a hooker!"

Silas's jaw dropped as Razvan choked back shocked laughter. "I take it you ladies had a good time?"

"We didn't actually 'buy' a hooker," Akasha countered as she set her friend down. "We just had to pay her for an interview."

Suddenly, she leapt into Silas's arms. He reveled in the heat of her body against his, wanting nothing more than to tear her clothes off and be inside her again. She moaned and kissed his neck. Yet again, Silas cursed the Elders and Selena's vindictive manipulation.

Razvan ruined the euphoria. "It is about time to go."

"Damn it!" Akasha growled.

Silas reluctantly released her. "Xochitl, may I have a word?"

When the girl trustingly approached him, Akasha stared at him with accusing eyes. *I'm sorry, but this is the only way,* he told her silently. But that didn't stop the guilt from roiling in his heart as he took control of her best friend's mind.

Xochitl lapsed into unconsciousness at Silas's slightest urging. That wouldn't work with Akasha, so they'd have to blindfold her. She didn't take kindly to the idea.

"I don't fucking think so," Akasha told him, speaking slower than usual.

Her eyes were rings of violet around huge pupils and she squinted at him. She must have gotten stoned along with

Xochitl. Though, her friend's condition indicated that it wasn't affecting Akasha as much.

Silas sighed. "I am sorry lass, but the Elders strictly forbid mortals knowing where they reside. We must cooperate with them in everything if we have any hope of leaving alive."

He didn't tell her about his recent decision. If they were sentenced to death, he'd pull Xochitl out of her hypnosis and try to get her to use her powers to destroy the Elders. It was a dangerous plan, with too many opportunities for disaster, but it was all he could think of. He'd do anything to keep Akasha alive and unharmed and to do that he must survive, at any cost.

Heart aching, he pulled her into his arms and stroked her soft curls, inhaling her delicate scent and repeated his promise to her before they'd first made love. "I will not let anyone hurt you again."

There was a knock at the door. Their escort had arrived.

Razvan opened the door to reveal a vampire Silas hadn't seen for nearly four hundred years. He sneered at Silas, baring fangs. "McNaught."

"Michael," Silas replied calmly, refusing to display his annoyance. "You have moved up in the world, I see."

Michael smirked. "Higher than you. You could have had such privileges if you hadn't left my mistress. Perhaps we will petition the Elders for your property when you are deposed."

He gestured to Xochitl's sleeping form. "She would make a great tool for our Order." His eyes raked over Akasha with an insolent leer. "And perhaps we may find a use for this morsel as well."

Silas bared his fangs and lunged forward, but Akasha squeezed his hand so tight it hurt, holding him back. Instead, he growled, "I can, by law, demand satisfaction for your insulting behavior."

Michael's face immediately paled, "A duel?"

He nodded, a predatory smile playing across his lips. "It is my right as a Lord."

The vampire swallowed. "We should depart."

"Yes, that is exactly what I thought."

They settled Xochitl in the limo and blindfolded Akasha. Razvan leaned back in his seat and chuckled. "So Selena *is* here. That makes it personal, not to mention very interesting. I wonder how she was able to press for a trial, the vindictive wench."

"No, it is more than vindictiveness," Silas struggled to conceal his dread. *She wants to stop the prophecy.*

"Who's Selena?" Akasha interrupted, voice laden with suspicion.

Silas stiffened, and Razvan snickered at his discomfort. "She was Silas's lover, until he discovered how insane she was."

He felt Akasha go rigid beside him and reassured her. "It was almost four hundred years ago, lass. She only wanted me for my psychic ability. She claimed to have powers of her own, but it turned out that she was a deranged leader of a strange cult. She was obsessed with my visions of the future, convinced I would bring them 'salvation.'"

"And if Michael's blathering was any indicator," Razvan added, lighting his pipe. "It appears her cult is still in operation."

The partition window rolled down and Michael snapped, "We are not a cult! Our Order knows more of the truth than the rest of you foolish lesser blood drinkers!"

He carried on a zealous monologue until they arrived at their destination.

Silas led Akasha carefully down the stone steps to the secret antechamber while Razvan carried Xochitl. Silas shuddered as he remembered the first time he'd been here, when he first gained the status of a Lord. The ancient faces of the Elders were cold and condescending then. He couldn't begin to imagine what they'd be like now.

Chapter Thirty-six

Light pierced Akasha's skull when the blindfold was removed. She blinked as her eyes scanned her surroundings. They stood in a huge circular stone chamber. Crudely carved staircases on either side curved up to a recessed area that was shored up by the last four feet of a ten-foot stone wall. The wall served as a podium for the twelve Elders, or in this case, judges. Six vampires lined the wall below them, arms folded. Bailiffs, apparently.

The derisive way the judges looked down on them from such a height reminded Akasha of the trial scene from *Pink Floyd's* "The Wall." Or maybe that was just the weed. Why did Xochitl have to insist that she had to eat a brownie too?

"Awaken the creature," a thick German voice commanded from above, jerking her out of her reverie. "We shall hear her sing."

Xochitl awakened, took in her surroundings and started singing "The Time Warp" from *Rocky Horror Picture Show.* Akasha couldn't suppress her laughter. Obviously the circular room reminded her of something else. The perplexed looks of the judges made her laugh harder even as her mind screamed at her to stop.

A judge in the middle actually pounded a gavel and yelled, "Silence! I demand to know what is the matter with those females!"

At last, logic overcame the drug and Akasha sobered.

Razvan calmly explained the reason for her and Xochitl's inebriated conditions, which brought a few chuckles from the room.

"You said her power was in her voice," another judge declared with a thick British accent. "I can feel it. Have her sing some more. This power seems to be harmless, though enchanting."

"'Kash, where are we?" Xochitl asked, giggling nervously.

Akasha glanced at Silas helplessly. Guilt gnawed in her gut for taking advantage of her best friend.

Tell her it's a dream, lass, he told her silently. *The Elders will take care of the rest.*

It took three of the Elders, with Silas, to lull Xochitl into a hypnotic state where she could sing for them and answer their questions without remembering anything later.

The room was captivated as Xochitl sang. Akasha hoped the power of her friend's voice would sway the judges to their side and not frighten them. When Xochitl sang the last note, the vampires shook off the spell and began the questions.

Akasha's heart wrenched in sympathy as they interrogated Xochitl mercilessly about what she was and why was she here.

When she began to cry after answering, "I don't know!" for the umpteenth time, Akasha lost patience and approached the Elders, fists clenched in fury.

"Leave her alone, already!" she yelled, ignoring the outrage on the vampires' faces. "Can't you see she's innocent of whatever it is you think she's done?"

"It is not what she has done that concerns us. It is what Lord McNaught will do with her that is the problem," a voice from behind her announced.

Akasha whipped around to see that another vampire had joined the obnoxious Michael. She was stunningly beautiful, tall and statuesque, with a silken mass of vibrant red hair. It had to be Selena.

She wondered why Silas would have left such an elegant woman... until the bitch opened her mouth.

It was apparent that Selena was acting as prosecuting attorney. Her accusations, which she based heavily upon her psychic visions, made her sound more like a televangelist than a lawyer.

What was most absurd was that she claimed Silas plotted to use Xochitl to raise an army to take over the vampire race.

"You saw the power of her voice!" Selena's hair flew around her shoulders in a red cloud as she whirled to point at Xochitl. Like a siren leading sailors to their deaths, so this creature will control us all!"

Razvan was acting as their defense and he rebuffed her statements with his typical mocking humor. "I see your taste for melodrama has not diminished over the centuries, Selena." Turning back to the Elders, he stroked his goatee. "I can say with utmost confidence that though I am captivated with Xochitl's talented voice, I feel no compunction to obey her in anything. Do any of you?"

The Elders shook their heads firmly as Akasha smiled in admiration at his tactic. If any had answered otherwise, they would have appeared weak.

Razvan won the round and the crazy Selena was shunted to the side as Michael took up the questioning. Unfortunately, Razvan's arguments against Selena's visions made Silas's own visions useless for his testimony.

"But you are forgetting the most important thing," Razvan's voice lost its humor and grew firm. "Silas was instructed by Delgarias himself to guard Xochitl and her friends."

"We have been unable to verify that," the Lord of Rome shook his head and added scornfully, "Besides, I find it hard to believe the Thirteenth Elder would have done such a thing without informing us." His cold eyes declared the topic closed.

The Elders moved on to the subject of the risk of Akasha's involvement with the government, which then brought about a recount of her capture and rescue.

The way they covered it up by looking like terrorists made a few of them chuckle and Akasha received a few respectful nods at her courage. Razvan glossed over the fact that they let Holmes live. So far, none had caught the omission.

The trial took on the atmosphere of a typical courtroom drama. Perry Mason reruns had always bored Akasha.

Maybe the brownies she'd eaten helped as well, for when she was questioned and cross examined, she answered everything with a cool detachment. The knowledge that her life and the lives of those she loved hanging in a precarious balance seemed distant and unreal. She didn't notice the respect and admiration in the vampires' eyes as she faced them fearlessly.

But when they moved on to Silas, her panic returned. Without the reasoning of Delgarias's command to support him, he had no real justification for Marking so many mortals. Michael did his best to cast that in a bad light.

Akasha's fear shifted to irritation as Michael taunted Silas relentlessly, circling him as he pelted him with accusations. Silas took it all stoically. His chiseled features were stamped with the cool indifference that only the nobility could exude. His emerald gaze remained fixed upon the judges and he answered the questions concisely. Michael's presence seemed no more to him than the buzzing of an insect.

Being ignored aggravated the prosecutor. He began to punctuate his accusations by poking Silas in the chest with a slender finger. Akasha moving closer, grinding her teeth in outrage. This had gone too far. Her gaze shifted to the Elders to see that they had no intention of interfering with the abuse. From the amused expressions on their faces, they were just going to watch and see how it played out. Fury roared through her.

How dare these assholes make us travel thousands of miles for the purpose of degrading us for their own sick sense of entertainment? Blood roared in her ears, drowning out Michael's tangent. Her vision narrowed to that finger poking into her lover's broad chest and the sadistic glee in the tormenter's face. She had to make the son of a bitch stop.

"Admit it, McNaught," Michael said. *Poke, Poke...* "You intended to destroy us all." *Poke... poke... poke...*

It happened in seconds. Akasha calmly reached forward, grabbed the offending finger and broke it, smiling at the satisfying snap.

Michael howled in pain and rushed at her.

She stepped aside, grabbed the back of his head and slammed his face into the stone wall.

The impact shattered the vampire's skull and he fell to the floor. His face was a mess of blood, bone shards and gobbets of brain leaking out. His torso barely moved up and down as he breathed. Michael was still alive. *Damn it.* Cries of shock and outrage rang out and she was seized by two of the vampire bailiffs.

Silas's eyes blazed green fire as another pair of bailiffs gripped him. The remaining two hovered uncertainly near Xochitl. She held a ball of flame in her palm. Her eyes darted around frantically as if she were trying to decide whom to throw it at.

As pandemonium broke out in the courtroom, Silas fixed terror-filled eyes upon Akasha. "What have you done, lass?"

We're screwed now. Akasha realized. And it was all her fault.

Chapter Thirty-seven

We are going to die, Silas realized.

The Elders themselves descended the podium steps to surround them. He froze in the guards' grips when he looked down at Michael's mutilated face.

Akasha was strong, he knew, but seeing the destruction she was capable of filled him with alternating washes of fear and admiration.

His eyes sought hers as he took in the sight of her beauty once more.

"You will pay for this, you little monster!" Selena shrieked as she grabbed a fistful of Akasha's hair.

Silas growled in rage. The guards held him back from charging her.

The Elders' voices were a cacophony of shouts. Some rushed to pull Selena away from Akasha, others surrounded Xochitl, and a few approached Silas.

The Lord of London's eyes locked on his and he muttered, "That is some pair of wenches you have there, McNaught."

The Lord of Tokyo glared. "Whatever games you've been playing will stop now, Silas. Your creatures must be put down at once."

Silas felt the Elders building their will and linked his mind to Xochitl's. *Burn them.* He commanded.

Xochitl's power gathered in a hair crackling rush. She raised her arms, which became engulfed in purple flames.

Xochitl, stop! Silas heard in his mind the same time a voice boomed, "Cease!"

A figure materialized in the chamber, bringing everyone to a stunned silence. It was the thirteenth Elder. Silas sighed in a mixture of relief and irritation. *It's about bloody time.*

Delgarias walked with liquid grace over to Xochitl. He knelt before her and said, "My Queen, it is an honor to see you again."

Xochitl smiled. "Uncle Del? Where've you been?" She blinked at him.

Startled gasps from all around nearly shook the chamber. Silas's jaw dropped.

Uncle Del? What did *that* mean?

Delgarias smiled fondly at her and patted her on the head, muttering something under his breath. Xochitl yawned, then sank to the floor, curled up in her coat like a cat, and fell asleep.

"Uncle Del?" everyone else all whispered. Confusion lay in the air thick enough to choke on.

Marcus, the Lord of Rome spluttered, "Your Eminence, what is the meaning of this? Why have you come?"

"I have been here all along," the Elder replied. "I was going to wait until closing arguments to reveal myself and say what needs to be said, but this one," he gestured languidly at Michael's prone form, "forced my hand."

"You cannot be serious!" Selena shrieked, still trying to grab Akasha. "Surely you saw that this abomination caused this... this disruption."

Delgarias chuckled, but his eyes remained cold. "Selena, you may be mentally ill, but it still should be obvious that Michael's injuries are your fault."

He cast a chiding look at the Elders. "Michael's behavior was inexcusable. One of you should have stopped him, but instead you watched in amusement as if it was a play. Silas could have called him out for a duel right then and there; but he was going to be polite and wait until the trial's conclusion to settle such matters, as a proper Lord would."

Delgarias inclined his head toward Silas and continued. "However, his chosen one decided to spare him the prolonged indignity of Michael's antagonism. She punished him herself. This woman should be praised for such good service to her master, not be restrained like a criminal. By the way, she could escape those two easily, and is only remaining still because she feels she's displeased Silas."

The Elders' faces fell with guilt. Akasha, on the other hand, fumed with rage, her eyes practically shooting violet sparks. Silas tensed.

She thrust the vampires that held her away, sending them flying into the stone wall. "He's not my 'master.' He's my boyfriend! And what do you mean? How can you be Xochitl's uncle?"

Delgarias's laughter was rich and tangible. He inclined his head respectfully. "I apologize, young general. I was merely falling back on our antiquated terminology. I meant no disrespect and did not mean to imply you were a subordinate. And I am not really Xochitl's uncle, merely an old friend of her mother." His gaze grew distant. "And her aunt."

"General?" Akasha's question was echoed by the rest.

The thirteenth Elder smiled. "We come to the crux of the matter. Selena was right about one thing. An army will be raised, but not by Silas, and *not* to destroy our kind. Silas was right to Mark Xochitl, Akasha, and the others. Not only was he obeying *my* command, but he was also obeying a prophecy older than myself." Delgarias pulled back the sleeve of his black robe. "Let us form a viewing circle and I will show you."

The vampires stepped closer. Each pulled up their left sleeve. Marcus of Rome sank his fangs in Delgarias's wrist, Ian bit into Marcus's wrist and so on, until they'd formed a chain. Silas drank from Razvan's arm, and all were swept into a vision.

Delgarias walked in the world with two moons. "Aisthanesthai," He said in their collective mind. "This world is called Aisthanesthai, and this happened eighteen years ago."

Delgarias watched an angel, looking down upon a battlefield strewn with dead angels. Suddenly, the angel's thoughts became clear to them all.

The princess looked down upon her decimated kingdom. Her people fought valiantly against Mephistopheles, but they could not win. Luminites, though fearless, are incapable of destruction. Tears ran down her pale cheeks as her vision swam with bloody wings and severed limbs. Thankfully night had fallen, obscuring the tragic sight.

Her people were all dead. She was the sole survivor, but at what cost? She'd faced Mephistopheles, but instead of killing her he'd thrown her down and raped her, the blood of her kin dripping from his body onto hers.

Kerainne gagged. She must leave this place before he returned to take this land and merge it to the world he was creating, a world wrought of evil magic and the blood of innocents.

"Princess!" A voice pierced her wall of silence. "You live! The Prophecy speaks true!" Delgarias hurried towards her. His velvet robe nearly tripped him.

"Oh, Revered One," she whispered and collapsed in his arms, not caring how he came to be here.

His tall form supported her. He took in the aching sight of her bruised body and her torn wings. The pearl and gold feathers were covered in dirt and blood.

"We must leave now, Kerainne. The Prophecy has spoken. Your unborn daughter must be safe and hidden from Mephistopheles."

"I'm going to have a baby?" She looked down at the blood slithering down her ankles and clutched her womb.

"Yes. And Mephistopheles will know if we don't hurry. She will be the savior of this world and others. So the Prophecy has told me. You must go to the only place where there is no magic. Mephistopheles cannot find you there."

Kerainne's lower lip trembled. "The Earth realm?"

Delgarias nodded. "This world is not safe for her now. On Earth she'll remain undetected until the time comes for her to return. There she will gather allies for a future conflict. We must delay no longer." He pulled her forward.

"Enough." Delgarias commanded, and the chain was broken.

The chamber reverberated with shocked questions. Other worlds? Angels? Mephistopheles? It was too much information with too little explanation. Silas smiled ruefully in remembrance of his earlier meeting with Delgarias.

And now the Thirteenth Elder was bombarding his cohorts far worse. Silas could see that many of the vampires were terrified at the idea that they were not alone in the universe.

"Long ago, how long I do not know," Delgarias began. "Magic existed in abundance on Earth. Dragons, luminites, faelin, and even leprechauns dwelled here, along with powerful human sorcerers. Our world was linked with others through many portals and the hub of Earth's greatest magic was the city of Atlantis."

Gasps and murmurs broke out among the audience. Delgarias waited for the noise to die down before continuing. "Then Mephistopheles came. No one knows what he is, or how his power came to be, and no one so far has desired to speculate. All that mattered was that Mephistopheles strove to be a god and he found a way to create his own world by destroying and then absorbing parts of other worlds.

"Atlantis was among the first of his conquests. When he took that fair city, much magic died. Most of those born with magic in their veins fled earth to avoid the mass persecution of humans."

"This is all *very* enlightening, Monsieur Delgarias," the Lord of Paris interjected sarcastically, but what does this have to do with us?"

"Weren't you listening?" Anastasia, Lord of Moscow hissed. "This Mephistopheles is that creature's *father!*" She pointed at Xochitl.

"Yes, he is." Delgarias said. "And in a way he is ours as well. He created vampires, you see, to be his first army. It did not work out, however, for we displeased him and he banished our kind to the earth realm, once it was rid of all magic."

Razvan nodded. "It appears there is some truth to the old legends."

Silas glanced at Selena. She was glaring mutinously at Delgarias. Silas had thought she'd be pleased with the announcement that her "god" and the other world was real, but she was furious. *Why?*

"Indeed." The Elder interrupted his thoughts. "And the time will soon come when war will break out among the worlds, and Mephistopheles will have to face his creations once more. For by his act of raping a luminite, he has sown the seeds of his destruction."

The chamber resounded with more questions. Selena whispered furiously at Michael. Silas used the distraction to take Akasha from the guards and move in front of Xochitl, who still slept through the whole thing, despite the quickly rising noise.

"Silence!" Delgarias commanded. "We would be here for years if we were to discuss everything this girl is and what she will do... and I do not want to tamper with the Prophecy by revealing too much to potentially wrong ears." His voice echoed in irrefutable command. "Only know that you must all leave Xochitl alone. The time will come when those selected must obey her call. She will travel across this world and others and perhaps even through time itself to gather her allies.

"And please end this ridiculous trial. Drop all charges against McNaught and let him take his charges home. Dismiss them now, or challenge me."

He stepped forward, his glittering eyes narrowed on each in challenge. Lightning crackled from his fingertips.

Everyone, even Silas, shrank away.

The Elders had left their gavels up on the podium, so the authority was subdued as they intoned in unison, "So be it. The case is dismissed."

For a moment Silas, Razvan, and Akasha stood still, absorbing the shock of being out of harm's way... and Delgarias's unsettling news.

Razvan was the first to recover. With a gentleness that Silas didn't know his maker possessed, he lifted the sleeping Xochitl into his arms.

Akasha threw her arms around Silas and whispered in his ear, "When we get home, can we do it in the garage first?"

Chapter Thirty-eight

Akasha squinted in the June sunlight and fidgeted with the white graduation cap. The damn thing refused to stay put.

"It's not fair that we have to wear white, while the boys get to at least wear blue." Xochitl complained for about the tenth time.

Akasha laughed. It really *was* funny how pissed off and uncomfortable her Goth friends looked at the pristine white graduation gowns.

Beau laughed and threw his arms around them, looking quite handsome in his royal blue gown. "Just feel glad you didn't go to Lake High. Their colors are supposed to be green and gold. I hear the girls there are wearing piss-yellow gowns."

Aurora smiled up at him. "You say the nicest things, Beau. Let's go smoke a bowl before the ceremony starts. Ya comin' 'Xoch?"

Xochitl shook her head so fervently that her cap fell off. "No, after that weird trip I had in Amsterdam, I'm never touching weed again. I must be allergic to it or something. Besides, I want to wait for Sylvis."

When Beau and Aurora left Xochitl turned to Akasha. "It sucks that Silas wasn't able to come."

Akasha shook her head sadly. She'd told them he'd had a business emergency. "He should be out later for the party, though."

Xochitl nodded, tears in her eyes as she watched parents embracing their classmates. "I wish my mom could be here for this."

Akasha put her arm around her. A lump formed in her throat as they watched the families gathering in the parking lot, laughing and smiling together while they headed toward the lawn.

And here we are; two orphans with nobody. She shook off the melancholy thought. She had everything a girl could want. Love, money, and the promise of starting her dream career. Xochitl was no lost cause, either.

She was going to be a famous rock star, and would someday save the world. And with her exquisite looks, she would find love in no time. They didn't need huge families smothering them with sloppy kisses and giving them flowers and useless paper cards. Still... it would have been nice.

Xochitl saw Aurora's and Sylvis's parents approach and ran to greet them. Akasha lifted the hem of her gown to follow.

She paused when she spotted a silver-haired man getting out of a blue pickup that looked a lot like the new one she bought for hauling parts.

There was something familiar about him... something about the set of his broad shoulders and his stride. He headed her direction carrying a dozen white roses. The man stepped onto the lawn, and she could make out his grizzled features. *It couldn't be!*

"Max!" she shouted in disbelief and threw herself into his arms.

"Spark Plug!" He picked her up in a bear hug and twirled her in the air, dropping the roses. Neither of them cared.

"How did you get out?" Akasha asked when her feet returned to the ground.

"Your young man had a great lawyer," Max said with a grin. "His lawyer convinced the parole board to spring me early and got them to agree to let me come to Idaho. McNaught then told me he took care of them government spooks too."

She laughed into his hazel eyes, her own growing misty. Silas was her magic man. She now understood what that *Heart* song was all about. "Yeah, he did."

"All I care about is if he's treating you right," Max said gruffly.

"You know I'd gut him like a sixteen pound trout if he didn't," she told him with a straight face. "So was that my truck you drove here?"

Max nodded. "Yup. Silas said you wouldn't mind since you only use it for haulin' parts. Does that mean you're still wrenchin,' girl?"

Akasha nodded, fighting a girlish urge to jump up and down. "Did you see that lovely green Roadrunner in the parking lot? I rebuilt her myself."

"I did." His proud smile warmed her. "You've done a beautiful job, Spark Plug."

Xochitl returned with Sylvis and her parents, and Akasha introduced him with a vague explanation while Max picked the roses up from the grass.

"I'll tell you more about him at the party tonight," she whispered to Xochitl as they headed inside.

The ceremony was a drawn-out assembly-like affair with all the accolades going out to the popular kids and a few of the more dedicated nerds. Still, Akasha was filled with triumph and pride as she and her friends collected their diplomas. She could swear Max's applause was the loudest.

The party was a sumptuous affair that Akasha had planned herself. She hired caterers and Xochitl's band to play and invited all of the outcasts in the senior class. It touched her to see them smiling, finally welcome somewhere.

To their surprise, a few popular kids crashed the party and Akasha welcomed them as well. Their curiosity about the "freaks" was so transparent that it was hard to keep a straight face as she greeted them and gave them a tour of the house.

Max stared in awe at *Rage of Angel's* performance. "Those kids are going places," he said as he handed her a bottled Coors.

She nodded and looked out the window for the tenth time. It was finally getting dark.

"That's the trouble with dating vampires, Spark Plug," Max remarked as he opened his own beer. "They're always late to these sorts of things."

Akasha whipped her head around so fast her neck popped. "You *know*?"

He winked and clinked his bottle against hers. "I've seen a lot of weird shit in my biker days. Don't tell him I know. It wouldn't do to aggravate the ancient bloodsucker."

Silas came in and Akasha fought back a squeal of delight as she embraced him.

"Thank you so much for getting Max out of prison," she whispered and pulled his head down to devour his lips.

The band stopped playing and Beau nearly dropped his bass. Xochitl and Sylvis dissolved into giggles. Aurora set down her drumsticks and dug into her pocket, frowning.

"I knew it!" Beau shouted. "I knew you two were an item! You owe me twenty bucks, Aurora."

Aurora rolled her eyes and handed him the money. "I hope you two are deliriously happy."

Akasha laughed and squeezed Silas tighter as many girls looked on in naked envy. Akasha's lips curved in a wry, secret smile. *Although they likely would react differently if they knew that he'd been my guardian.*

Max coughed.

"I hate to be ungrateful, McNaught, but I can't rest easy until I know your intentions towards my little girl. She's the only daughter I have." The retired biker's tone boded ill if the response was not to his liking.

Silas alternated between accusing looks at her and guilty ones at Max. She decided to take pity on the vampire.

"Don't get crabby with Silas, Max." She fixed her mentor with a stern gaze. "He proposed already, but I don't want to even think about marriage until I finish college and get my business off the ground."

Max nodded. "All right, I suppose that sounds like a wise decision. Just what kind of business were you planning on starting?"

Akasha's heart lit up with joy. "I'm going to call it 'Resurrection Wrenches.' It will be a full service automotive restoration and repair shop that will be open at night."

Her mentor smiled in approval. "Well, that sounds like a promising idea. I'm proud of ya, Spark Plug."

"One more thing, Max," she said.

"Yeah?"

"I'll need a partner." She winked at him and held out her hand.

Max's eyes grew misty before he ignored her hand and crushed her in a bear hug. "You got yourself a deal, girl."

Razvan came in, followed by a vampire with waist-length black hair and a face full of piercings. He gestured for everyone to be quiet.

"This is Dominic Slade," he announced. "He owns a club called 'The Mortuary' in Seattle. He would like to hear *Rage of Angels*."

Xochitl and Beau screeched and jumped up and down. Aurora's eyes were the size of distributor caps.

"An audition? *Now*?" she squeaked.

Sylvis shrugged and giggled nervously. "Why not? Everything is set up."

They whispered together for awhile before returning to their positions. Dominic sat down in a chair before the stage with a look of feigned boredom plastered across his features. Akasha wasn't fooled. She could tell that he was fascinated with them already. His eyes followed Xochitl with an intensity that was laughable.

"Do you know any Seattle bands?" he asked.

Xochitl exchanged grins with her band mates. After some silent communication they played *Metal Church*'s "Beyond the Black." The song was so hardcore that Silas and Razvan looked scared. The other guests were stunned silent. Dominic, however, had misty eyes.

"I've never heard anything more beautiful in my life! Could you play 'The Dark'?"

Rage of Angels' career was sealed. Akasha relaxed in the circle of her lover's arms and smiled at her friends as she thought: *So this is what "Happily Ever After" feels like!*

Epilogue
Four years later

Silas laid out the wedding photographs, ready to place them in the white leather embossed album. If he didn't get them organized, no one else would. Akasha was out at her favorite tavern playing darts with Max. Silas was still exhausted from the honeymoon and happy to stay at home to attend to this poignant chore.

They'd spent a month in Europe. Silas even worked up the courage to take Akasha to his homeland of Scotland. It was a bittersweet experience, made better with her fascination. She was moved to tears when he showed her the ruins of his castle. But his new wife was a delight when she bought him a kilt and devoured haggis like a native.

Many Lords had insisted they enjoy their hospitality, but Silas and Akasha snatched as many nights alone as they could. The other vampires were incessant with their questioning him and Akasha about the prophecy, Xochitl, and the coming war.

Nothing had happened so far, besides Xochitl's band becoming a world-wide phenomenon practically overnight.

However, Silas had a deep feeling they were languishing in an eerie calm before a storm. Something was going to happen, he knew it in his bones and the feeling was growing so intense that his chest was tight and it was getting increasingly difficult to breathe.

He turned his attention back to the photos. Here was one of his bride looking mutinous as the wedding coordinator adjusted her gown. His heart warmed. It was hard to believe that after five centuries, he finally found the love of his life.

Here was another picture of her, forcing the paparazzi away from Xochitl and the band. Her spine was straight and head was up in a distinctly militant pose, just like the general that Delgarias said she would be.

His brow furrowed. Someday Akasha would lead a war, at Xochitl's side. She didn't seem to be alarmed by this portent and Silas didn't know if it was because she didn't believe it, or if it was because she didn't understand how bloody and awful war could be. Silas had fought enough battles to understand what war could do to a person's body, mind, and even soul. He wished with all his heart that he could protect her from that knowledge, even as he knew that she was strong enough to handle it. Hell, she was the strongest person he had ever met.

The phone rang, startling him. The photo album slipped off the desk as Silas reached to answer.

"McNaught Finance." He tried to hide his irritation as he caught the album before it crashed to the floor.

Razvan's voice was grave on the other line. "Selena has taken Post Falls."

Silas paced back and forth behind the desk, his fingers absently twisting the phone cord in his fingers. "What? That's right between our territories. What in the hell possessed her to try a crazy move like that? She knows we have immunity. Well, keep an eye on your end and we shall do the same. I had better tell Akasha."

"Tell me what?" Akasha demanded from the doorway the moment he hung up.

Silas raised a brow. He was so shocked with Razvan's news that he hadn't heard her come home. He sighed. "Selena has taken Post Falls as her territory."

"Why the fuck would she *do* that?" Akasha asked. "I know she's crazier than a shithouse rat, but I didn't think she was stupid. She knows we have immunity. We could go hunt her down and kill her right now!"

"Actually, we cannot." Silas sighed. "Razvan told me Selena and her cult have moved into one of the newer suburban developments. There's no way we can destroy her without risking injury and the awareness of all the mortals living nearby. And we do not have immunity from revealing ourselves to humans."

"Damn it!" She slammed her fist down on the mahogany desk. "I hate that fucking bitch!"

Silas winced at the sound of cracking wood. He was fond of that desk.

"I think she came here to taunt us in revenge for making her look bad at the trial as well as to be close to the area," he said with a calm he didn't feel. "She knows the prophecy is centered around us. And I'm sure she knows that important events will be happening soon. She cannot resist keeping her dirty fingers out of it."

Akasha clenched her fists. "If she sticks her nose in too far, I may just have to smash it… and a few other parts she may value."

"What the hell is going on?" Max demanded, coming into the room.

Akasha and Silas exchanged guilty looks.

She gave her husband a level gaze. "You might as well let me tell him. He knows what you are anyway. And no, I didn't tell him, he was smart enough to figure it out on his own."

Silas sighed. "Very well. I suppose that's where the immunity comes in." His eyes narrowed on the retired biker.

"Although I would like you to tell me how you've discovered my secret."

Akasha turned to Max. "Do we still have a half rack in the fridge?"

Max nodded, eyes darting between her and Silas.

Akasha grinned at her mentor and business partner. "Good, let's head on downstairs. Talking is thirsty work and this is gonna take awhile."

***

"Push!" Joe Holmes shouted encouragingly to the panting woman on the bed.

The surrogate mother complied with a groan and clung to Lillian's hand like a lifeline.

Holmes's daughter gripped her hand back and gave her a tight smile of encouragement before looking back at the monitors.

"They're both still going strong."

"Splendid!" Holmes crouched between the woman's legs, heart pounding in anticipation. "It's crowning!"

Moments later a mass of slimy, squalling flesh slid into his gloved hands.

He didn't lay the infant on the woman's chest like they did in maternity wards nowadays. It wouldn't be good for the surrogate to form a bond.

Instead, he wasted no time in cleaning up the crying baby and ensuring that its airways were clear.

"Well?" Lillian inquired pointedly as she handed the surrogate a glass of water.

"It's a girl."

The baby's cries eased as she stared up at Holmes. One tiny hand gripped his finger tight enough to hurt.

"She has her mother's strength." The question was, would she have her father's taste for blood or vulnerability to sunlight? Or at least, as he hoped, healing powers and longevity?

The surrogate rose slightly from the bed to wipe sweat soaked strands of hair from her forehead. "Thank you so much, doctor, for giving me the chance to make amends, to do something good." She clasped her St. Christopher Medal. "I hope the baby is healthy and her parents are happy with her."

With that, she slumped back against the pillow, passed out from exhaustion.

Just in case, Lillian added a little morphine to the woman's IV so she could rest easier. "Will the baby's parents ever know she exists?"

Holmes tamped down a pang of guilt. Although he'd lied to this woman regarding their reasons for needing her to be a surrogate, he'd paid her twice what surrogates usually earned and helped ease her conscience on her past transgressions.

I've done something good, he told himself. I've achieved a scientific breakthrough.

"Perhaps in time," he answered at last. *Though I pray they never find out.*

I hope you enjoyed Wrenching Fate, if you'd like book 2, Ironic Sacrifice for free, Sign up for my newsletter!

Teaser for Ironic Sacrifice

Spokane, Washington

"Oh God, please, make them stop!" Jayden dug her fingertips into her temples as if she could tear the horrid visions out of her skull.

Long after the police officer left, the imprint of him invading his daughter's room every night and the sound of her terrified whimpers was irrevocably burned in her memory. For the rest of her life, along with her worst visions, it would flash behind her eyes like a bad commercial, leaving behind a chill in her soul and a bitter taste in her mouth.

Again the temptation beckoned to end it all, to climb over the Division Street barrier to the dam churning the waters of the Spokane River and jump, drowning the visions permanently.

Oblivious to curious onlookers, Jayden sank to her knees on the cracked sidewalk.

The visions were getting stronger. The cop's hand barely grazed hers when she handed him her driver's license after he checked her ID. Immediately she'd been pelted with vile images. It had been agony for her to keep a straight face as he interrogated her. She wanted to hit him— no. She wanted to tear his balls off and make him suffer a thousand-fold for what he did to that innocent child.

But there was nothing she could do. He was a man of the law while she was just a crazy homeless twenty-three year old woman. Once he confirmed her age and finished harassing her, the policeman left, free to rape and molest again while Jayden Leigh was trapped with terrible revelations of suffering that she could do nothing to prevent or free herself from.

"Are you all right, dear?" A gentle hand touched her shoulder and for once Jayden didn't get a vision. Although for a moment it seemed she could smell fresh baked bread.

Jayden looked up into the compassionate blue eyes of an elderly woman.

"Yeah," she croaked, licking dry lips. "It's just a... migraine." She fell back on the usual excuse for these situations, though she was tempted to shriek the horrible transgressions she witnessed.

The woman nodded, brushing a snowy lock from her forehead. "Don't you fret, dearie. I've just the thing for that!" she declared, reaching into her gargantuan red leather purse.

Jayden began to protest, but the matron cackled, "Ah-ha! Here you are, dear. Keep the bottle. My doctor gives me plenty of pills as it is."

Jayden smiled at the Excedrin. If only a little pill would cure her problem. Or perhaps it could, if she took the whole bottle.

"And take this too. It looks like you've fallen on hard times." The kindness in the woman's voice was enough to make Jayden's throat tighten with humble gratitude and the barely suppressed desire to cry on the stranger's shoulders and pour out her sorrow.

"Oh no, Ma'am, I couldn't." She tried to return the twenty-dollar bill, but the woman had already walked off and was getting into her Buick.

Her eyes brimmed with tears at the generosity. She pocketed the pills and money, picked up her bottle of cheap Chardonnay and resumed walking to her car, where she lived. She could always jump into the dam tomorrow. After all, it wouldn't do to waste the wine.

***

Sleep came hard that night. It wasn't the wailing of police sirens, or the rumble of semi-trucks on the freeway, or even the sounds of a couple screaming at each other a block away. Something else drowned those incessant city noises. A voice in her head sobbed despairingly, *"Why? Why? Why!"*

That voice had grown so loud that she could barely hear anything else. And still the keening cry rose higher… *"Why? Why? Why!"*

A real headache was dangerously close.

"Why indeed?" she murmured as she uncapped the wine bottle and took a deep drink. She knew perfectly well what the voice was asking.

Why have I been reduced to this pathetic state?

Jayden still did not have an answer.

Only three months ago things had been normal. *Or had they?* She'd had a decent job that fit with her college schedule, taking care of people with developmental disabilities. It fulfilled her hungered spirit and was a step closer to becoming a counselor, a secret dream she'd nursed since childhood. Jayden had been working in the group homes for almost a year when she began having the visions. They were quick and faint at first, making her blame her imagination even though her instinct argued furiously. *Just too much work,* she would tell herself. *All I need is a break. Things will get better when the semester ends.*

But the next day the visions would come back stronger and soon the breaks did little to hold them off. Jayden became convinced that she was losing her mind. It was beginning to look as if she was going to end up like her mother after all. Stark raving mad in a psychiatric ward, heavily medicated in a padded room until, unable to take it any longer, she died a slow painful death of a broken heart and shattered mind.

Shortly after summer break began, Jayden's supervisor fired her for being unproductive and upsetting the clients.

The next month, her landlord evicted her from her apartment. By then Jayden was half-insane from the severity of the visions, so she didn't really care.

Mechanically, she'd packed what little belongings that would fit in her little Toyota and left the apartment. She then withdrew the rest of her money from the bank and closed the account. Going back to school in the fall was not an option.

Besides the hassle of showering, going to the bathroom and having to move to a different location every night, living in her car was kind of liberating. She didn't have to pay bills or work or answer to anyone. The self-delusion only lasted a week when Jayden saw how quickly she was running out of money. She tried a few times to get a job, but every place she walked into and every person she encountered gave her such a cacophony of visions that she soon gave up, realizing that she would probably never be able to exist with the rest of humanity ever again.

Now it was early October and she almost froze to death every night.

"Why? Why? Why?" the voice cried again, despite all the wine she drank to muffle it.

"I told you already, I don't know!" Jayden growled. "Besides, *why* doesn't matter anymore. What I need to figure out is *what* the hell am I going to do?"

She put on her headphones and turned the volume up on her MP3 player, seeking solace in the music of her favorite band. For a blissful half hour, *Rage of Angels'* latest album blocked out the voices until she turned it off, mindful to conserve her batteries.

Her heavy eyelids drifted closed.

Glowing eyes… Blood-dripping fangs… A dark shadow closes over the figure of a woman, about to drain away her life. Jayden's voice screams, "No! Take me instead! I want to die, I need to die." Mocking laughter rings in her ears, "An ironic sacrifice I do say. Very well, a life for a life."

The shadow gently engulfs her and she begins to drown in thick velvet blackness. The sinister voice echoes, "A life for a life… A life for a life… a life for a life."

The piercing trill of a car alarm shunted Jayden from the dream.

"Damn it," she groaned and pulled the blankets over her head. Even nightmares were preferable to her miserable consciousness.

As she shifted in a fruitless attempt to seek comfort, Jayden realized that she had to pee. Cursing again under her breath, she sat up and pulled her shoes on. It was freezing cold outside. She shivered and her breath came out in big puffs of steam. She hurried into the alley to find a safe spot to relieve herself. When the street was out of view she crouched and unzipped her pants.

Just when she finished, a scream of terror tore the air close by, making her jump. Jayden yanked her pants up, zipper forgotten, skin prickling with acute alertness.

"No. Don't you dare touch me!" a woman demanded haughtily. She had to be only twenty feet away.

Jayden knew she should get the hell out of there and drive as far as her near empty gas tank would take her, but her legs propelled her relentlessly forward. Her heart pounded with a heady mixture of terror and anticipation as she came upon a scene that had only before existed in her dreams.

The woman was a tall leggy blonde in designer clothes. Jayden fleetingly wondered what such a classy lady was doing in a dark seedy alley. But then a vision assailed her. This woman had been so spoiled all her life that it was sickening. Her love for herself and utter scorn for all others rose up more noxious than the scent of her expensive perfume. Scenes of her temper tantrums flitted through Jayden's mind. She didn't really start to hate the woman until she saw her kick a bum on the street.

"H-how did I get here?" the woman demanded shrilly, trying to hide her fear. "I don't belong in this filth!"

"As a matter of fact, this is *exactly* where you belong," another voice replied. His voice was deep, smooth as velvet and faintly accented.

Jayden's eyes shifted to the dark form looming before the woman. It looked like a man, but it wasn't a man. This thing was far older and far more terrifying than a mere mugger. She started to take another step closer, but then it spoke again. His voice was so rich and enchanting that it held her motionless.

"I have brought you here, Charise, because it is time for judgment to be passed upon you."

Charise's eyes widened in terror. She gasped and put a dainty hand to her throat as if she were rehearsing for Broadway.

The creature nodded. "Yes. I know of your crimes. I know everything. And it is I who will decide your fate. In fact, I already have."

"What is it then?" she whispered.

"Death."

Slowly, he cupped her face in his hands. She shrieked and tried to scratch out his eyes with her long manicured nails, but the man easily restrained her, seizing her anorexic-thin wrists with one hand and tilting her neck to the side. His eyes began to glow with an unholy light, reflecting on his bared fangs.

Jayden saw the monster for what he was immediately and at the moment she didn't take the time to examine the impossibility of it all. She just flat out accepted it. *Vampire.*

"Wait!" she cried out, surprising herself.

Those glowing eyes now turned upon her, freezing her heart. Jayden stumbled back with an icy intake of breath.

"Yes?" The whisper was silky, invoking tendrils of fire in her belly despite the chill of the night and its events.

"D-don't k-kill her," she found herself stammering. "T-take me in-instead. I *want* to die."

The vampire laughed. Its mocking tone struck a sharp chord within her soul. This laughter had haunted her dreams many times before.

"You know what I am, don't you?" he asked, amusement lacing his voice like spun sugar.

Jayden nodded.

"And you know this woman for the foul selfish creature she is too, don't you... Jayden?"

She had felt his mind whispering against hers since their eyes met, but the shock of his learning her name almost stole her breath... or perhaps it was the intimate way in which he spoke it.

"Y-yes. I saw," she admitted, unwilling to show her fear of him.

"She deserves to die. Surely you cannot argue with that."

"I am not one to pass judgment," Jayden stated plainly. "Nor, do I think are you... Razvan." The ancient, foreign-sounding name came to her like a curveball.

The woman stared at them both dumbly. Her gaping lips opened and closed like those of a dying fish. She didn't even bother struggling in her captor's grip.

Razvan chuckled and twirled his short black goatee with one long finger, regarding Jayden like she was an amusing new toy. "And you offer yourself in her place, you say?"

"Yes," she whispered.

Again, the rich mocking laughter rippled across her body, touching her in places that should never be touched.

"A very powerful psychic I have come across," he said musingly, and crooked a finger, gesturing her to come forward.

Unbidden, her feet carried her forward. It was a powerful mind trick. Jayden realized with trepidation that the vampire could probably make her do anything he wanted against her will, as if she were a puppet. When she was inches away from him, he raised a hand and lifted a lock of her dirty hair, then let it drop.

"A poor girl for a rich one, a vagabond for a socialite, a truth for a lie," he murmured in a voice that brought goose bumps all over her flesh. "An ironic sacrifice, I do say. Very well, then. A life for a life."

Those familiar words made her heart jump into her throat.

The vampire turned his attention to the other woman, whose wrists he still held. "You know that this woman is sacrificing herself for your worthless hide, right?" he asked her.

The blonde nodded rapidly, her relief apparent as the vampire released his grip.

"And you are grateful, yes?" Razvan prodded. His tone oozed with false sincerity as he circled around her like a stalking wolf.

She nodded again. Her facial muscles twitched strangely. Jayden realized he must be now immobilizing her with his preternatural power.

"Then say it!" he ordered harshly.

Cerise flinched, but obeyed. "I-I'm grateful!" she half-shouted.

"No, you stupid bitch, I don't want or need your gratitude, but *she* does." He inclined his head to Jayden. "Now thank her."

The woman slowly approached Jayden, eyes full of awe. "Th-thank you."

Jayden nodded.

"Now kiss her hand." The icy command was irrefutable.

Charise took Jayden's hand, face screwed up in disgust at the dirt and grime that covered the flesh, and quickly brushed her lips across it. Jayden was confused about Razvan's motives for such a pointless demand. Maybe he just wanted to be cruel. One glance at the wicked glee in his eyes confirmed her suspicion.

"Very good, Charise," he said in a way a teacher congratulates a pupil.

Then, quick as lightning he pinned her against the brick wall. Jayden thought he had changed his mind about letting Charise go, but it appeared she was wrong.

"Now you are going to redeem yourself, yes?" he whispered. "I am certain you will, Charise. I am certain you will treat every person you encounter from this day forward with respect and dignity. Do you know how I know this?"

"H-how?" she stammered.

"Because, my dear, if you don't... if you remain the same self-centered trollop that I summoned into this alley, I will know and I will bring you here again. And trust me, you will not be so lucky as to survive the encounter. Now go!"

She didn't move, only stared dumbly.

"Quickly!" he growled, "before I change my mind. I am getting very hungry."

Charise ran. The sound of her clacking high heels echoed down the alley long after she was out of sight.

"Now, Jayden, where were we?" Razvan turned to her.

Oh God, she was going to die now. Jayden gazed up at the vampire, desperate to study the last thing she would ever see.

Razvan was taller than she, about six feet. His hair was long and dark and fell in rich waves to his shoulders. His eyes were like perfectly carved onyxes and when she met them it was like looking into eternity and slowly slipping over the edge. She shook herself, unwilling to fall under his spell, which he was surely trying to exert upon her, and turned her attention to the rest of his face. It was all harsh masculine planes and angles, with a firm jaw under a goatee and high, almost hollow cheekbones. The brows were thick and arched in such a way that he would always look malevolent. It was the same with his lips; they were so sharply sculpted and tinged with cynicism under a rakish mustache, it was doubtful that they could ever portray a smile of joy or honesty.

"What is the matter, Jayden?" Razvan asked suddenly. "Don't tell me I've now frightened you speechless. Not after you so boldly confronted me."

"No. Nothing's wrong," she said too quickly. "Well, besides the fact that I'm about to die. It's kind of a large thing to grasp, if you don't mind."

His smile faded, eyes turned serious. "Don't worry. I will give you time." He held out a hand. "Come."

She frowned in confusion. Was he toying with her? Unease trickled down her spine like rivulets of ice water. "What do you mean? Aren't you going to kill me now?"

Razvan shook his head. "No, I think not. You amuse me too much right now. And I would at least prefer to have you fed and bathed first."

Her cheeks grew hot with embarrassment. She didn't think about how badly she must smell to him, having not bathed in a week.

"Well?" He raised a brow.

Shivering in apprehension with a touch of excitement, she placed her hand in his. It was cool to the touch, but not as cold as she had expected of an undead creature. His other hand clamped about her waist as he pulled her body against his. The shocking intimacy made her tremble.

Suddenly, they both began to rise up into the air. Jayden clung to him in support, but as their ascent quickened, the wine, malnutrition, lack of sleep and shock got to be too much for her. Blackness closed over her as she slipped into unconsciousness.

About The Author

Formerly an auto-mechanic, Brooklyn Ann thrives on writing romance featuring unconventional heroines and heroes who adore them. She's delved into historical paranormal romance in her critically acclaimed "Scandals with Bite" series, urban fantasy in her "Brides of Prophecy" novels and heavy metal romance in her "Hearts of Metal" novellas.

She lives in Coeur d'Alene, Idaho with her son, her cat, and a 1980 Datsun 210.

You can follow her online and keep up with her latest news and releases at http://brooklynann.blogspot.com as well as on twitter and Facebook.

Keep in touch for the latest news, exclusive excerpts, and giveaways! Sign up for Brooklyn Ann's newsletter!

Works:

SCANDALS WITH BITE

BOOK 1: BITE ME, YOUR GRACE (April 2013)

Dr. John Polidori's tale, "The Vampyre," burst upon the Regency scene along with Mary Shelley's Frankenstein after that notorious weekend spent writing ghost stories with Lord Byron. A vampire craze broke out instantly in the haut ton.

Now Ian Ashton, the Lord Vampire of London, has to attend tedious balls, linger in front of mirrors, and eat lots of garlic in an attempt to quell the gossip. If that weren't annoying enough, his neighbor, Angelica Winthrop, has literary aspirations of her own and is sneaking into his house at night just to see what she can find.

Hungry, tired, and fed up, Ian is in no mood to humor his beautiful intruder...

BOOK 2: ONE BITE PER NIGHT (August 2014)

He wanted her off his hands... Now he'll do anything to hold on to her... Forever.

Vincent Tremayne, the reclusive "Devil Earl," has been manipulated into taking rambunctious Lydia Price as his ward. As

Lord Vampire of Cornwall, Vincent has better things to do than bring out an unruly debutante.

American-born Lydia Price doesn't care for the stuffy strictures of the ton, and is unimpressed with her foppish suitors. She dreams of studying with the talented but scandalous British portrait painter, Sir Thomas Lawrence. But just when it seems her dreams will come true, Lydia is plunged into Vincent's dark world and finds herself caught between the life she's known and a future she never could have imagined.

BOOK 3: BITE AT FIRST SIGHT (April 2015)

When Rafael Villar, Lord Vampire of London, stumbles upon a woman in the cemetery, he believes he's found a vampire hunter—not the beautiful, intelligent stranger she proves to be.

Cassandra Burton is enthralled by the scarred, disfigured vampire who took her prisoner. The aspiring physician was robbing graves to pursue her studies—and he might turn out to be her greatest subject yet. So they form a bargain: one kiss for every experiment. As their passion grows and Rafe begins to heal, only one question remains: can Cassandra see the man beyond the monster?

BOOK 4: HIS RUTHLESS BITE April 2016

The Lord Vampire of Rochester doesn't do a favor without a price. And now it's time to collect

Gavin Drake, Baron of Darkwood is being pestered by nosy neighbors and matchmaking mothers of the mortal nobility. To escape their scrutiny, he concludes that it's time to take a wife.

After witnessing the young vampire Lenore's loyalty to the Lord of London, he decides she is sufficient for the role.

After surviving abuse from rogue vampires, Lenore Graves wants to help other women recover from their inner wounds. She befriends mesmerist John Elliotson and uses her vampire powers to aid him with his patients. When the Lord of London declares that Lenore is the price the Lord of Rochester demands for aiding him in battle, she is terrified. Will all of her hard work be destroyed by Ruthless Rochester? Yet she can't suppress stirrings of desire at the memory of their potent encounter.

After Gavin assures her that the marriage will be in name only, Lenore reluctantly accepts Gavin's proposal. Determined to continue her work, she invites John Elliotson to Rochester. As they help women recover from traumas, Lenore explores her own inner turmoil and examines her attraction to her husband.

Gavin realizes his marriage is a mistake. His new baroness's involvement with the mesmerist is dangerous. He knows he should put a stop to Lenore's antics— yet her tender heart is warming his own and tempting him to make her his bride in truth.

As Lenore and Gavin's relationship blossoms, the leader of a gang of rogue vampires embarks on a quest for vengeance against Gavin… using Lenore as his key.

Book 5: Coming Soon!

BRIDES OF PROPHECY
BOOK 1: <u>WRENCHING FATE</u> (February 2014)

She's haunted by her past.

Akash Hope trusts no one. Her parents were shot down by uniformed men, which forced Akash to spend most of her life on the run.

She's so close to getting out on her own, making her own dreams come true when he shows up and disrupts everything.

Her new legal guardian.

His kindness makes suspicious, while his heart-stopping good looks arouse desires she'd kept suppressed.

He promises her a future.

Silas McNaught, Lord Vampire of Coeur d'Alene, has been searching for Akasha for centuries.
He's perplexed to discover that the woman who has haunted his visions is anything but sweet and fragile. Her foul mouth and superhuman strength covers a tenderness he's determined to reach.

While government agents pursue Akasha and vindictive vampires seek to destroy Silas, they discover the strength in their love.
Can they survive the double threat?

BOOK 2: <u>IRONIC SACRIFICE</u> (October 2014)

Jayden Leigh wants to commit suicide.

Her clairvoyant powers have become so intense that she lost her job and home. Death is the only way to make them stop. Opportunity presents itself when she comes across a sinfully handsome vampire ready to make a kill. Jayden begs him to take her instead. A blissful death in his arms, or the visions ravaging her mind? She'd gladly take the vampire.

Razvan Nicolae is captivated with the beautiful seeress who sacrifices herself for a stranger. Killing such a pleasing asset doesn't interest him. If he could get her powers under control, she could be the key to finding his missing twin.

Controlling her visions and working for a seductive vampire? Razvan's offer is like a dream come true. But her dream turns into a nightmare when a mad vampire cult leader seeks to exploit Jayden's powers to stop an ancient prophecy.

As Jayden finds herself at the center of a vampire war, she realizes that the biggest threat isn't losing her life, it's losing her heart.

BOOK 3: <u>CONJURING DESTINY</u> (October 2015)

Famous rock star, Xochitl Leonine, has dreamt of a world with two moons where a black cloaked man beckons her. One Halloween night, she meets the mysterious stranger of her dreams... literally... and their shared dance becomes a rendezvous in a place of endless night.

Zareth Amotken has no idea how important Xochitl's heavy metal band is to her. As an immortal sorcerer, he doesn't care. He has one goal: to find the prophesied savior of his world. Her voice holds the power to bring back his world's vanished sun.

Xochitl's compassion urges her to help in any way she can. Yet learning the mysteries of her past causes conflict with her future in music. Her destiny in his world and her obligations to her band pull her in opposite directions. How can she long for one while the other is so dire?

As Zareth introduces her to his people and teaches her to control her powers, she aches for his enchanting kiss. Zareth tries to resist, for their passion will unleash serious consequences, both political and magical.

As the time to fulfill her destiny draws closer, she must choose between her heart, her duty, and her friends. The wrong choice could ruin everything.

But if Zareth's evil half brother succeeds in taking control of her for his own ends, he will take away her choices... and destroy the world.

BOOK 4: <u>UNLEASHING DESIRE</u> 2016

A setup so perfect... it might just be fate.

Radu Nicolae has spent centuries in a guilt-induced hibernation beneath the ruins of his family castle. The only time he awakens is to feast on the occasional vampire hunter. When Lillian Holmes invades his lair, trying to kill him for a crime he did not commit, he decides it is time to rejoin the world. As he feeds on the inept, but delectable hunter and sees her memories, he realizes that he is being used as a weapon to murder her. Radu does not like being used.

Agent Lillian Holmes, of the Abnormal Investigation Unit, is sent on a mission to kill the vampire who murdered her father. But when she tries to stake Radu, he awakens. When his fangs sink into her throat, she thinks she's a goner. To her surprise, she wakes up a prisoner. Furthermore, Radu did not kill her father. The AIU killed Joe Holmes and sent Lillian to Radu to die.

Together, they strike a bargain: Lillian will help Radu travel to the United States to reunite with his long lost twin brother. In return, he will help her take down the men who killed her father. As their relationship deepens on their journey, so does the danger. Not only must they keep government agents from finding out that Lillian is alive, but she also has a secret that will rock the foundations of the vampire world.

Book 5: Coming 2017

HEARTS OF METAL (Heavy Metal Romance)

Book 1: KISSING VICIOUS (August 2015)

Aspiring guitarist Kinley Black is about to get her first big break—as a roadie for Viciöus, her favorite heavy metal band, and for the rock god she always dreamt might make her a woman.

The Roadie

At 15, aspiring guitarist Kinley Black wished she were a boy. At 16, after hearing Quinn Mayne sing, she wanted him to make her a woman. Now, at 22, her dreams have come true. Quinn's band Viciöus needs someone to lug their amps around the country, to strive and sweat with the guys. She just has to act like one of them.

And the rock god

Quinn had to admit the new chick could pull her weight, but that didn't mean his road manager made the right choice. Taking a hottie on a heavy metal music tour was like dangling meat in front of a pack of feral hounds—and Quinn could be part dog himself. But more surprising than her beautiful body are Kinley's sweet licks, so that no man could help but demand a jam session. Quinn will soon do anything to possess her, and to put Kinley in the spotlight where she belongs. And to keep her safe and sound from the wolves.

Book 2: WITH VENGEANCE (2016)

Katana James is about to become the studio guitarist for her favorite heavy metal band ever—and meet the musicians, music, and man of her dreams.

SHE MEANS BUSINESS

Twenty-three year old Katana James can shred on the guitar. Not that anyone would know, as she's spent most of her time working on a popular news and gossip website for Heavy Metal fans since her own band broke up. But her dreams are in reach when she gets an audition to play with her favorite band, Bleeding Vengeance. Kat won't let her gender, her anxiety disorder, or even the pranks of a malicious stalker stand in her way. The only thing to threaten her focus? A growing fascination with the group's brilliant, mysterious bass player.

HE OFFERS PLEASURE

Klement Burke has always been the heart, soul and brain of Bleeding Vengeance. He's the kind of rock star who stays in the shadows, a perfectionist more interested in satisfying his brain than other parts of his body. Until he auditions Katana James. At first it seemed a perfect idea, as he's been aware of her talent for some time. But meeting her in the flesh ignites thoughts far from professional. Despite the conflict of work, the odds against her falling for a geek like him, and a secret he's been hiding, his heart, body and soul now belong to Kat.

Book 3: <u>ROCK GOD</u> (2016)

CPSIA information can be obtained
at www.ICGtesting.com
Printed in the USA
LVOW11s2047080317
526552LV00004B/797/P